NO
WAY
HOME

CHRISTY
COOPER-BURNETT

Black Rose Writing | Texas

ISBN: 978-1-68433-502-2
PUBLISHED BY BLACK ROSE WRITING
www.blackrosewriting.com

Printed in the United States of America
Suggested Retail Price (SRP) $18.95

No Way Home is printed in Calluna

*As a planet-friendly publisher, Black Rose Writing does its best to eliminate unnecessary waste to reduce paper usage and energy costs, while never compromising the reading experience. As a result, the final word count vs. page count may not meet common expectations.

For my son and mom for your unwavering love and support.
Thank you to my friend Ambie, for helping me put the parsley on the plate.

NO
WAY
HOME

NO
WAY
HOME

PROLOGUE

Piedmont, Oklahoma 1867

I feel the panic inside me rising. Unable to control the fear, I snap at Marcus, "Shut up, I need to figure out what's wrong!" He stares but offers no reaction, which isn't surprising. Why should he care? He has no choice—he'll be staying here. I, on the other hand, should have left by now. I try the transponder a few more times with no luck. It shows no signs of life.

Oh my God, this can't be happening.

I'm stranded two hundred years in the past with no weapon, no supplies, and a prisoner who's more likely to abandon me than offer any help.

My breathing is uneven, my heart pounding. I don't know what to do; there's no protocol in place for equipment failure. It's always been a given I'd get back to my present day; I've transported prisoners many times in the last ten years with no problem. And I'm a good transporter, I keep my emotions out of the job. Yet here I am, a forty-year-old woman from 2070 Los Angeles in the middle of nowhere in 1867 with a twenty-three-year-old cyber-criminal who thinks of me as the enemy.

And not one idea about how to get home.

I can't count on my prisoner to be much help. I spent the last day prepping him for his exile here, and I wouldn't describe him as resourceful.

I pace back and forth for a few minutes trying to calm down, when Marcus announces that he is leaving. I'm not sure if I'd be better off with him here or if I should be relieved he is going, providing one less complication to worry about. I eye the backpack slung over his shoulder. I remember every item in there—I inspected the contents earlier today. He sees me looking at him and stands up straighter, grabbing the shoulder straps of the pack firmly.

I raise my eyebrows and tilt my head. "Please, at least a bottle of water?"

"No way." Backing away and smiling, he laughs and gives me a weak salute before jogging toward town.

What a little shit he turned out to be.

And just like that, I'm alone.

ONE

Piedmont, Oklahoma 1867

Gazing out the window of the cabin to the miles of dry plains in each direction, I wonder how the hell I ended up in this place. That's a rhetorical question; I realize how I got here—I just don't understand why I'm not home yet. My thoughts turn to my son, Michael, as they do every day, trying to imagine what he's doing, praying he's safe. I'm not adjusting as well as I had hoped after six months here, but that isn't surprising. Never a big fan of change, a life-altering transition with no warning is not something I was prepared to handle. I've always been a strong person, but this experience has turned my entire world upside down, and quite frankly, I'm pissed off about it.

The only silver lining in this situation has been finding a friend, Annabelle. We've grown close, despite her being someone I would not be friends with in my real life. She annoys me most of the time but is a welcome confidant. So I tolerate the minor irritations and thank the heavens for someone I can trust. Finding Annabelle was a fluke really, we were never meant to meet. I am in Piedmont getting supplies and she is in the same store. I notice her immediately. It is hard not to; we are wearing identical dresses in different colors, mine brown and hers blue. I remember thinking how odd that our wardrobe is not just similar, but exact replicas of each other. This is unusual because it is not an era when garments are mass produced. Clothing is handmade at home, or in a tailor's shop, if you're lucky enough to afford that luxury. Something about her isn't right, but I can't put my finger on it. When she leaves the store, I follow her outside and sit on a bench, watching her talk to another woman. Her hand moves to her waist resting on her midsection several times, while she adjusts her waistband. Someone else might never detect it, but I do. It stands out to me as a gesture I have made on more than one occasion. I conceal my transponder in a hidden pocket sewn into the band of my skirt. It is an old habit learned over ten years, to check the device; make sure it's there, still secure. As Annabelle walks away, she catches her foot on the corner of a board on the sidewalk. She lets loose an impressive string of obscenities under her breath after recovering her balance, and in that moment I realize who she is. So I get up to pursue her.

"What are you hiding in your dress?" I ask, trailing behind her.

She turns to me with a frown on her face. "What? Nothing. I don't know what you're talking about."

She continues to walk faster, but I catch up, grabbing her arm to turn her toward me.

"I think you do. Is it your transponder? We need to talk. My name's Christine Stewart from Los Angeles, ID number 56022. Does that mean anything to you?"

She stares at me for a moment before a smile forms.

"Oh my God. Are you serious? Holy crap. I didn't realize anyone from our timeline was here. Annabelle Harris, ID number 98421, from Chicago. When did you transport here? Were you assigned to take me back?"

"No, I'm not here to take you home. I arrived a month ago, you?"

"The same. April 2, to be exact. So, if you aren't here to retrieve me, are you saying you're stuck here too?"

"Yes," I say, my shoulders sagging.

And that's how our friendship began. We traded stories about our time here, complaining about the lack of, well, everything. Finding each other gave us both hope that we could somehow find a way home.

Annabelle and I were both only supposed to be here for twenty, thirty minutes tops to make our drop-offs and be on our way. I still don't know what went wrong, I only know we can't get home. Annabelle rents a room at a boarding house working as a schoolteacher. She was slated to transport in two hundred fifty miles from Piedmont, near Boonesville, Arkansas, population under one hundred people in 1867. But she came in several miles off course from her intended transport site, which happens sometimes. Her prisoner deserted her on their first day there, leaving her nothing but a small pouch of water. By day three, unable to find more water, she was dehydrated and exhausted. Panic set in, motivating her to walk, looking for Boonesville or any other signs of life. Finding a trail, she collapsed there later that day.

A family traveling with a wagon train found her, headed from Little Rock, Arkansas to California and they allowed her to join the caravan. Among the travelers was a teacher bound for Piedmont to start a new school, whose family had paid travel passage. Annabelle was reluctant to leave her drop off point but had no other choice, and she resolved to stay with the travelers only until they reached the first town. She planned to leave the wagon train then and figure out what to do next. That changed when a smallpox outbreak swept through the wagon train during the second week on the trail, leaving one third of the people sick or dying. The teacher was among those who became ill, and with that Annabelle saw her opportunity. Vaccinated against smallpox as a child, she knew she would not get sick. She told the family who rescued her she was a teacher, and when the first teacher succumbed to the disease, Annabelle continued on to Piedmont to fill the open position. At least until she could plan her next move. No one on the wagon train cared either way; they focused everyone on surviving long enough to reach California.

Three weeks after rescuing Annabelle, they dropped her off outside Piedmont to make her way into town. Taking over the schoolteacher position, she was only a week into the job when we met.

My story is somewhat different. I'm living with a man who found me on my third day here. That isn't as scandalous as it sounds.

John Harding, the man who took me in, lives on a small ranch two miles outside town. I had no choice, I had to stay somewhere; I would not make it here on my own—that much was obvious even after only a few days. I don't know how he explains me living there, and to be honest, I don't care. I imagine he tells people I'm a sister or cousin or some other relative. This isn't a time when a man and woman can live together unmarried, so I suppose he has to explain me somehow. Since I rarely speak to anyone besides John and Annabelle, I haven't had to answer for much—at least not yet. Annabelle, though, has spun a web of lies so thick I don't understand how she keeps it straight.

So, now I focus on surviving each day and trying not to give myself away in a hundred different ways every time I open my mouth. The work required to survive here is astonishing. With no running water, buckets must be hauled from a stream half a mile away. I cook over an open fire and prepare everything to eat from scratch. Caring for the animals is a huge job that takes a few hours a day and is not for the faint of heart.

Every day, thoughts of how to get back to Michael and what I can try next to make that happen consume me. I'm so tired of being here, so over this, that I worry about losing my self-control. Before coming here my life was one of convenience, but the way I'm living now is so far removed from that, my memories of it are fading.

It's not entirely bad, though. Although my survival here depends on the generosity of a stranger, life is much slower paced, and I must admit that's nice. Clocks no longer rule the day, and my priorities have shifted—to staying alive. Even though I was tossed into this unprepared, I've kept my wits, mostly. Realizing early on that if I allowed it, I could slip into a state of panic I might never recover from. So, I do what I must, to fit in and survive. I have no other choice.

When I met John, I told him I was traveling with my family and my father's business associates from New York to stake out future properties here in the West. Indians killed everyone I was with and they took me hostage, but I escaped. That's when he found me. It's a weak story with holes big enough to drive a tractor through, but I had to come up with it on the spot. If he doesn't believe it, he never lets on, and I've become very good at avoiding the topic. Now that fall has crept in, I worry about how I'll pull through this. I used to trust I would not be here for long, so that wouldn't matter. However, it's been six months and reality has set in. Self-preservation has taken over, and I've considered long-term survival here. I sometimes get angry when I realize what I'm doing; it feels like giving up on getting home. Half the time I'm calculating how to get out of here, while the other half I spend thinking of how to endure.

Now stories are circulating about Indians moving near here. Stories I don't want to admit may be real. The thought is scary as hell, as it's already so frustrating to be in a position to have to worry about this. John owns one rifle, usually by his side, so unless he's standing right next to me when I need one, I'd be out of luck.

Pulling my gaze from the window, I glimpse around the room, rubbing my arms to warm up. Out of habit, I walk to the loose floorboard in the room's corner and take out my transponder, my most guarded possession. I unroll the worn cloth it's wrapped in, turning it over in my hand. No change since the last time I examined it. Although it's my key to getting home, I don't know what to do with it at this point. I only dare keep it out for a minute; Annabelle is the only person who can see it, or that could be the end of us both. I return it to its hiding place, careful to make sure the board is secure.

As the wind whistles through the gaps in the windowpanes it reminds me how exposed I am here. If I ever need to run there is nowhere to go; no brush for cover, no river to float away on, only rolling plains on all sides. When the wind bends a tree branch, scraping it against the window, I get goosebumps. I'm so jumpy today, probably because I don't enjoy being in this house alone, and I use the word house loosely. More of a shack, constructed from logs and mud with drafts everywhere, that it's still standing defies logic. The knock on the door jolts my thoughts back to the present, and I see Annabelle on the porch. I open the door, and in typical Annabelle style, she offers no greeting. Pushing her way through, she jumps right into whatever is on her mind.

"Have you tried it today?" she asks.

"Yes, no change. Yours?" I'm hopeful for a minute she's come to tell me something's changed.

"Same with mine. Dammit. Hey, did you hear yet? Indians attacked the Millers' place. They found Jacob dead, and Sarah and the girls are missing."

"What? Oh my God. We need to get out of this hellhole. I don't understand why no one from home has been here yet."

Annabelle nods. "I don't think I can keep this act up much longer. It's a struggle to remember who I'm supposed to be half the time. And Doc told Mr. Tyler that there's a fever and stomach illness going around, sore throat and intestinal pain. Six people have died. Could it be cholera? Or scarlet fever? I've been trying to remember when those outbreaks started."

"I don't know, maybe. Or just a nasty strain of the flu. Although that isn't much better, that could easily kill us too. One more reason to get out of here."

"And go where, Christine? Do you suppose there's another town somewhere that might be safer? Trust me, I've been out there, and this town is as good as they get. Besides, what if we need to be here for them to find us? Don't get me wrong, I want to go home. I miss Joe and the girls so much I can't stand it! And these kids at school, they're Stepford kids, some are really spooky. This life has defeated them. You're lucky you found John, who was willing to take you in, no questions asked. Or very few, anyway."

"Oh yeah, I'm so lucky. He bathes once a week, Annabelle, and I have no privacy here whatsoever. Thank God the bathroom is outside."

Wow, that's a sentence I never thought I'd hear myself say.

"Besides, I'm certain he's waiting for something romantic to happen between us, but I'd rather suck broken glass through a straw than sleep with him."

Annabelle laughs and shakes her head. "Right, whatever. I'm only saying it's semi-safe here. I get the old man Tyler hitting on me every other day, and it's appalling."

"I think we need to keep going back to my drop off point. What if the longitude and latitude influence our trackers?"

She knows what I mean, no need to elaborate. I take the time to study her face and notice her eyes have dark circles underneath and she's clenching her jaw. When she begins to bite her bottom lip, I can tell she's near the breaking point.

"Listen, Annabelle, people are trying to fix this. There are people back home who worry about us, who must be working around the clock to get us home. They must be! The CCEA would not leave us here. Let's continue to do everything in our power to help them do that. If that means going back to that drop off spot every day, then that's what we do."

We do this regularly. When one of us is falling into the abyss, the other pulls her back. And one of us is always leaning over the edge lately.

"Okay," she says. "So, let's go tonight. We can go right after dusk, when your bunkmate is out doing whatever he does when he sneaks off every day."

"Are you crazy? With people being killed and kidnapped by Indians? We can't go running around at night. We need to be smart about our safety. If we don't survive, there is zero chance of ever getting back home. And you know very well he doesn't sneak off, he feeds the animals. And please stop calling him my bunkmate, it sounds so creepy."

"Yeah, you're right, it sounds kinda creepy. Tomorrow at the latest, okay? I'm looking over the edge of the cliff here."

"Okay, let's go for water and I'll say we're going to bathe, that'll buy some extra time. I'll make it work. You'd better start back. It will be dark soon, and it's not safe to be out alone."

"Yeah, I get that. I'll be back tomorrow at noon. And Christine? Check it again tonight, just in case."

I roll my eyes. "I always do. You don't need to remind me every day."

I stand in the doorway and watch her ride away on the horse, disappearing over the horizon. I hope she can hold it together until we figure something out. She can be so impulsive, the last thing we need is to let something slip, making someone curious. I sense we're getting close to something happening, and we need to prepare for anything.

An hour later I hear the horses get restless and the dog barking, which usually signals John's arrival home. I see him riding up with three rabbits strung on the side of the saddle.

Great rabbit again.

At least there's food for a few days.

"Hi," I say as he comes through the door.

"Hello, was everything quiet here today? No problems, I assume?"

"Yep, no problems. Annabelle came for a visit; we decided to go for water tomorrow around noontime."

"We have enough, it's almost full. I need you here to pick vegetables and make certain the new garden's ready to plant. And it is not safe for you to be out by yourselves with Indians advancing so near."

And here we go.

"I can do both, John. I'll get walnuts and berries while I'm there. Besides, we want to bathe. I will do everything before I leave. We'll be fine, and if we see anything out of the ordinary, we can come home."

He turns away and busies himself with the rabbits. I realize he swallows much of what he wants to say to me, but let's be real—I am not his wife, nor am I his lover. And I'm not accustomed to getting permission from a man when planning my day.

And if I get lucky, I won't be coming back tomorrow.

I spend the following afternoon with Anabelle, swimming and picking nuts and berries. It doesn't matter how often I bathe here—I never feel clean. I want my hair to smell like jasmine again, so I continue to dream about shampoo and body wash while I float in the river, enjoying the sun. I know John isn't coming home until late today, so we're in no hurry to leave.

I'm lost in a daydream of Aruba when Annabelle glides over to me and puts her hand over my mouth. Gesturing for me to be quiet, she points to the other side of the riverbank.

Indians!

I see six of them on horseback riding along the crest. We turn to hide in the cover of the tall grass at the river's edge. It's at that moment my horse moves out from the trees to graze in the open meadow. The movement catches the attention of the Indian in the lead, and he turns his horse in our direction, guiding it into the shallow river. The others follow him, and I steal a glance at Annabelle.

She looks terrified.

The leader stops ten feet from us, while the rest stay behind him, their horses prancing and kicking up water, as we stare at each other. I don't break eye contact with him because I'm frozen with fear, but I also think he'll regard that as a sign of weakness.

Of all the ways I could meet my demise, this wasn't even on the long list six months ago.

They've only been in the water for maybe sixty seconds, but it seems so much longer. I remember reading somewhere that time slows during periods of intense fear or stress, and now I can confirm that. He glances around the river, and I'm sure it's obvious to him we are here alone.

There are two horses grazing and ours are the only clothes on the rocks. Neither Annabelle nor I have moved a muscle. He says something to us, and we do not understand what he's saying. I'm not sure how to respond, so I smile at him, just pushing the corners of my mouth up slightly.

That's friendly, right?

He doesn't react, and I worry that I have offended him. I sense we're in a standoff to see who breaks first.

Here goes nothing.

I take a deep breath and grab Annabelle's hand underwater while I inch backward. I remain crouched to stay covered, moving toward the rock where our baskets of berries and clothes are. As we progress, he signals to the Indians behind him with a wave, and they turn to ride up the bank of the river. He stays a heartbeat longer than the others before finally twisting around to ride after them. He glances at us once more when he reaches the crest, and with a slight nod of his head, guides his stallion up and out of sight. I watch them ride off, turning to look at us one last time. We wait until they leave then leap up to the rocks, where we get dressed. We run the mares home without slowing. I jump off even before my horse has stopped. I fling open the front door and it hits John, dumping a pot of water he's carrying.

"What the hell!" he says, jumping back to avoid becoming wet.

"We ran into Indians at the river," I say between gasps of air. "There were six of them, and we were swimming, and they were as close as you are."

"Are you both all right? Did they hurt you? I told you, you cannot be out unaccompanied!"

John turns to hug me, then moves to the windows to peer out each of them.

Annabelle wastes no time searching the cupboards for whiskey. She pours us both a cup, and I take two shots to calm myself. I tell him the details of what happened, but downplay it. I don't want to hear any more about it. This will already cause problems with him and I know we must make it back to the drop off point by any means.

"They left us alone, John," Annabelle says. "I think they were more curious than anything else. It was just spooky to see them up close."

John glances back and forth between us as if we've gone crazy. "I know you two harbor secrets, and both think yourselves untouchable, but I must insist concerning this subject. I forbid you to travel to that river alone! That is the end of it and the matter is closed for further discussion!"

Untouchable? I don't have words to express how vulnerable I am in this place and time.

Annabelle stifles a laugh and I nudge her, giving her a look that suggests she stop.

"John, I am grateful for everything you have given me, but you've got no right to forbid anything. I am fine, Annabelle's great, they only spooked us, as she said. I won't let this keep me from the river, or anywhere else. Please, say so now if that's an issue. I will take my things and leave."

He considers that for a moment, shaking his head. Picking up his hat, he starts across the room for the exit, stopping short halfway there.

"You needn't leave, but I shall. I will return home tomorrow." The slamming door rattles the whiskey bottle on the table.

"How adorable, your first fight," Annabelle replies, laughing and pouring another shot.

"Oh, shut up already. If I'd known that's all it would take to scare him off overnight, I would have done it months ago."

We touch glasses in a cheer and drink while discussing plans to travel back to the walnut grove the following day.

TWO

Piedmont, Oklahoma 1867

The next morning John isn't home yet, not that I mind. It's crowded here most of the time, though it's only the two of us. Having not lived with a man for ten years and not being romantically involved makes it more awkward. Add to that the fact that I moved in here as a stranger, and you get the idea.

John had to teach me how to do almost everything when I arrived. I have never taken care of animals such as chickens, goats, or horses. To be honest, I'd never seen most of those creatures up close and personal until I landed here. The only animal I have ever loved enough to take care of is my dog Max. I rode a horse once when I was a kid, but that was only a pony at a petting zoo. Not quite the same thing as saddling up a mare here. Now I tend the animals, make bread from scratch, grow vegetables, and cook the meals, all of which are major accomplishments for me. I have also learned how to sew a little, which would floor anyone who knows me back home. But this is not home, and despite these newly gained skills, I miss my real life.

After drinking two extra shots of whiskey last night, Annabelle fell asleep and is still passed out in the rocker. I woke up at dawn this morning to an eerie quiet, as John typically wakes before dawn and is outside puttering around when I rise for the day. I was accustomed to the noises of a big city, and I now know that white noise helps me stay asleep. However, I'm thankful for the time alone to clear my head and nurse my hangover.

We had fun last night; it was by far the most relaxed I've been since getting here. The whiskey helped, and I ended up confiding in Annabelle about my divorce and my life back home. She told me about her husband Joe, daughters Willow and Heather, and life in Chicago. She also divulged more about the trip here from Arkansas, and I have to give her mad respect for resourcefulness. Alone and with nothing, she made her way to Piedmont to land a job, rent a room, and survived, despite the odds. By the time I met her, she was thriving. Well, thriving is probably too strong a word—I'm uncertain anyone could truly thrive in this environment. However, she made some kind of existence for herself on her own. Which is more than I can say for myself. I'm not confident where I would be if John hadn't come along to rescue me. Would I be as healthy and safe as I am? I doubt it.

I finish my coffee as I watch Annabelle snoring softly in the rocker. Her curly blonde hair cascades over the back of the chair and I wonder if maybe I haven't given her a fair chance. I like Annabelle, despite her tendency to annoy me occasionally, but it definitely took time for her to grow on me. I look forward to seeing her, and if I'm being honest with myself, without her I'd have gone mad after my first couple of months here.

She's my best friend in the world. Who am I kidding? She's my only friend.

Craving the caffeine, I make myself a second cup of coffee even though it's easily the worst I've ever had. I go to my floorboard hiding spot and unwrap my transponder. I sit on the floor staring at it for a while, not knowing what else to do. At first, it gives me a sense of comfort to see it, like a small bit of home. Then I remember how ticked off I am that it's not working.

Piece of crap, why won't you work?

I shake it in anger, and I think I feel it vibrate just for a second or two.

Did I imagine that? What the hell?

I shake it harder, and the green light flickers slightly.

Oh my God, oh my God, oh my God.

My heart races and I can't breathe properly. I glance at Annabelle; she's still asleep. I turn the power on, and it whimpers a little, struggling to warm up. This is the most promise the device has shown since I've been here.

This has to be a positive sign!

Annabelle and I both carry the same transponder, and we try them every day without fail.

And now my device is trying to start on its own. I want to see if hers is doing the same, and if so, that means we may go home.

"Annabelle," I whisper, my voice breaking. "Annabelle, Annabelle, wake up!" When I find my voice, the sound fills the room.

"What the hell?" Annabelle sits straight up, then plants her feet on the floor to balance the rocker. "Why are you screaming? Oh my God, my head," she says, rubbing her neck.

"We need to leave for the walnut grove right away! Where's your transponder? Do you have it with you?"

"Huh, what? Of course, I always bring that with me. What is up with you, you're acting like a crazy person? I need some coffee before we go anywhere. As bad as the coffee is here, I'll be happy to have a cup this morning. Seriously, what is in this whiskey? I never feel this crappy after a few shots."

"Stop talking and listen to me! My transponder is vibrating and flashed on for a second."

I hold it up to show her, struggling to convey my urgency to her.

"What? Are you being serious right now?"

"You cannot believe I would joke about this?"

"Holy crap! Do you think it's working again? Why would that happen if it wasn't working?"

"I have no idea. Give me yours, let me try it. If yours is doing the same, that will tell us something."

Annabelle pulls her transponder from her waistband and hands it to me. I press the menu bar, and it flickers the same way mine did. This is definitely a good sign.

"I don't understand why they're only flickering and not turning on. Let's get back to the drop-off point. This is way more than they've ever done before, so that must mean something. We may only have one opportunity at this, and I don't want to screw it up."

My gaze wanders around the cabin and I realize that I have nothing of mine to take with me. All I own are the clothes on my back.

How pathetic is that?

I have no way to leave John a note, and even if I could, I'm not sure he knows how to read. I guess when I don't come back this afternoon, he'll go looking for me. It won't be hard for him to figure out where I went; I only go to town or to the river, and always with Annabelle. I'm so glad he got mad at me and took off last night. If he were here now, I never would have taken my transponder out this morning and tried it. I don't know long this will work. This could very well be our only chance. And by the luck of the draw, it might just work out.

We get our horses saddled up, grin and then laugh. This is it, the day we've hoped and prayed for going on almost seven months. I nudge my horse with my heels, and we exit through the gate. We take off, riding at top speed until we reach the grove of walnut trees near the river.

We look around before getting off the horses, the memory of yesterday and the Indians still fresh in our minds. We scramble to the ground under a tree and unwrap our devices, expecting the moment of truth. I squeeze her hand tightly for a minute.

"Are you ready?" I say, grinning.

"Is that a real question?"

Annabelle giggles and is acting more confident than me. I tuck my transponder into my dress as I stand.

"Just give me a second, I need to make a pit stop before we leave. I'll be right back," I say, already hiking my skirt up as I walk to a group of dense bushes about fifty feet away.

"Wow, Christine, now? You can't hold it?"

"No!" I call over my shoulder, "Two cups of coffee means I can't wait," I mutter to myself under my breath.

"Okay, hurry, let's get out of here. Oh my God, we're finally leaving!"

I glance over to see her do a fist pump in the air and give a little whoop which makes me laugh. My hands tremble as I struggle with the yards of fabric on my skirt. If today is our ticket home, then my nerves will fade—but I find it hard to shake this feeling of urgency, something tells me we need to hurry.

What if it doesn't work, and we've gotten our hopes up for nothing?

I can't even consider that possibility. Still crouching behind the bush, I pick up the sound of the horses neighing and fidgeting. I think little of it until I listen to Annabelle. She keeps repeating no, and I sense the panic in her voice building. I move to bolt upright, but my instinct tells me not to, so I remain hidden. I plant my hands in the dirt, steadying myself to peek around the brush and then freeze—Indians. But not the same sort as yesterday; these cause the hair on my neck to rise. Mohawks trail into long ponytails wrapped in cloth, their faces painted with bright colors. The tomahawks are all I need to convince me; they're not here on a friendly visit like the last tribe. There are four of them circling her, and as she tries to sprint, they grab for her.

They pick her up, laying her over the horse stomach down. She cries and swivels around frantically, looking in my direction. I recognize the exact moment she spots me; I see it on her face. They don't realize I'm here yet, and she will not give me away.

Oh God, I'm not sure what to do. If they take her, she's as good as dead.

I begin to rise but she rocks her head.

"No, don't do it or we're both lost!"

They don't understand what she is saying, and I'm sure they don't care. Tears fill my eyes, and I stay concealed, only my head peeking out because I realize she is right—the only chance for survival is to remain out of sight. There's nothing to be done to save her by myself. I have minimal training in hand-to-hand combat as all transporters do, but I'm not stupid enough to take on four men with tomahawks. With no weapon and being outnumbered, it's futile. I tremble and tamp down my rising nausea. Annabelle fights every step of the way; knowing she will not make it out alive if they take her.

Good girl. Keep fighting while I try to come up with a plan.

She lifts her head and speaks softly.

"My girls, promise me you'll look after them."

Tears flow down my cheeks as I nod to her. When one glances my way, I lunge behind the thicket, but I'm too slow. He's already seen me.

Shit. Fight or flight.

It only takes a split second for my instincts to kick in, and I run. Still clutching the bottom of my skirt, I spring up and tuck as much as possible into my waistband.

Annabelle screams, "Go, Christine! Run and don't look back!"

I have my lightweight work boots on, and I can run in them. I train in long distance when at home, so I hope I'm able to outlast them, if nothing else. I start toward the river and make out the sound of their footsteps driving me forward with everything I have. Reaching the edge of the bank, I slide down, hiding in the tall grass. The wind is swaying the plants, camouflaging me.

I sneak out the other side, where we came in earlier today. We had meant to tie the horses here, allowing John to find them after we left, but forgot in the excitement. I struggle up the hill, clawing at the dirt and shrubs, trying to gain traction. Hearing a noise behind me, I panic, my adrenaline surging. I reach for a rock, but it gives way and I tumble into the shallow part of the water. I spot one wading in after me and two more catching up. Scrambling upright, the fear takes over, and I steady myself in a battle stance. He looks confused at first, and then a small smile creeps onto his face.

You assume I'm an easy mark, huh? Well, you can kiss my entire ass because I refuse to go down without a fight.

He starts toward me, and just before he reaches me, I fall on my back and use my boot to kick him where it counts—hard. His eyes roll into his head as he buckles over and folds into the river.

That had to hurt.

As I leap up and race to the opposite side of the water, I spot the other two pursuing me, and I run into the grove of trees. I double back in the river's direction, hoping they'll continue their search forward. I stop to catch my breath and listen for noise, when a branch snaps behind me. I twist around ready to attack again, only to eye a deer dart through the woods. I tuck the loose parts of my wet dress in and push forward.

I reach the end of the trees, where it opens to a grassy meadow. Afraid to risk crossing that, I turn into the woods and keep running. I pause again, and I know they're coming—they're close. I realize that I haven't truly run in six months, and I'm paying for it now; it will be impossible to keep up this pace and escape. I need to find a safe spot to hide.

The Indians are not worried about being quiet, knowing I have no chance. They are going to catch me and scalp me. Or drag me somewhere and kill me there, after doing Lord knows what to me.

I get out of my damp clothing with a single tug to allow me to run faster, then spot a dead log jammed up against a clump of brush. Rot hollowed out part of the timber, so I climb through. Kicking a section of the rotten wood out quietly, I continue crawling through, securing myself just inside the huge thicket of scrub.

It's so dense I have a difficult time getting in, but the thought of them chasing me provides excellent motivation. Ignoring the scratches, I prop the pieces of broken log up where I kicked them out to conceal the hiding place even more. I pull my dress over my head, knowing my pink bra and underwear will stand out through the green and brown brush. Thank goodness my clothing is brown too.

Just be quiet and still.

I curl up into a tight ball and use the fabric as a filter to mask the noise of my labored breathing.

The bush is so thick I only detect slivers of light here and there. My heart is pounding as they draw closer. I don't dare move a muscle, breathing as shallowly as imaginable. I hear them rushing past me and overhear voices in the distance even five minutes later. They must have doubled back, unable to locate me.

Either they think I've gotten away, or realize I'm hiding.

Too afraid to leave, even with my legs cramping, I stay put, not willing to take a chance on being discovered. I focus on something else and wonder if it's possible for Annabelle to have escaped while I was being chased. I only hope by running I could draw them elsewhere long enough for her to free herself. If three of them are after me, that would leave only one of them guarding her. If I know Annabelle, she made the most of that opening.

As dusk sets, I consider moving, but not convinced it's safe yet, I stay put. I continue to hear noises and I can't be sure it's not them. I will worry John when he sees that I'm not home yet, and he'll figure out something is wrong.

Please God, let him locate Annabelle in time.

I understand the odds are against that, but I have to keep up hope—that's all I have.

I'm cold, uncomfortable, and scared, but if I fall apart, there's a good chance I will die here today. The thought of never seeing my son again makes my stomach twist, and at that moment I vow to do whatever I have to, to survive this. If I play it smart, I might wait them out; they can't keep searching forever.

Right?

They'll abandon the search eventually, allowing me to make a break for the ranch. If I had a horse, it would be much safer—and faster. I decide that when I take off, I'll go search for my mare. If the Indians are lingering nearby, it's unlikely they will hang out at the river.

They will search in the woods. They won't think me brave enough to go there again, making a hunt safe. I won't leave here without trying to help Annabelle; I know she would do the same for me.

How could I live with myself if I got home, and she didn't?

I change my position every half hour to relieve the cramping and stop my feet from falling asleep. But with little room to move, it makes no real difference. As I wait, I consider how asinine it was to send me here with no contingency plan in place for emergencies. I was given no supplies and no weapon. They provided the person I escorted here with money, medication, food, water, and a blanket. It's absurd, the more I consider it. Would it be too hard to equip me with a few necessities in case of a delay getting home? My mind continues to wander, while I fall in and out of sleep. Dehydrated and exhausted, I no longer have any feeling in my legs or feet. As I drift into a state of semi-consciousness, my thoughts take me back to my first day here.

THREE

Piedmont, Oklahoma 1867 / Los Angles, California 2070

The day I end up stranded begins like any other travel day I've had in the past ten years. Marcus and I arrive on the outskirts of Piedmont, Oklahoma on a warm spring afternoon in 1867. There's a breeze rustling the leaves in the grove of walnut trees we've descended in. The first thing I notice is how peaceful it is; the chirping of birds the only sound. I listen for a minute, scanning the landscape to be certain we're alone. The tall grass and wildflowers almost appear fake, they're so vivid. Then Marcus jolts me back to reality with his moaning.

"What am I supposed to do now? You're dropping me off in the middle of freaking nowhere with nothing!"

He looks as if he might lose his dinner.

Did he sleepwalk through the last day of training and prepping?

"Marcus, we've been through this. I am not leaving you empty-handed. Let's run through your survival pack together. The nearest town is only three miles south of here, you can do that by nightfall easily."

"Easy for you to say. You get to go home. I'm stuck here—wherever the hell here is—and how am I expected to make it there, walk? Oh, hell no! I make one mistake and I'm kicked out of society, just like that."

He snaps his fingers for effect, as if that's how it all happened—accused and carted away to never-never land with no notice.

"Marcus the laws are very clear, and everyone, including you, know of the consequences. If you hadn't bailed out of your historical training, you'd know more about where you are and what to expect. I will not debate this with you anymore. Do you need to go over your pack or the survival guidelines again or not?"

"No, I know the damn rules, I went to all the friggin' classes."

"All right, if you aren't willing to let me review anything with you, then I'll have to take off. Good luck, and I mean that. You'll be fine, you're a smart guy. I think you will have a decent life here if you embrace it and give in to the process. Just don't fight it and you'll make out okay."

He scoffs and spins away from me.

Good God, I hope he's not crying again.

I use my handheld transponder to scan the chip inserted under the skin of my left wrist and wait for the familiar dizzy feeling that signals my departure.

Only nothing happens.

I try again, and then twice more. Marcus turns to glare at me, waiting for something to happen. I look at my transponder, and it isn't registering as on.

Shit. This can't be good. What the hell is going on?

I try rebooting it but it won't even flicker on. I struggle to maintain my composure, but I feel the fear written all over my face. Marcus chuckles, then straps on his survival backpack.

"Oh my God, are you serious? Your thing isn't working? Sucks to be you."

He laughs again, and it makes me want to slap the grin right off his face.

I feel the panic inside me rising. Unable to control the fear, I snap at Marcus, "Shut up, I need to figure out what's wrong!" He stares but offers no reaction, which isn't surprising. Why should he care? He has no choice—he'll be staying here. I, on the other hand, should have left by now. I try the transponder a few more times with no luck. It shows no signs of life.

Oh my God, this can't be happening.

I'm stranded two hundred years in the past with no weapon, no supplies, and a prisoner who's more likely to abandon me than offer any help.

My breathing is uneven, my heart pounding. I don't know what to do; there's no protocol in place for equipment failure. It's always been a given I'd get back to my present day; I've transported prisoners many times in the last ten years without a problem. And I'm a good transporter, I keep my emotions out of the job. Yet here I am, a forty-year-old woman from 2070

Los Angeles in the middle of nowhere in 1867 with a twenty-three-year-old cyber-criminal who thinks of me as the enemy.

And not one idea about how to get home.

I can't count on my prisoner to be much help; I spent the last day prepping him for his exile here, and I wouldn't describe him as resourceful.

I pace back and forth for a few minutes trying to calm down, when Marcus announces that he is leaving. I'm not sure if I'd be better off with him here or if I should be relieved he is going, providing one less complication to worry about. I eye the backpack slung over his shoulder. I remember every item in there—I inspected the contents earlier today. He sees me looking at him and stands up straighter, grabbing the shoulder straps of the pack firmly.

I raise my eyebrows and tilt my head. "Please, at least a bottle of water?"

"No way." Backing away and smiling, he laughs and gives me a weak salute before jogging toward town.

What a little shit he turned out to be.

And just like that, I'm alone.

I sit under a tree trying my device every few minutes until it gets dark.

Now what am I expected to do?

I climb the walnut tree I've been sitting against and lean backward on a huge branch. I continue to look at the transponder, afraid to miss it turning back on. As night descends, the darkness becomes claustrophobic. With no city lights, the stars are all visible, but they do little to illuminate my surroundings.

I listen to what I suspect are coyotes howling in the distance, but how would I be sure of that? They don't exist in 2070 Los Angeles, but they sound similar to the coyotes in movies, so I err on the side of caution, staying put. It's warm out, so I'm as comfortable as I can be, given the circumstances.

Frank must be working on the problem with technical support. Everyone will be in a panic at base when I don't show up in the jump room as scheduled, prompting them to do a forced transport. Frank is my unit supervisor and friend of many years. He's the person who gets us through orientation and preps us for travel. I reflect to this morning, when I left. He told me I was in for a treat—I'd be traveling to the wild west, his favorite era. I didn't share his enthusiasm then, and I sure as hell don't now. But I never get nervous when he transports me, and today was no exception. I shake off the memory, struggling to figure out what I should do before they transport me home. I can't hide in this grove forever, but I don't see what else I can do but stay here and attempt to get my transponder to work.

At first light, I scale down and stretch my legs after a fitful night of dozing. Dehydrated and hungry, my stomach growls loudly. All I had to eat yesterday was a doughnut for breakfast and a few leaves of lettuce in an attempt at lunch. I walk out of the grove where the trees thin out and open to a small grassy area, where I hear running water.

Yes!

I jog toward the sound and discover a modest river behind tall grass. I sneak along the edge of the shore to inspect, confirming I'm alone. Even in my period clothing, I realize I'd have a hard time blending in here and I can't risk a chance of being seen by anyone. We wear brown or black work boots as our pioneer dresses are long enough to cover them, and I'm thankful for that as I start down the muddy bank. I recognize I should boil the water before drinking it, but with no pot or means to start a fire, this will have to do. I locate a spot where it flows over a narrow grouping of rocks and dip my hand in for a drink, letting the cold water quench my dry throat. I stay hidden in the grass for a moment to be certain it's safe to backtrack along the path I came in. Once in the grove, I locate the tree I spent the night in. I head there only because I have nowhere else to go.

My walk from the river has made me realize my clothing has become a burden. The yards of heavy fabric are difficult to move in, so I tear the fluff out from underneath, which makes it only slightly better. Why the wardrobe department deems it necessary to put a petticoat under these skirts, I will never understand. I'm usually only in period clothing for two hours at a time, making it somewhat bearable. Now I've been stuck in this costume for almost two days and it's wearing on my last nerve.

I sit down, lean against the tree, and try the transponder again.

Nothing.

I don't understand why someone isn't doing a forced transport home; my device doesn't need to be online for that. There are fail-safes in place for many emergencies, including equipment failure. Our scanners, injected just under our skin, have tracking chips so we may be located up to three hundred miles away from our drop zone. If they come searching for me, they can pinpoint my location easily. Maybe I should wait a day for my travel time to catch up to home time before I overreact?

That must be it since I lose time when I transport.

If that's the case, no one will realize there is a problem yet. I'll suck it up for another night and they'll do a forced transport. I give myself a mental pep talk, convinced I can do this. I found a water source and I can hike this stupid dress up and sleep in a branch again. Okay, not ideal I get it, but what other choice is there? I can't breeze into town and announce I have no money but need a room and some dinner for the night. That won't happen, and Marcus could give me away somehow.

I spend most of the day in the grove of trees, trying my transponder every fifteen minutes.

I find wild strawberries and blueberries growing near the river and walnuts from the trees. I try to make my version of trail mix, but I struggle with getting the nuts open. My first couple of attempts to crack them with my boot only turns them to dust. I can't find a rock bigger than a pebble, and I'm not strong enough to break them with my hands. As my frustration comes to a head, I throw one at the tree with such force that it cracks just a little, enough for me to pry it open. While I eat the walnut, my panic subsides as I continue to convince myself that I'll only be here a day, tops. I consider shortening my costume to make it easier to move in, but I'm not uncomfortable enough to accept that risk. If anyone were to discover me like that, it would raise a lot of questions I'm not prepared to answer.

The next day, I'm stiff from spending the night in a branch. I decide to modify the dress later to prepare for what will be my last day here. I haven't seen or heard anyone since I've been here, so I feel confident that my spot remains safe.

I venture down to the river again for water and berries and to take in the sun's warmth.

The morning moves on and my mood vacillates between complete boredom and extreme anxiety.

I mess with the transponder a dozen times with no change. As the sun sets, my hope sinks with it.

Something is very wrong; they should transport me by now. I think of Michael and cry.

Does he know there's something wrong?

He'll be so worried when he finds out I haven't made it back.

I pace back and forth and work myself into a state of panic again. I've never been so helpless and I don't know what to do next. I'll have to move from this tree. I don't look forward to sleeping clinging to a branch for another night; if I do, I won't be able to walk in the morning.

I'm too old for this crap.

I should also think about the immediate future as I can't live on walnuts and berries.

Wrapped up in my thoughts, I take a minute to realize that I hear something—a branch snaps, and then again. I twist around to see a man on a horse looking at me.

Dammit.

This won't turn out good. Even with all my worrying, I hadn't thought about what I'd do if someone found me out here. Which means it's time to wing it, starting now.

FOUR

Los Angeles, California 2070

I wake up to the alarm beeping and the dog climbing out from under the covers to sit on my chest and lick my face.

"Noooooooo, get off me you little beast," I say, laughing and pushing him off.

Five o'clock in the morning and I feel as if I fell asleep an hour ago. Only three days until I start my vacation.

I can do this for two more days.

I'm treating my son Michael and myself to a trip to Aruba, although I may be a tad more enthusiastic about it than he is. I'm not sure it would thrill me to go on a trip with my parent when I was his age, either. The older he gets the less time we spend together, so I've been looking forward to this break. An entire week in the sun at a five-star resort is just what I need. I saved for a full year to pay for it, and as a birthday surprise for him I purchased a ticket for his girlfriend Maddie. I won't be bringing anyone; none of my friends could swing the time off work. And to be honest, I don't have that one friend, that long-term BFF that most women do. The dog snaps me out of my pity party by scratching at the bedroom door, ready to run out to see if Michael's awake yet.

"Okay buddy, hang on, I'll let you out."

I open the door to the smell of burning toast. I can't understand why he insists on using that old toaster when the Chef-Aid will make him whatever he wants.

"Okay, run get him boy."

The dog scampers off in search of Michael, happy at the prospect of a treat. At twenty years old—almost twenty-one—as he reminds me often, Michael has grown into a charismatic young man that any mom would be proud of.

Where did the time go?

It sounds so cliché, but it's true; they grow up in the blink of an eye. He works for the same agency I do; the CCEA, Cyber Criminal Enforcement Agency. I am a prisoner transporter, a glorified chaperone, really, and Michael works in detainee control.

In the early decades of the twenty-first century, prison overcrowding became a serious problem. Looking to develop a plan to ease that, it didn't take the government long to figure out the issue. Cyber criminals were becoming a significant contribution to the problem. A government-funded research facility had been working on time travel for several years, perfecting it in 2060. Six months after introducing the concept, the new law passed in the United States. We would transport criminals hundreds of years to the past. Exiling them to a timeline where no cyber technology exists removes them as a threat to our present day. The rest of the world followed our lead soon after, and now it's common practice in most countries.

I've traveled all over the country in many time periods, but they always confine my travel to the United States, as countries only transport within their own borders. Which is fine with me; I have no desire to traipse all over the globe. Every day there are dozens of transporters doing drop-offs around the world, and we don't know our destinations until the day we travel. It sounds like a great way to get a glimpse into history, but I have seen nothing of real interest in the ten years I've been doing this. They allow us no contact with anyone other than our prisoner while there, and we may not stay long enough to sightsee even if we wanted to.

I glimpse at myself in the bathroom mirror on the way to the shower, and I'm not impressed. I look like I didn't get any sleep at all, and my shoulder-length dark hair is giving even the worst case of bedhead a run for its money. Nothing a hot shower and a little makeup won't cure, so I step into the enclosure, ready for the steaming water to revive me.

"Shower, on."

The water pours out of the overhead nozzle, and I tell the system how I want the temperature adjusted. Having my house outfitted with SmartTec is the best decision I've ever made. I love the convenience of not even having to turn a knob. Once done, I towel off my hair, get dressed, and perform some magic with my makeup. As I step into the kitchen, I hear Michael laughing and scolding Max for stealing his toast.

"Coffee?" I ask.

"Already made it, Mom," he says, nodding toward the counter.

"Only a few days until we're out of here kiddo."

I can't keep the excitement out of my voice, and I can tell he's trying to muster up some enthusiasm for my sake.

"Uh huh, yeah, I'll start packing tonight," he says without looking up from his phone.

"Hey son, if Maddie were to join us, you guys wouldn't run off and leave me alone for the entire trip, would you? I mean, would you be willing to spend some quality time with me during the day at least?"

"What, huh? Mom, we'd totally hang with you. Wait, why are you asking me this?"

Now I have his attention.

"Well, I bought an extra ticket, and she's coming to Aruba. I thought it would be a nice birthday gift for you. Twenty-one years old is a milestone, right?"

"Are you serious? Oh my God, you're the best!" He rushes over to hug me and my heart melts.

"Yes I am, and don't forget that, Son. Let's go, we'll be late unless we take off right now."

I order a doughnut and a cup of coffee from the Chef-Aid.

"I'll be in the car."

"Yep, gonna brush my teeth, be right out."

I watch him start down the hall and stop myself from reminding him to floss. Old habits are hard to break. He taps his phone and I hear him talking to Maddie about the trip as I grab the dog's food from the counter.

"Here's your breakfast Max, try to be a good boy. See you in two days."

He wags his tail and paws the air. I put his food dish down, which he ignores, so I drop him a pinch of doughnut and he trots off, happy with his treat. I juggle my coffee and pastry, checking my phone while I walk to the car. I punch in my alarm code and get comfortable in the seat.

I finish my breakfast while I wait for Michael to come out. I haven't eaten a doughnut in ages.

I'm sure one isn't going to kill me, right?

Once he settles in, I begin my obligatory speech.

"Okay, you remember I'm traveling today, so call your Aunt Kat or Frank if anything comes up. There are plenty of recipes programmed into the Chef-Aid, and you can always choose the shortcut and just ask it what's available with what we have on hand. No parties, make sure you program the security system at night and please let Max out before bed."

"Mom, I realize that you think you need to do this every time you leave, but seriously? You don't. I know how to use the Chef-Aid, I'm not gonna starve. Also, not an idiot, I'll lock the house, and you know Max will want to sleep with me, so I'll put him out. He's not getting into my bed unless he's pee-proof."

Did he just roll his eyes at me?

"You said nothing about the parties."

"Please tell me you're kidding. I'm almost twenty-one, not fifteen. I don't need to throw a party when you go out of town."

"Just checking. This is my only chance to get your full attention, when I have you trapped in the car with me, so I prefer to take advantage of that."

He looks at me and shakes his head before putting his earbuds in and turning to the window.

I've been dismissed.

We pull into the parking lot ten minutes later. It's an imposing building. Only employees and prisoners ever go in—and prisoners don't come out unless they're in a body bag. It's a state-of-the-art facility, but they designed it with no attempt at aesthetic value. Even the landscaping looks utilitarian. Our tax money at work, no doubt.

A real positive the modern world offers is the crimes that once overran society have decreased. Drug dealers, thieves, pedophiles, murderers, and rapists, they've all seen their time come and go. Probation doesn't exist, and early release and plea bargaining are all things of the past. If we convict a criminal of a serious or violent crime, we jail them for life—end of story.

Gangs and drugs were so out of control by 2050 the public didn't feel safe. With the rise in cyber-crime in our highly technical society leading to the overcrowding, time travel as a solution made sense. Once the government decided exiling cyber criminals was a solution, they analyzed risks and secure transport sites. We ran family histories through the database to ensure prisoners were not placed near relatives. A dozen other major issues were identified and resolved, though the law was not without controversy. Human rights activists protested, so to ease that pressure, the authorities made one concession. They would assign transporters to bring the detainees to their destinations, and that's where I come in.

I park the car and finish the last of my coffee before getting out.

"Okay honey, be back in two days, be safe. Love you."

"Yep, love you, Mom. Be safe too and don't worry, everything will be fine. Remember, I take my promotions test this afternoon, so no calling me to have lunch or anything, I'll be studying."

"Oh, God forbid I should want to buy my son lunch."

Twenty minutes ago, I was the best mom in the world. His words, not mine. Now I'm forbidden to call him for lunch. Or anything.

Fine.

"I'm serious Mom, I need to study until the last minute."

It's my turn to roll my eyes. "I heard you Michael, don't worry, I'll do my best to resist hunting you down for a free meal."

I lean over to hug him, but all I get is a quick squeeze on the shoulder as he exits the car.

He heads toward the detainee population unit, where the prisoners are confined until their transport day.

"Please feed Max," I yell after him.

He doesn't break stride or turn around, just lifts a hand in a wave. All right then, off I go.

I walk to the employee entrance and lift my palm to the screen.

"Entry approved."

The sugary, condescending voice always irks me. I open the door and the noise level increases. People are walking in every direction, talking or laughing, the paging system directing employees. It would seem to an outsider that a lot of us don't know where we're supposed to be and they must tell us where we're expected. As the door closes behind me, I look at Frank coming down the hall toward me.

"Hey doll. See Med Check, then orientation at zero nine hundred hours in Station Twelve."

"Good morning to you too, Boss."

"That *is* my good morning greeting, it's more than most people get, so consider yourself special."

I head for the lockers to change into my uniform and put my employee ID necklace on.

We're not allowed to wear our uniforms outside the facility; it's a security thing. Some prisoners are not thrilled about being exiled hundreds of years into the past, and their families are just as angry. We don't need to announce the fact that we're transporters. All that does is give someone the chance to kidnap or hold us hostage, hoping to bring their family member or friend back. It's happened before, hence the rule. I go to Med Check after changing, sign in, and wait my turn.

"Christine Stewart?" A bored-looking aide calls me to a rear room. She leads me to the scanner and waits until I am secured inside.

"Stand still please until the scan is complete."

I'm doing very well, thanks for asking. Not friendly, this one.

"How's my blood pressure?" I ask after the machine does its once-over on me.

She pauses a minute, for dramatic effect, I think. "The physician will review your results with you when she gets here," she deadpans as she closes the door behind her.

The doctor arrives in a few minutes, reading my chart.

"Hi Christine. Everything looks good apart from your blood sugar, which is elevated. What have you had to eat today?"

Wow, I can't get away with anything.

"I had a doughnut earlier with my coffee. Well, more like half a doughnut. The dog had some too."

She is not amused.

"That would explain it. I assume you realize that excessive sugar isn't recommended on a transport day?"

"Well yeah, I guess I didn't think about it, I was in a hurry. How high is it?"

"You're registering at ninety-six."

"Ninety-six? Is that what we're calling high these days?" I laugh a little because it sounds reasonable to me.

"I did not say high, I said elevated. Optimal would be at seventy-five for you as your normal register is between seventy and eighty. Let me present this to the chief of physicians to determine if he'll clear you for transport."

For a level of ninety-six? Is she kidding me?

"I mean isn't that a healthy-ish reading? I understand lower would be better, but that's not dangerously high is it?"

"Any abnormality needs clearance no matter how minor, and I don't agree; ninety-six is significant when compared to your previous range. We require you to maintain excellent health to withstand the stress transporting places on your system. We take that seriously."

Clearly.

"So, do I wait here for word?"

"No, we'll page you once I have an answer," she says, taking notes on her handheld computer.

The paging procedure. I should have guessed.

I walk out of the medical wing to find Frank. He's in his office on a call and gestures for me to sit. He punches the end button a little too hard as he ends the call.

"Really Stewart, a doughnut? On a travel day? You're killing me here."

"That didn't take long. Jeez, it was one flippin' doughnut Frank. You'd think I shot pure sugar into my veins or something. All I did was have breakfast," I say, irritated.

"Well thanks to your 'breakfast', I have to delay orientation until I'm assured you can work today. Everyone wants to thank you, so I'd stay out of sight if I were you."

Great, looking forward to the other transporters on my ass.

"I'm certain they will, Boss. I'll make it a point to stay under the radar until then."

I go to the break room, researching Aruba online. I may as well use the downtime doing something useful.

Two hours later, the page finally comes through. "Christine Stewart, report to Med Check nine." I start for downstairs again, eager to get on with my day.

"Hi, I'm Christine Stewart, someone paged me."

The aide looks at me as if I am the stupidest person she has ever met.

"Yeah, I remember, I checked you in earlier and just put out the page. Follow me."

She's obviously a people person.

The doctor doesn't force me to wait long and appears concerned.

"So, I will order you something to help lower your sugar, and if it comes down within the hour, you will be clear for travel. But if not, I cannot allow you to transport with your level at ninety-six."

"Okay," I say, knowing that arguing is pointless.

I take the injection like a trooper and they have me wait in the lounge. An hour goes by before my new friend the aide motions me to the back and directs me to the scanner again. She reads the results and makes a note on the wall computer.

"Am I down to normal?"

She gives me straight up stink eye and tells me the physician will assess the findings with me when she gets here.

Still a charmer, I see.

After ten minutes, the doctor appears and clears me. I approach orientation Station Twelve and peek through the window in the door. I watch Frank and four other transporters milling around looking bored and pissed off. I steel myself for the onslaught, and right on cue, my entrance sparks the comments I knew were coming.

"A damn doughnut, Stewart? What were you thinking? Any idea how late we are?" McCarty barks.

If I hear 'doughnut' one more time today, I will not be responsible for my actions.

"Yeah, thanks so much for making us sit around for an extra three hours," Bosch says, pocketing her phone and scowling at me.

The others glare at me.

"Okay, settle down people, it's over, let's move on," says Frank as he gives me his own version of a dirty look. "Everyone in position, I'm calling them up"

Frank uses his handheld to give the all clear to bring the prisoners up. They shuffle in one by one with their guards, each looking miserable. They find seats and wait, staring at Frank.

"Welcome to orientation, people. Today you are being transported to your assigned destinations with your transport escorts. You'll each be appointed a transporter to accompany you to your destination and go through your on-site walk-through once there. You will each receive a pack which includes basic survival gear, emergency food and water, medical supplies, and money. You will leave here in period-appropriate clothing. Do not complain about the clothes—you need them to blend in. Do not whine about your geographical or time-period placement. It is all preset by the system and we can do nothing to change it. The department who *can* change it for you won't, so don't ask. Questions?"

The prisoners sit still, and no one says a word.

"Excellent. Moving on, then. You're required to go back a minimum of three generations. You are not to contact any of your relatives, your relatives' spouses, or any other members of your immediate or extended families. While you won't go to an area where any of your known relatives are living, you may not travel to locate them. You also may not be within one hundred miles of any major historical event. This means political or otherwise. You can review your individual paperwork later for examples, each of you have specific off-limit events and areas for your new timelines. Under no circumstances are you to interfere with any historical event or do anything that could change our current timeline. You have all had trackers injected in undisclosed areas of your body while we sedated you for your sterilizations. They are only removable with a surgical extraction device. So, do yourself a favor and don't cut holes in yourself trying to discover where the surgeons inserted it. If you contact anyone in your family, or you are within the aforementioned one-hundred-mile restricted area or event, you will be transported further back in time and to another area. With no notice."

Frank pauses for effect, taking the time to look around the room at each of the prisoners.

"Let me say again, with no notice. The enforcement team will not hesitate to transport you. And trust me, they'll find out, they always do—the system tracks you twenty-four-seven, three hundred and sixty-five days a year. You cannot procreate, because as I just mentioned, and you all know, that was done when you first arrived here. You may request an anti-anxiety injection should you feel you require it. You need to see a med aide for that, so please inform your transporter ASAP if you choose to exercise that option. Okay, let's go to your assigned transporters so you have your placement information. Please sound off when you hear your name called so we know who you are."

Frank looks at the prisoners to make certain they are still paying attention.

"Thomas, Dillion, we assign you to Officer Williams, going to Smithfield, New York, 1751. Cooper, David, you are assigned to Officer McCarty, heading to Charles City, Virginia, 1621. Burnett, Darryl, you are going with Officer Paxton to Houston, Texas, 1820. Simpson, Marcus, you're with Officer Stewart, leaving for Piedmont, Oklahoma, 1867. And last, Taylor, Christopher, you are appointed to Officer Bosch, transporting to Green River, Wyoming, 1868."

The rebuttals start as soon as he reads the first assignment. It doesn't faze Frank; he's accustomed to it and continues to read right through his list. The prisoners continue to protest and are getting louder by the minute. Frank slaps his hand hard on the desk in front of him, startling the room into silence.

"I will only say this one time, so listen up. If you are belligerent, I will consider you combative and you will be sedated. No questions asked, no second chances. This is happening today, whether you like it or not, so I would suggest you settle down and pay attention to the rest of the orientation. The things we review with you could very well save your life. After this you are going to the History Lab to receive a brief education on your placement site. This is invaluable information on how to blend into your new world and help handle any emergencies, should they arise. As I mentioned earlier, you are each getting a handout with some basic rules you are to follow once you arrive at your destinations. Read through it and make your transporter aware of questions. You have thirty minutes to read the pamphlet. After that we will watch a film, so you understand the importance of keeping your mouths shut once you arrive at your assigned destination."

As it settles down, I look at my prisoner.

Is he crying? Great.

He looks young, and they are always the hardest to transport. His entire life will be shit after this, and he's realizing that. I walk over to him and sit down.

"Read your pamphlet and let me know if you need guidance or have questions, okay? I'm here to support you. And don't sleep during the film—it's important."

He looks away for a minute.

"Listen lady, I don't need your condescending ass preaching to me like you're my mother or something. Just leave me the fuck alone, and I'll do the same."

Well, okay then. He wants to do it that way. Let's try a different approach.

"Listen to me carefully, asshole. I'm here to help you through this, whether you believe that or not. I am trying to make sure you don't get yourself killed in the first twenty-four hours of your placement. If you choose to blow me off, fine—but I guarantee you'll regret that decision later. In the meantime, you will treat me with respect. If you continue with your crappy attitude, I'll have Frank call to sedate you right now. He has zero tolerance for disrespect. Do you really want to wake up in Oklahoma alone and without a clue what to do? Make your choice now. I can be your best ally, or I can order your injection and you can piss away your only chance to survive this in one piece."

He looks at me with wide eyes, and then the tears roll down his cheeks.

"I'm only twenty-three, man, this isn't fair. My whole life is over. I'll never see my family again, or my girlfriend, and what the hell am I supposed to do in Oklahoma, for fuck's sake?"

"You need to accept this, no matter how difficult. This is happening, so wrap your head around it and absorb all the information available. You will use all of it once you're in Oklahoma."

He drops his head into his hands and wipes his eyes.

"Yeah, whatever, I'm fine. Just let me be and I'll do everything I'm supposed to."

"Okay, make sure you do, Marcus. And stay attentive during the film. You'll have plenty of time to feel sorry for yourself later."

I settle into a chair in the back of the room with the other transporters, ready to watch the film I've seen many times before.

FIVE

Los Angeles, California 2070 / Salem, Massachusetts 1692

The prisoners finish reading their pamphlets and sit staring into space looking shell-shocked.

None of them have questions, they rarely do. Is there a way to prepare traveling back in time, leaving everything you've ever known behind? This is the stage when they realize there's no road out of this and they ready themselves for the inevitable.

If they think they're freaked out now, the film will send some of them over the edge. A program like this has obvious psychological effects on the individuals being transported, and the government needed to understand where things worked and where they might go wrong. So, when the program was in its development stages, they selected a few transporters and detainees as test cases. These cases were recorded and analyzed later. Transporters stayed with their prisoners for a few days and wore body cams integrated into their clothing for observation. The missteps reported in those cases are what we use today for training. The orientation film outlines how matters can go very wrong, quickly. It remains the most extreme case to come out of the tests.

The transporter in the documentary is Erin Hawkins. I don't know why her name is burned into my mind the way it is. Maybe it's because the footage has such an effect on me every time I see it. She had a body cam embedded in the brooch she wore on her period dress, and she recorded most of her life there, although it was edited down. It had been an excellent idea to record events, as we needed to learn how people reacted to transporters and prisoners, and how they both handled themselves. No matter how much preparation, there would be snags to work out. We expected issues we hadn't thought of or planned for. To give the detainees the strongest chance for survival, everything was reviewed and dissected.

Things with Erin and her prisoner started out as expected. They jumped to the assigned destination in Salem, Massachusetts in 1692 without incident. The woman Erin transported was named Sarah Good. She was a brilliant mathematician and computer sciences professor at an Ivy League university, but she was difficult to manage. Erin spent the entire first day there trying to acclimate Sarah to her surroundings by reviewing survival techniques and period etiquette. It became a lesson in futility, as she remained uncooperative and unresponsive.

Erin tried her best to make Sarah comply with the guidelines, but on their second day there she realized that her prisoner had no intention of cooperating. She had no choice but to release her and allow her to find her path into town alone. Erin's orders were to follow at a distance and record as much of the experience as possible. She was to have no direct contact with her prisoner once she released her. Erin made her best effort to document as much of Sarah's daily life as she could, but she didn't make it easy. She spent a good deal of her day in the woodlands, living in a homeless encampment. It proved difficult for Erin to follow her there without raising suspicions about herself. In retrospect, Sarah was not an ideal candidate for the trial run because of her unwillingness to cooperate. That defiance was the catalyst for some of the most horrific moments in our nation's history.

Erin stayed at a local inn in Salem Town, while Sarah lived on her own on the Salem Village side of town. While technically these two were the same municipality, Ipswich Road separated the areas. They could not have been more different. Salem Town was prosperous, while Salem Village was mainly full of poor farmers, beggars, and the homeless.

Sarah was ill-prepared for her life there, despite Erin's best efforts. The towns were both occupied by devoutly religious Puritans who looked down on beggars and the destitute with a deep-seated disdain. She would move from house to house begging for food with the other homeless people. After several days of this, Sarah realized what she would be in for here, and she made it known—she was not happy about it. On day three, she found Erin walking through town, and the sight of her triggered something in Sarah. Medical would later refer to it as a break with reality because of extreme stress. That's an understatement. Erin watched her approach and did her best to avoid her, however she kept advancing and reached her before she could make her getaway.

"Hey, I can't stay here! You need take me home, or somewhere else. I'm a respected, tenured professor, for God's sake! I have rights! Give me that damn transponder!" she screamed as she lunged for Erin. Erin avoided the lunge and took two quick steps backward.

"Madam! Leave me alone at once or it will force me to call for help!"

"Good! Call anyone you wish, let's tell them all who we are and what we're doing here!"

"Sarah, keep your voice down, you will get us killed, for God's sake!" Erin whispered, but the microphone in her brooch picked it up.

"Don't tell me to be quiet, I'm done going along with this bullshit!"

Erin turned to walk elsewhere, when Sarah ran after her and stood in front of her.

"Listen to me, goddammit! I demand to talk to someone from home. I want your supervisor here, right now!"

"And I'm advising you for the last time, get out of my way and leave me alone. You will regret doing this, Sarah, and there will be nothing I can do to save you. Don't you realize that? God, don't be so shortsighted. You're starting to draw attention to yourself, and that's the last thing you want here. I will transport home either way and leave you here to deal with whatever mess you've created."

"Screw you, Hawkins."

"Just remember, you did this to yourself, Sarah."

With that, Erin moved around Sarah to stand closer to the circle of people forming as they continued to grow louder. She realized if this were to spiral out of control, she would need to move quickly. Luckily, she'd had the sense to keep her transponder tucked into her undergarments—she didn't dare leave it at the Inn where it might be discovered.

"Well? What's wrong, transporter Hawkins? At a loss for words? Fine, I'll tell them. She,"—she walked up to Erin and pointed at her, her finger grazing Erin's neck—"is from the future. I am too. That's right. We came here together from the year 2070! She transported me and now she's recording all of this so they can study it later. Well, I refuse to be a guinea pig for some bullshit psychological experiment where we are tossed back in time like a damn bag of trash! Do you hear me, Hawkins?" she screamed.

That did it for Erin. Sarah put it out there, no taking it back now. Most people in the crowd appeared confused, a few were whispering among themselves.

She turned to Sarah and said, "Leave me alone, witch! Don't touch me! Someone please, help me and get this witch away from me!"

She took a few steps back, continuing to ask for help.

Someone yelled out, "Witch!" Another cried out, "Devil!" The crowd jumped on that, and inside of one minute they were chanting. "Witch, witch, witch!"

"What the hell are you idiots talking about?" Sarah shrieked. "Get us out of here, Hawkins!"

Erin said nothing. How could she? If she aligned herself with Sarah now, they were both dead. She was under strict orders and was trying her best to adhere to them. Reassigning her prisoner was not something she could do, and Sarah had placed herself in this situation by breaking the rules.

The crowd worked itself into a frenzy within minutes. People pumped their fists and chanted "Devil!" and "Witch! over and over, getting louder with each passing minute. Sarah looked at the gathering crowd frantically, then reached under her dress to pull out a mini lighter. How she got that past all the checkpoints, we never figured out. To bring back anything other than your survival pack is prohibited.

She held the lighter up for everyone to see.

"Look, here's proof that I'm telling the truth! This is technology from the future that starts fire."

When she flicked it on, the people gasped and she charged a man in the huddle, touching the flame to his jacket. Flames started to form on the bottom hem of the garment, and the woman next to him appeared to faint before someone caught her. Women wailed and men lunged forward to tamp down the flames. The man stood looking at his clothing, stunned. Matches wouldn't be invented until the 1800s. This was like nothing these people could imagine.

"Devil fire!" someone shouted. "She's a witch!"

Many of them were crazed by this point. Sarah stood in the middle, surrounded by out-of-control people screaming, and she gawked at them as if she was oblivious to it all. The entire incident didn't take over ten minutes to escalate from her stopping Erin to this. She scanned the gathering and her body cam caught it all. The constables arrived, and the townspeople demanded Sarah's arrest as a witch. No one wanted to touch the lighter out of fear, so it remained on the ground, right where Sarah had dropped it. They arrested her, but as soon as they turned to move her, she snapped out of her stupor and began to kick and scream.

"I'm from Los Angeles in the year 2070, and so is she!" She twisted her head to find Erin, but she had already slipped behind the first layer of bodies in the crowd.

"No, you can't do this! Search her hotel room, you'll find her transponder, then you'll know I'm stating the truth! I'm not a witch!"

A few people turned to look at Erin. She stood up straight and lifted her chin.

"You may examine every corner of my room if you wish to. I have nothing to hide! She is clearly a witch—you've seen what she did."

The people started to stir again, when someone cried out, "Search her room!" Others started to join in, yelling out, "Let her prove she isn't a witch too!"

"You will not treat me this way. Send the constables if you wish and come with me right away to inspect my accommodations."

She started to walk away, followed by three men trailing behind. They arrived at the Inn a few minutes later, where she opened the door to her room and swept her arm out in front of her, motioning them inside.

"Please, search whatever you'd like. I assure you, you will find nothing extraordinary. I do not know that woman or why she tormented me, but she's evidently doing the work of the devil."

"You don't know her?"

"Certainly not! She appears to be a vagrant, and I am only visiting your town, having arrived just yesterday."

"What business brings you to Salem?" he asked, rifling through the desk as the other two search the suite.

"I am traveling to visit my sister in Boston, she is birthing her first child soon, and I am to help her get settled. I only stopped here for a day or two. I was feeling ill and thought I might rest and hire a coach for the remainder of the trip."

"Why are you traveling alone? Where is your husband?"

"My husband in an officer in the Third Massachusetts Regiment and is preparing for the possibility of resistance from the Indians. His duties require that he remain at his post until the threat has passed. I am perfectly capable of traveling alone to my sister's home, Mr. . . . . . I apologize, what was your name?"

"Smith, Albert Smith. I am the governor here in Salem. And you are?"

"Mrs. John Hawkins. I trust that this satisfies your examination of my belongings? As you see, nothing here should give you any cause for concern. That woman is obviously disturbed."

"Yes, things seem in order here, my apologies, madam. I must ask you to remain in Salem for a few days though. That woman will go to trial tomorrow at the Court of Oyer and Terminer, and I'm certain that we shall expect your testimony."

"I understand, and I'm at your call should you require my testament. I'm just relieved that they have taken her into custody where she can do no more harm to anyone."

"We'll be on our way and be in touch with details as needed."

"Thank you, Mr. Smith, I will await word from you."

The two men left, leaving Erin unsettled. She was shaking so badly that when she took her brooch off and angled it toward herself, the video trembled forcefully.

"This is Agent Hawkins, January 12, 1692, Salem, Massachusetts. If anyone is monitoring, please notify me, I'll leave my transponder on. I'm not sure what you want me to do here, please advise."

The recording picked up the following day as Erin walked out of the Inn. People gathered outside town hall where the courtroom was on the second floor.

Mr. Smith approached her quickly.

"Mrs. Hawkins, I was coming to see you. The hearing starts this morning and requires you there for your testimony."

"Of course, Mr. Smith."

Erin watched the townspeople move to the watch house where the constables had held Sarah, the day before. She saw two men half dragging her to the courthouse. She looked like she had aged ten years overnight. Her hair was matted, her dress torn at the shoulder. What had happened in there? Sarah saw Erin and started to mouth something, but stopped, tears filling her eyes.

They took her into the courthouse, and Erin followed the crowd inside. She took a seat in the back so her body cam would record as much of the trial and surroundings as possible. They packed the courtroom to the brim, standing room only. They shackled Sarah to a chair that had a wood railing built around it. She stared out blankly and seemed disassociated from the whole event.

The lighter had been her undoing. She could have talked her way out of her meltdown by acting like a crazy person; irritating but harmless. But the lighter set her fate on a path there was no recovering from.

Chief Magistrate William Stoughton hammered his gavel, bringing the crowd's attention to the front of the room. The crown's prosecuting attorney, Thomas Newton, looked thrilled. He paced back and forth a few times for dramatic effect before he spoke.

"We are here for the trial of Sarah Good. She practiced witchcraft in public, in the presence of many witnesses, when she created a fire with this machinery."

He lifted a glass bowl that contained the lighter. The court erupted into gasps and yells of "Witch! Devil!"

Sarah stared at the prosecutor her eyes wild.

"I am not a witch! You people are crazy! It's only a lighter for fuck sakes," she shrieked.

"Guard! Silence the prisoner!" he shouted.

The guard walked to Sarah taking a short whip with him. You could hear Erin's gasp on her microphone as he lashed her across the back several times. As she wrenched forward in pain, he punched her in the face. Her screams echoed through the courtroom as people called out, "Whip her!" and "Beat the evil out of her!" He lifted the whip to her once more as Prosecutor Newton watched with no emotion. Sarah passed out after a few minutes and lay hunched over the edge of the wood railing. Her chest rose and fell faintly, but that was the only sign she was still alive.

"Please, ladies and gentlemen, if we can proceed." Magistrate Stoughton banged his gavel once again, and people started to quiet down. "I understand that everyone would prefer to be here for this hearing, however, I must insist that we remain civilized and keep order."

"Thank you, sir." Newton rose to resume his pacing. "If I may continue, several witnesses saw her perform witchcraft in audience. Your Honor, why do we need to exhaust the town's resources with a hearing? Why do we desire to waste the time of these respectable citizens?"

He swept his hand across the crowd. "Twenty townspeople saw what she did. We have the instrument she used, unlike any other we have ever seen. It is the work of the Devil! We must destroy this apparatus and hang her before the sun sets today, to protect the residents of this township!"

The place exploded once again. People jumped up this time, leaning over the barricade between the prosecutor's table and the audience seats. The magistrate pounded the gavel on the desk, quieting the crowd. They all knew his next words would be pivotal in the outcome of this so-called trial. Sarah moaned and appeared to stir.

"Well, you drive an excellent point, Mr. Newton. While this seems a clear-cut case, it is my duty to see she receives a fair trial."

"Your Honor, I have witnesses to testify to the fact that this woman is a witch! You have here the very object she used to light an innocent man on fire!"

Stoughton glanced at Sarah, then at the prosecutor.

"And what does Ms. Good say, Mr. Newton? Does she confess to the crime we accuse her of?"

The prosecutor snapped his fingers at the guard and pointed toward Sarah. He grabbed her hair to pull her head up. Her face was bloody and swollen. She moved her eyes to look at Newton.

"Well, tell us, are you a witch? Do you profess to your crimes?" Newton asked.

Sarah didn't break eye contact with him.

"Screw you, you piece of shit. I hope you die screaming. Go to hell, all of you!" she shouted.

She spit at the prosecutor's feet and laid her head down on the balustrade. There were gasps from the crowd as they started to murmur. The prosecutor watched Stoughton looking at Sarah in disbelief. He sat up straight and cleared his throat.

"I agree with Mr. Newton; I see no reason to continue. The prisoner is seemingly not interested in defending herself, and the evidence is clear. I do not feel the need to hear testimony. I am prepared to hand down the sentence."

The audience burst to life anew. People were clapping and shouting their approval. He held his hand up and the courtroom went silent almost immediately.

"I condemn this prisoner to death by hanging at Gallows Hill, enforced tomorrow at dawn."

Newton smiled and nodded to him.

"Praise you, Your Honor. You've done the town justice here today. We must be diligent in removing threats to our decent citizens. Guard, please remove the prisoner from court and secure her in the watch house until we carry her sentence out tomorrow."

Newton faced the courtroom.

"Let this be a lesson to you. I shall deal swiftly and severely with all found to be a witch. I will try as well, any person hiding or protecting someone who is practicing witchcraft."

Sarah looked up, locking eyes with Erin. Her expression said it all; she was resigned to her fate. The guard wrenched her from the seat and headed her out of the courthouse. As she passed through the aisle, people spit at her or threw things, and all of them yelled "Witch!" or "Devil!" at her. Her gaze never left Erin's as they led her from the courthouse.

SIX

Salem, Massachusetts 1692 / Los Angeles, California 2070

Erin turned to watch Sarah being led from the courtroom, her body cam recording the anguish on her face. The angry crowd followed them to the street and to the watch house, shouting all the way. Transporters may not contact base for any other reason than emergency transport. To do that, we send a distress beacon that alerts them to begin a forced exit. I've often wondered why Erin didn't use that. To see her prisoner being whipped, beaten, and dragged away—it must have been surreal. She received accolades for her bravery and composure under extreme circumstances upon her return, but in that moment, she had to be feeling some of the agony that Sarah was.

As I look around the room at the current group of prisoners, I see it's affecting them. A couple try to maintain a brave face, but most stare at the screen looking horrified. Frank stops the film for a ten-minute break, and most of the prisoners stay in their seats, talking amongst themselves. I am sick to my stomach, as I always am when I see this film. I think about what I would do in Erin's place; I don't feel I could watch Sarah being beaten and arrested for witchcraft without intervening. I often wonder if base answered her request for guidance, and if so, what did they tell her to do? Carry on and let it play out? I guess I'll never know, though I'm certain I could not lead the crowd in the direction she did. It must weigh on her heavily to recognize that she was the catalyst that began the Salem witch trials. Easy for me to say as an outsider, I know, but I just don't think I'm wired that way. Hopefully I won't ever need to find out. At the time she did not consider the impact of her actions. But once home, history had changed, and she learned of the atrocities during debriefing.

Ten minutes later, Frank calls the room to order, and the film picks up with Sarah being led out of the watch house the next morning. Erin's body cam follows her as she's brought to the center of town, a handful of people trailing her. More people wait at Gallows Hill. Two men push and pull her up onto the platform where they wrap the noose loosely around her neck, her torn clothes exposing her wounds. He must hold her up, as she cannot stand on her own.

The man at the podium holds up his hand, silencing the crowd. It becomes eerily quiet almost immediately.

"We are here today to carry out the death sentence of this witch!"

As he points to Sarah, the man keeping her upright lifts her face up to the people. Her eyes roll into her head, and she coughs softly.

"Do you confess your crime? Confess, and we will show mercy."

She takes a moment to open her bruised and swollen eyes.

"I confess nothing. But if you think I'm a witch, you must also conclude that I can curse you. And I will, believe that."

She drops her head back down and the crowd murmurs. Several people step out of the group and walk away hurriedly, not wanting to take a chance on being cursed for taking part in the hanging. The man holding her looks unsure, but the other continues unfazed.

"Very well then, we will show no mercy. You will hang and burn at the stake."

The remaining crowd cheer and whistle. The man holding Sarah pulls her upright and tightens the noose around her neck while the other walks to the lever that will drop the planks she is standing on. The man standing near the lever who seems to be running the show nods toward the other man, who lets go of Sarah. The other man pulls the lever and her body drops for an instant before being pulled up violently. The rope goes taut around her neck.

At that moment it's as if they flip a switch on inside her; she kicks and twists, trying to loosen the rope, but with her hands bound behind her it's impossible to make any difference. It seems like an incredibly long time before she's still again. The man at the lever twists the rope pulley to lower it, dumping her unceremoniously onto the platform. As if she is only a bag of trash.

It's a sickening sight to see, and the enormity of what they just saw seems to sink in with the prisoners. Some lay their heads down on their arms on the table, while others shake their heads and look aside. They load her onto a cart and wheel her off the platform and across the dirt to a pile of wood. They throw her on top of the wood heap and toss a torch on top. People pull their clothing over their faces to mask the smell of her burning flesh. Erin stays to document until the last of the crowd has dispersed. She turns off her body cam as she walks away from what is left of the wood pile.

"Okay people, heads up please."

Frank turns the lights on, walking to the front of the room.

"I hope this impressed on you why you should not run your mouth off when you get to your assigned location. I will say it once again—where you're going, they do not tolerate different. They fear the unknown and they will not hesitate to torture or kill you because you make them uncomfortable."

Christopher Taylor, Nancy Bosch's prisoner stands up to yell at Frank. "That was so fucked up. I can't believe the government allowed that to happen! Is that what the transporters do? Throw us to the wolves like that if there's trouble? Man, I say we get away from them the minute we can. If that's the way they're gonna do us, what the hell good are they?"

"Read your pamphlets, people. Transporters can have no contact once they release a prisoner; she followed protocol. That prisoner had only herself to blame for what happened. Her transporter tried to warn her twice, and she just wouldn't let up."

Frank lowers his eyes as he speaks. He can't hide what he is feeling; he finds the film as disturbing as everyone else who sees it does.

The only good thing to come out of this—it gets the message across to prisoners. Keep your mouths shut. People fear what they don't understand, and fearful people react rashly.

"Okay, let your transporter know if you have questions, and when you're ready, your next stop is the historical training lab. You'll spend the next two hours with your coach, who'll give you a rundown on your time and location; what to expect, cultural information, etcetera.

After you finish up there, you'll go to concessions, where we issue your survival kit. Your transporter will review each item with you, so you understand what they are and how to use them. After that, the cafeteria and a one-hour lunch. From there you'll go to medical for vaccines, and next to your one-hour family visit with your four chosen family members. Once that visit has concluded, your final station will be uniforms, where you will change into your period-appropriate attire. Then you're ready for the jump room and travel prep. Questions?"

The room is so quiet you can hear a pin drop. They all continue to stare at Frank, reality setting in. I walk over to Marcus and sit next to him.

"Do you have questions for me yet?"

"I don't know. It's a lot to absorb to be honest."

He looks so young; he's not much older than Michael. I shake my head to snap myself out of it. I can't let myself feel sorry for him and still do my job.

"Let's hang out here for a minute and review your packet, see if any questions come up. Make sure you're familiar with your restricted areas and events. I'll be right up front, and if nothing comes up, we can continue down to the history lab."

"Yeah, okay."

I walk up to Frank, who's swiping the computer screen on his desk.

"So, is everyone pissed off at me because I made the egregious error of eating a doughnut this morning?" I ask, half sitting on the corner of his desk.

"Well, I'm not sure any of them will want to join your fan club anytime soon, if that's what you're asking."

"Yeah, well, it's an exclusive club, so who says I'd welcome them, anyway? Michael's taking his promotion test today, so he has banned me from calling him for lunch. You want to get something to eat with me while my guy is in History Lab?"

"You know I would doll, but I'm buried under this budget approval and I have to leave on time today or Linda will shoot me. We're going to dinner with her sister and her new husband tonight. I can't wait. He seems like a prick who I will need to smack into next week. Why don't you ask Bosch to go?"

I scoff at him as I glance over at Bosch who's sidled up to Paxton, laughing and batting her eyelashes at him.

"Frank, you know I'm not great with girlfriends," I answer with a heavy sigh.

He looks at Paxton and Bosch and grunts before stabbing a finger at the screen and resuming his work.

"Fine, I guess I'll go back to the library and hang out there, out of sight from my admirers."

"Yeah, might be good to give them some space until they forget your 'egregious' error," he says without looking up.

My prisoner waves at me and I make my way over to him.

"I guess I don't have questions."

"All right, to the history lab then."

I raise my hand to let Frank know we're ready to leave for the first floor. He picks up the phone and signals back to me it'll be one minute. A few minutes afterward, the guards arrive to shackle Marcus.

"What the hell? Why do I need shackles?"

"It's policy, we restrain all prisoners outside this secured floor, for your safety and ours."

"What a bunch of bullshit."

"Nevertheless, we aren't leaving this room without shackles."

The guard puts the shackles on him, and I lead him out of the room to the elevator. We arrive on the first floor and make our way to the historical training workshop. I sign us in, and we wait for them to call us. Ten minutes later, a woman walks into the waiting room with a handheld computer.

"Simpson, ID number 16859?"

"Right here," I reply, standing up.

I pull my charge up, as he doesn't seem very enthusiastic about introducing himself.

"Hi, I'm Taylor, I'm your coach today."

"Hey," he says, not bothering to look up.

"Okay, you'll be here two hours, so I will finish up your file and I'll be back before your session is up," I say.

He doesn't acknowledge me, so I tell Taylor to page me if there are any issues, and watch as he follows her through the doors of the holding area. I run down to the cafeteria, but nothing looks good. The now infamous doughnut has given me heartburn.

The gift that keeps on giving, how fortunate for me.

I sit at a table near the window and surf the net. Lots of things to do in Aruba, it turns out and I reserve a zipline adventure for the three of us. I DocuSign Marcus's paperwork and travel disclaimers and still have about an hour left before I need to go to the lab to pick him up.

I move through the cafeteria line to buy some antacid, trying to kill time, and call my sister to remind her I'm traveling today. I feel short-timer syndrome coming on, that excitement you have when only days away from vacation. I just want to complete this transport and go. I wouldn't even take on a transport this close to vacation, but Martinez broke his arm, so he'll be on restricted duty for a while. I won the lucky draw and get to go in his place.

I hear my name being paged to report to the historical training lab.

Great, why did he get out early, I wonder?

I open the door to the lab, and Marcus and Taylor are already in the waiting room.

"What's up? Why's he finished so early?" I ask Taylor.

"Mr. Simpson isn't interested in learning about his time placement, so he's opted out of historical training."

"Really, Marcus? Are you certain? This information is useful later."

He glances at me and shakes his head.

"Yeah, I'm positive. I can handle it on my own."

"All right, but I think that's a bad decision. Let's go up to concessions then."

I lead him to the elevator, and we ride up to the third floor to concessions. I log us in and wait to pick up his pack. The clerk heaves the knapsack over the counter and pushes it toward me.

"Here you go. One survival pack for prisoner number 16859—Simpson, bound for Oklahoma, 1867."

"Thanks," I say as I hoist it over my shoulder.

"What the hell is that?" he asks, sneering at the pack.

"This is what passes as a backpack in 1867. It's not that bad, at least it's leather."

He scoffs as I lead him to an empty table and open the pack.

"Okay, let's go through these things one by one so you understand what they are and how to use them."

I go through the pack, checking the contents. It has all the basics including emergency water and purification apparatus. We always send high calorie protein bars, food replacement capsules and a few dozen one-dose broad-spectrum antibiotics. They added flint and a wool blanket to the list last month.

"Marcus, there's one hundred dollars in period money in here. That's a lot of money in 1867."

"What do I need antibiotics for?"

"Well, what if you have a cut and it gets infected? Or you step on a rusty nail? Who knows? But if you ever need them, you'll be glad you've got them, I'm confident of that much."

"Yeah, whatever."

"Okay then, if you don't have questions, we can go down to the cafeteria for lunch."

We make our way to the cafeteria and I bring him through the line. I order a salad but only pick at it; the damn doughnut is still giving me a little heartburn, even after the antacid I bought earlier.

So, this is forty? One doughnut wreaks havoc on my stomach for the better part of the day? How delightful.

My alarm dings on my watch phone to signal the hour is up.

"Let's go. Up to medical for your vaccines."

"What do I need vaccines for? I don't want any injections."

Ummm, so you don't die? Jeez, does this guy have to argue every point?

"Because there are diseases in 1867 wiped out years ago. We no longer have any immunity to them. You need protection to stay healthy. Some of them will kill you unless you get inoculated."

"What the hell? I can get sick and die there? I don't have enough to worry about? This is so fucked up."

"You're not listening to me—I said *unless* we vaccinate you, which we're on our way to do right now. So, nothing to be concerned about. Our medical technology is light-years ahead of anything they had in the 1800s. A couple of injections and you're good."

We get back in the elevator to travel to the eighth floor, where we sign in and wait again for someone to call him in. Twenty minutes later, the aide calls us in to a room. The nurse is already there waiting with the vaccines.

"Hi, I'm Cynthia, I'm giving you your vaccines today. We give all pharmaceuticals in an injection in your arm. You will feel a small prick and that'll take care of it. The doctor has ordered ten drugs, given in five injections, some of them taken together. Okay, so let's roll your sleeve up and get this done, yes? Ain't nuthin' to it but to do it!"

She grins at Marcus and reaches for him when he jerks his arm back and tucks it close to his side.

"Hang on, I wanna know what I'm getting. Don't I have a right to know that?"

Cynthia glances at me and I nod my head impatiently.

"Um, sure. You're receiving scarlet fever, tuberculosis, typhus, smallpox, measles, chicken pox, cholera and three strains of influenza. The flu comes in one vaccine. You also receive whooping cough, yellow fever and acute coryza, commonly referred to as a cold."

"I don't know what some of those are. I don't need them."

"And you don't want to, trust me. If you're assigned to the 1800s, you'll require them. Those diseases have the potential to kill you. Without vaccines you won't be able to tolerate even the smallest thing like a cold," Cynthia says.

I sigh heavily, my patience just about gone.

"Marcus, we're trying to give you the best chance for survival we can. Vaccines aren't an option, they're a requirement."

I can't remember anyone who ever objected to the vaccine process. I cross my arms over my chest and peer at him.

"I can have Cynthia here sedate you and give you the injections, or you can cooperate and just get on with it."

This guy is a piece of work. He sticks his arm out like a petulant teenager and glares at poor Cynthia. I look at her and roll my eyes, and she smiles at me as she injects him.

"There, that wasn't so bad was it? Now you won't die back there. Well, at least not from those diseases." She smiles and gives him a friendly pat at the injection site.

He pulls his arm back once again, frowning at her, "Not cool, not cool at all."

I purse my lips to hide my smile.

SEVEN

Los Angeles, California 2070

We complete vaccines with no further trouble and wait in a holding room for the next hour to be sure Marcus has no adverse or allergic reaction to the injections. Once we're given the all clear, we head to the elevators, where I've spent the better part of my day. Because we are alone for the trip up to the visiting center, I offer him some guidance.

"Listen, Marcus, this next part is difficult. I just want you to prepare for it. Saying goodbye to your family is tough. Who do you have scheduled in today?"

"My parents, my brother, and my girlfriend."

"Let me give you some advice. Keep it together, at least until you leave the room. That will be hard, I understand. But for your family's sake, try. You'll regret it if you break down and it'll torture them forever. Reassure them. You'll be glad you did later."

"So now you're an expert and gonna tell me how to handle myself with my family? You don't know crap about me or them, so don't stand there and pretend that you give two shits about what happens to us."

"You're right, I don't know any of you. But I am a mom, and if you care about yours at all, you'll trust me and do what I say for her sake. That's all I'm saying. Allow her and the rest of your loved ones a chance to move on with their lives. Don't taint your last memory of them and don't have them remember you in distress. Your mother will worry about you forever, and if you can ease that even a bit for her, wouldn't you do so? I'm being as transparent as possible with you. I'd want someone to do that for my son."

I've seen it too many times. People clinging to each other while the transporter calls guards in to drag the prisoner out, their visitors watching. Every time it happens, they want to go back later, to tell their families they will be fine, to reassure them. But by then it's too late; they can't, that is the last memory they have of their loved ones. Maybe I feel sorry for this kid because he's so young. I try to imagine how I would handle myself if it were my son getting exiled, and the thought makes me sick to my stomach. I can't envision living my life without Michael.

We exit on the eleventh floor and arrive at the visiting center. I check us in, and we're led to a private room where Marcus's visitors are waiting for us. The CCEA require transporters to stay with prisoners during the visit. We confirm they have smuggled nothing in and don't ask visitors to tweak history or contact relatives. This part of my day is always awkward and intrusive. It's such a private time between the prisoner and their guests. Yet there I am, looming in the room's corner. A huge black cloud, a reminder of what's coming.

The guard reviews the rules with us before we enter. He can't receive or give anything to his visitors. He cannot inquire about familial history or where previous generations lived. We allow no physical contact when the visit concludes. We enter the visiting room, and I see Marcus's parents have been crying. They both smile when they see him, putting on a brave face for his sake, no doubt. I ask the guard to unshackle him, and the minute he's free the girl who must be his girlfriend runs toward him and wraps her arms around his neck.

The guard tells me he'll be outside if I need him and looks at the family making sure they've heard him. Marcus unfurls himself from her and hugs his parents. The tears start again, and his brother turns to the wall, not wanting us to see him cry. Marcus sits between his mom and his girlfriend on the couch, each holding one of his hands. They all stay silent for a minute until his father tells him about what's been happening with family and friends since his incarceration. Laughing and joking they seem to have a nice visit. I notice his mother glancing my way out of the corner of my eye. I'm staring straight ahead attempting not to impose when I see her break away and walk over to me.

"Are you my son's transporter?"

"Yes, hi, Agent Stewart."

"Hello, DiAnna Simpson. Am I allowed, I mean, is it okay, if I ask you a question? What are the chances my son will survive there?"

She tears up, and I glance away. One, so I don't tear up, and two, to establish she isn't acting as a distraction so someone else can hand off paraphernalia to my prisoner.

Everyone is still in the same place, father and brother on one couch, Marcus and his girlfriend on the other.

"He'll be fine, Mrs. Simpson. He has completed his training and I've reviewed everything with him. We've vaccinated him against every deadly disease for his placement time and have given him the opportunity to have a good life. We'll arrive there safely. After that it will be up to him, but he's a smart guy, and I have no reason to believe he won't succeed."

I don't mention that he neglected to complete his historical coaching, I find it hard to kick someone when they're already down.

"I understand I may not hug you without the guards storming in and arresting me, or worse, but know that I want to. Thank you for helping my son. I have no idea if you're a mother or not but knowing that you're supporting him is a comfort to me. Thank you."

I smile and nod at her and she returns to her son. She holds his hand and smiles back at me. This is the first time I've seen Marcus laugh, which is understandable, and he seems relaxed.

The hour passes quickly, and the guard comes in, ending the visit. I see the panic on their faces as he moves to shackle Marcus.

"Wait, we have a few minutes!" Mr. Simpson starts toward his son, but the guard intervenes.

"No physical contact from this point forward sir."

He steps between them, snapping the shackles on.

His family hug and cry as he glances at me before turning to face them.

"Listen up, everyone. I'm gonna be fine. My transporter here has gone over everything with me, twice. I'm actually looking forward to this. It'll be an adventure, and you all know how I love adventures and how I never stay in one place for too long, right?" His girlfriend stops sobbing and is listening to him.

"I'm ready to go. I'll not only survive, but do something good while I'm there. Mom, Dad, Matthew—I love you all so much. I'll never forget you, and I'll think about you all every day. Mom, you've been the best parent I could have ever asked for. None of this is your fault. It's all me and my bad decisions and I accept all the responsibility for that. But I'll be fine, I promise you. I'm smart, and I give you my word to be safe and make you proud. Dad and Matt, take care of Mom and Ariel for me. Ariel, I love you, but I want you to move on. Find someone who knows what a catch you are and don't settle for some douchebag. Whoever she ends up marrying, all of you be nice to him if he's good to her. That's all I ask, be happy and go on. Do that and I'll be all right."

They've all stopped sobbing now and are sniffling. His mother smiles at him with her hand over her heart.

"I am so proud of you, son, and I love you so much. We'll take care of each other, and Ariel too—I promise you that. Please be careful. You needn't stand out, live a quiet, simple life. Be happy and safe. I love you always, and we'll meet again."

"Time to leave, Marcus," I whisper.

I guide him toward the exit by his elbow. He turns once more and grins at them.

"Off on my adventure! Woohoo!"

They smile at him through the tears, if only for a moment. I glance at them one final time before the door shuts behind me, watching DiAnna Simpson's husband catch her as her knees give way.

Marcus is silent, staring straight ahead as we approach the elevator. We're only inside for maybe thirty seconds when he screams and sobs. It's surprising because it comes on so suddenly and without warning.

"Hey, calm down! Medical will knock you out cold if you keep this up."

Either he doesn't hear me or doesn't care, as he continues to cry and ignore me. The sound of his wailing is jarring, and the only other person in the elevator backs up and presses herself to the wall, looking petrified. She pushes the emergency help button, and the lift stops on the next floor. The doors open to two guards waiting for us. As soon as they see him, one of them calls for medical.

I grab him and push him into the hall where a guard moves him to a bench handcuffing his shackles to the frame so he's immobile.

Dammit all.

I don't want them to incapacitate him. That's a rough transport for me, and it doesn't do him any favors either. I cannot wait with him until he comes out of it, so he'll wake up alone and confused in Oklahoma. I looked his mother in the eye and promised her I would get him there safely, and I intend to do that. Medical shows up within three minutes, and by the time they arrive, Marcus is sobbing uncontrollably and begging anyone who will listen to let him stay here.

The aide approaches me to tell me he's giving him a Mac-Pac, which will knock him unconscious for several hours.

"Do me a favor, please—shoot him a regular sedative. I'll calm him down after that. I still have to process him through vaccines and uniforms."

Okay, so I told a little white lie—we only have uniforms remaining, but they don't have to know that.

"If that's what you want, sure, but if he doesn't calm down within ten minutes, I'll have to Mac-Pac him. Regulation."

"Okay, fair enough,"—I look at his employee ID—"Miller. I owe you one buddy."

"I won't forget it either."

He puts the metal cylinder on Marcus's arm, and it shoots the sedative in. I have the guard unlock his shackles from the bench and lead him into the first empty room I find. I shove him into a chair and grab one for myself, sitting to face him.

"I'm not kidding Marcus you need to calm the hell down. I'm trying to help you here. Allow the meds a minute to kick in, and you'll feel better. Take some deep breaths with me. In through your nose, hold it for five seconds, and out your mouth slowly. Come on, let's do it together."

I breathe, and he takes a deep breath with me. I take him through the breathing exercise a few times until he does it without me having to prompt him. The meds are kicking in, he's relaxing, and the crying has subsided.

"All right, feeling better?"

He nods and slumps further into the chair.

"Let's hang here a few minutes before going to uniforms," I sigh, leaning back in my seat. "You did the right thing in there."

"Yeah. What did my mom say to you?"

"She wants you to be safe is all. I promised her I'd get you there, and I told her you'd been doing very well with all your prepping. She loves you more than you can imagine. So do her proud. Live a simple life as she asked you to. Do not draw attention to yourself, remember the film you saw earlier. Blend in and live your life."

"Will I ever talk to them again? How can I find out if they're sick, or pass away? How will they know I'm okay? My mom's going to lose her mind if she has to wonder how I'm doing. She calls me every day to check on me, even at my age. My dad will shut down and keep it all inside and give himself a goddamn heart attack. And what about my brother? God, I wish I'd done none of the stuff I did to end up here. I knew I was taking a chance breaking the law, but I never thought I'd get caught. I'm an idiot, and now I've screwed up their lives too. I really fucked up this time."

"I'm sure you regret what you did, but it's over and there's nothing to be done to change it now. Stop beating yourself up over something that's already history. You can't see them again, I won't bullshit you. But you gave them the best gift you could, which was to reassure them you'll be fine. Please, help me keep my promise to your mom. Calm down and get your act together. If the med team knocks you out, I won't be able to wait for you to come out of your unconsciousness in Oklahoma. Do you really want to wake up there alone? You need to be alert and on point when we arrive."

He cries, and I make him begin the breathing exercises again until he calms down.

He closes his eyes and I let him relax for five more minutes before I lead him to the hallway again. The med aide and guards are talking and laughing in the hall when we come out.

Miller walks over. "We all good here, sport?" he says, putting his hand on Marcus's shoulder.

He shakes off Miller's hand and glares at him.

"Okay, then I'm out of here, see ya. I'll look you up when I need that favor," he says, winking at me.

I don't respond, but his wink has made me want to clock him right in his perfect white teeth, further souring my already plummeting mood.

"Come on, we're running late, and everyone's pissed off at me for delaying orientation this morning," I say.

"We waited around in staging all morning because of you?"

"Yeah, don't ask. Let's get going before they send someone to look for us."

Back on our course again, Marcus is finally calm and compliant. We arrive in uniforms and check in. Ten minutes later we're led to a large area where a few other prisoners are in various stages of dress. A middle-aged woman approaches holding a bundle of clothing.

"Stewart and prisoner Simpson 16859, right?"

"Yes," I reply as she hands me the heap of clothing.

"These are self-explanatory: boots, pants, belt, shirt, vest, and hat." She turns to Marcus.

"We create the clothing to appear worn and dirty, for authenticity. Don't try to clean it before you go, or you will stand out." She looks back to me. "You know the drill, take him over behind any of the open dividers to change. Raise your hand when you're ready, and the guard will unshackle him and then re-cuff him once he's dressed."

"You,"—she points to him—"sneak nothing into the clothing. I'll know if you add anything, no matter how small. I worked in a Hollywood wardrobe studio for twenty-five years before I came here. Better than you have tried to bamboozle me with no luck."

I like her.

Once Marcus changes into his period clothes and is re-shackled, we start our way to the jump room holding space. Thanks to the sedative, he gives me no further trouble. I see the rest of the team waiting as I walk him over and secure him in a holding cell where he sags against the wall, looking dazed. Frank gives us our room line-ups and I go to the locker room to change into my transport clothes. Wardrobe has already sent them up and I find the garment bag with my name on it, hanging on my locker. I turn off my phone and toss it in my locker with my watch, uniform and employee badge. I enter the holding area, uncomfortable in my period costume, as I always am.

"Lucky you, going to the wild, wild west today Stewart," says Frank.

"Yeah. Yippee-ki-yay," I say while adjusting the transponder in my waistband.

"Room twenty-five for you two."

We stand in front of our room and wait our turn. We're third to launch so Frank gets to us within fifteen minutes. He waves a wand over Marcus to confirm he has smuggled nothing in.

He unshackles him, handing us both mouth guards while strapping us into our bays.

"See you in two days, cupcake. I'll check on Michael, maybe guilt him into going to a movie with me or something. Have fun."

"Thanks Frank." I smile at him, feeling lucky to have him as a friend.

Frank leaves the chamber, securing the lead-lined door on his way out and I hear him over the speaker a moment later.

"All clear. Transport in five, four, three, two, one."

The chamber goes dark, and then a million sparks of light move around, going so fast that it looks like one long stream running in a circle. I fade to black and my last thought is that I hope Michael does well on his promotions test today.

EIGHT

Piedmont, Oklahoma 1867 / Cotswold, England 1335

Bright sunlight streams in through the bushes and blinds me as I try to open my eyes. My feet and limbs are numb, and my neck is throbbing. I take a minute to realize where I am; the panic creeping in. I stay still for a full five minutes, listening for anything out of the ordinary. When all I hear are birds chirping, I push the loose piece of bark out of the dead log and crawl out of the brush. My legs won't work properly, the pins and needles sensation rendering them useless. I stretch on the ground. All I can do is lie on my side in a fetal position and cry. Everything hurts, and I can't move my neck to the right without shooting pain. I don't know how long I've been curled up in there, but it's daylight and seems to be early morning.

As I remember what happened, I think about Annabelle. I try to stand up, but my legs won't support me yet and I collapse onto the ground. Tears run down my cheeks as I consider what might happen to her. I reach back through the log into the bush to grab my transponder and turn it on. It flickers and vibrates like yesterday, nothing more.

I wonder about the possibility of other transporters being stranded. We've had to assume the entire system has been down. It was too coincidental to both have defective transponders. I bear no evidence of that, only my gut feeling. But I realize something is very wrong; there is no way it should take six months to repair whatever malfunctioned. The pain in my legs pulls me back to the present and I remind myself I need to move to the grove of trees to try the transponder. I want to be in the general vicinity of where I transported in, hopefully improving my chance of transporting out of here.

I can finally sit up and lean against the fallen log to stretch my limbs further. I appreciate I shouldn't stay here for too long—I've no idea if the Indians are still in the area—but I can't make myself move yet. I also know I should rush to the spot where I came into this time and try my transponder, but I need to tell John about Annabelle first. If there's any hope of getting her back, any possibility she's still alive, he needs to go after her.

I force myself up and hobble a few steps before being able to walk at a semi-normal pace.

I put my damp dress on, deciding that's better than wandering around in my underwear. I won't be able to run yet, so I say a quick prayer that I won't need to. I find my way to the river and stop for a much-needed drink of water. I start out again, and as I approach the grove of trees, I see my horse grazing.

I can't believe he's still here!

He must have gotten spooked and ran off during the commotion, making his way back here later. The Indians wouldn't leave a healthy horse behind by choice. I walk over to him and pet his nose as he nuzzles my hand. I hear something and turn to see John walking out of the trees into the clearing.

"Christine! Where have you been? Where's Annabelle? It worried me sick when you two were still gone yesterday! I've been searching all night."

"John!" I'm so relieved to see him.

"Have you seen any Indians? Have you found Annabelle?"

"No, I didn't see Indians, but it looks like there was a struggle under a tree." He gestures to the spot I last saw her. "Ten men are searching for you. Where is Annabelle? Why isn't she with you? Why did you leave your horse here?"

"Oh, thank God! Listen to me, Indians took her, but not the same type we saw here before; these were different. They had tomahawks, and they chased me. I had to hide in a dead log under some bushes all night, and they didn't find me! You have to rescue her before they kill her, please! You have to go look for her!"

"All right, let's go home and after I will track down the search party, we can concentrate on finding Annabelle. I am very glad to see you safe."

"I need you to listen to me carefully. I'm not going home with you. You need to track down the other searchers right now and help them find Annabelle. I'm staying here."

"Christine, I am taking you to the ranch. Other women are there, and men for protection. Get your horse and let's go. I promise you we will find her."

He turns to the horses, ready to mount his. I grab his shoulder and turn him toward me as my composure dissolves.

"Listen to me!" I yell at him, and he's so startled that he takes a step backward. "I am not going to the house. You need to leave right now and find Annabelle. When you find her, tell her to keep trying to get home, that I made it, and I'll send for her. Do you understand? Repeat it to me."

"Have you lost your mind? What do you mean? Where on earth would you be? You're making no sense at all."

"Please, if you care about me at all, you'll do this and not ask me questions. I don't have time to explain this to you. Even if I did, I don't know that I could articulate it to you. I can't even understand all of it myself. But Annabelle will figure out what I mean, and it's critical that you tell her what I've said. Do you understand?"

He stares at me like I've sprouted a second head, and who could blame him? I must sound insane to him.

"John? Please, promise me."

"Don't ask you questions? I can't even fathom where to begin with the questions for you, Christine. There are so many."

"You're not listening to me! I will not be here, John. We're wasting time with this back-and-forth bullshit. There's no time for this."

"You will not wait for Annabelle? Of course you will; you wouldn't leave without her. I am certain of that much. Please Christine, be here when I return. That's all I ask."

I take a deep breath and try to calm down, as this is going nowhere fast.

"I can't make you that promise, but thank you for everything you've done for me in the last six months. You didn't leave me here on my own, or worse. You're a good man, never forget that. But I desperately need your help right now."

"Christine, I want to help you, I do. There are many things about you that make little sense. The manner in which you speak sometimes, it's so

. . . strange. That you're a grown woman and could not cook or ride a horse when I found you. I cannot grasp what is happening with you. I have done my best to give you the time you seemed to desire until you were ready to talk about it. But this? You two are missing, and Indians take Annabelle. Yet you refuse to accompany me home to safety, and I do not follow what you mean by leaving. Where would you go? I demand some answers, Christine!"

"I realize this must seem odd to you. I just can't tell you everything, not because I don't want to, but because I can't. It would put you in danger or produce effects far, far beyond anything you can ever imagine. I know you don't believe my story about how I got here, and you're smart not to. I can tell you Annabelle and I are from roughly the same place. We're stuck here, and we want to go home to our families. We're not bad people, we've done nothing wrong, and this isn't our fault. I've never had to ride a horse, cook, or sew where I'm from. No one does. It isn't done where we come from; it's not how we live."

"'It's not done?' How the hell do you live? Do you employ servants that cook? And what effects? I don't understand."

"I'm so sorry, you deserve to know more, you truly do. I can't tell you more than that. Doing so might change history, and I can't risk that. I've taken an oath, and I must stand by it. I understand this makes no sense at all to you. Please, just know that it must be this way. If I could get around it and tell you everything, I would."

"You have a family at home, in New York? Where you're from?"

"I'm not from New York, John. I live in Los Angeles, in California. But yes, I have a son named Michael, and I miss him terribly. I'm not married. I mean, I was, but I no longer am. Please, I have to get home to my son. Help me do that, I'm begging you. I'm asking you to trust me, John."

My pleading has reached a near manic level which must show on my face, as he sighs and drops the reins to his side.

"You need her to keep trying to go home, you made it, and you'll send for her."

"Thank you, John! You do not understand how much this means to me."

I sigh with relief then hug him and kiss his cheek. I pull away when he grabs me and hugs me again. My eyes well up as I look at him.

"Thank you for helping me. Thank you for saving me when I was alone and scared. I can't thank you enough for everything."

He smiles and climbs onto his horse. I take a step back and turn to walk away, then think better of it. I watch him ride away until he is out of sight. I scramble to the tree I slept in all those months ago and take my transponder out, hesitating for a minute.

Should I wait to see if John finds Annabelle?

I toss that thought back and forth for a minute and decide that my best chance to help her, if she's still alive, is from home. I turn the transponder on, and it flickers weakly. I scan the tracker imbedded in my wrist, but the transponder doesn't ding as it usually does to let me know it registered. I try it again, and a weak sound comes out. I wait, but nothing happens, so I try it a few more times. Within a few minutes I am dizzy, a familiar sensation.

Oh my God, it's working!

The world around me spins, and I lie down to overcome the vertigo. My last conscious thought is to pray to God that John finds Annabelle alive.

* * *

I wake up, my head throbbing. I'm nauseated, and I feel as if I'm in a thick fog.

This is what it's like to be drugged.

I can't seem to string my thoughts together, and I'm so cold that my shivering causes my teeth to chatter. I hear whispering, but I can't be sure if it's real or if I'm imagining it.

Someone lays a blanket or something soft over me, and I try to open my eyes. Well, my brain tells my eyes to open, but nothing happens.

What the hell is wrong with me? And why is it so damn cold?

I'm sure I hear voices now and they're talking about me, wondering if I'm waking up. I struggle to remember where I am, evoking a vague memory of hiding in a bush.

Why was I in a bush?

No wait, I saw John, and then I was being transported.

I must be home!

I open my eyes as much as I can, which is minimal. My eyelids feel as though weights are attached to them.

I see people sitting on logs around a fire, the backdrop a thick forest. My adrenaline kicks in at the site of them.

Where am I? Who are these people?

One of the men gets up and comes over to crouch beside me. That kicks my brain into action, and I scramble up to a sitting position and push away from him. My boot heels send dirt and pine needles flying until I hit a tree that stops me.

"Whoa, easy, easy," he says holding his hands up in a surrender position. "We're transporters, just like you. I can explain everything, but let's bring you some water to help with your head. I assume you're feeling a bit dodgy at the moment."

Another man chimes in, "Dodgy, more like arse over elbow."

I'm groggy and thirsty, and I'm having a hard time figuring out what they're talking about.

Why do they both have British accents?

My stomach churns and I lean over to vomit. The tall one brings me water out of a tin cup that's rusted through. I drink from it anyway, as the water is cold and at least soothes my throat.

"Where am I? Who are you people?"

I stand up, but I'm too dizzy and start to fall over.

He catches me and sits me down against the tree.

"My name is Ethan, I'm a transporter from London, England." He gestures toward the other people. "This is Aidan, Malcolm, Estera, and Thomas."

They nod at me, and the female comes over to kneel beside me. "Hi, I'm Estera. Try to relax until your headache is better; I was in the same shape when I got here. It'll pass, trust me."

Her accent sounds French, but I'm uncertain.

"Where is here? Where am I? When am I?"

The tall one—Ethan—speaks up.

"We're in what will one day be modern-day Cotswold, England. We're on the outskirts of Cotswold in the year 1335."

"1335? What the hell? I meant to transport home. Why are you all here? I don't follow any of this. How did I end up here?"

"Ha!" A man stands up from the fire and laughs sarcastically. "No one knows why we're still here—everyone's guessing. You ask me, they don't give one shit about us; it's a right cock-up and they will answer for it if we ever get home!"

Ethan scowls at him. "Thomas, shut your mouth and let her get her head straight before you spew your crap." He turns back to me. "I know it's a lot to take in, just try to breathe and calm down and I can try to explain it to you."

I lean against the tree and struggle to make my head stop throbbing. No such luck. It throbs away, and I find it hard to stay alert.

"Why do I feel so shitty? And why did I wind up here?"

Ethan sits down next to me and Estera sits down beside him.

"I don't know for certain how this happened, we can only guess. Malcolm and I,"—he glances to the fire pit and a blonde younger guy gives me a nod—"we were messing about with the transponders, and wires crossed. Malcolm is a computer expert who I transported here, and I figured if anyone could make sense of it, it would be him. Estera transported here first, and now you. The best we can figure, you were trying to transport home, and we were trying to do the same thing and somehow our transponders linked. The other two, Aidan and Thomas, were traveling together and found us here by lucky chance two months ago."

"Wait, so she got here the same way? You're saying wires got crossed, and this is a damn accident? Oh, hell no. I just spent the last six months at my transport site, and now this? I'm worse off here than I was there!"

Estera leans over to look at me.

"Where were you before? In what year?"

"I was in Oklahoma in 1867."

"Oh my. Yes, that is better than this. I was in Marseille, France in 1710. Very civilized and aristocratic. Not at all like this place. Do you want to come with me, and I can get you some dry clothes? Your dress is damp, and you must be freezing. We have a shelter built just inside the woods here."

I take my time getting up and need a moment to steady myself before following her.

Am I truly in 1335 England? Please let this be a bad dream.

I follow her into the woods, and several feet in I see a shelter of sorts. It's made of logs and branches and lots of mud. Even so, I'm glad to see it, as five minutes ago I thought they might camp outside in the open. Estera pulls aside the hut cover, stooping to get in. It's warmer inside, and I notice that they've built a fireplace out of rocks. She takes a piece of flint off a rock and lights a log and a pile of sticks inside the fireplace.

"The fire will help once it gets going. Here,"—she hands me a worn long dress—"I stole this when we were in town a few days ago to use as an extra. Someone had it hanging out to dry. It should fit; we look about the same size."

"Thanks," I say as I take my dress off. "How long have you been here?"

"Hmmm. About three months, I guess. We've tried to figure out what to do about the transponders. Clearly, we've had no luck."

"What do you think is going on? With me stuck in America and you here, it must be a global outage."

"It appears so. We have met no other transporters, and I had met none in France either. Thomas and Aidan found each other, then found us. We weren't sure if only we were affected. We still aren't sure if it is everywhere."

I'm about to ask her more when the four men come into the shelter.

"So," Ethan says, sitting on a log. "Tell us about Oklahoma and what you've been doing there. Are we the first transporters you've seen?"

I think back to the last time I saw Annabelle, strapped onto her horse and surrounded by Indians. I glance at each of them for a moment before I take a deep breath and tell them my story.

NINE

Cotswold, England *1335*

As I finish telling them my story, I look around the hut at the five people there. Yesterday I had only seen one person from my timeline in the past six months, and now I'm part of a group of six. Hard to believe the difference a day can make.

"Where is Annabelle now, still in Oklahoma?" Estera looks at me, waiting for an answer.

"I have no clue. The last time I saw her, the Indians tied her up on her horse. When I got to where I last saw her, John was there looking for us and a search team was looking elsewhere. He wanted me to go home and wait while they continued to search for her, but I decided my best chance to help her was from home."

I wipe the tears from my eyes with the back of my hand and continue.

"I considered that maybe no one at base knew of what was happening; perhaps they just assumed we disappeared or something. I didn't know if it was only Annabelle and me who couldn't leave. We talked about it many times, but had no means to discern if it was unit wide, worldwide, or what? It was difficult to figure out why they weren't doing a forced transport, was it the area or year we were in, an anomaly only affecting us? We considered other transporters being stuck, but it was too overwhelming to imagine, and we also had no way to find out. I had to conclude if that were the case, base would have fixed the glitch by then. So, I tried my transponder again, as we did every day, and it worked, sort of. I presumed I was transporting home, but obviously I ended up here."

Ethan frowns at me. "A search party was looking for you and Annabelle? You had relationships—friendships—with other people? People from 1867?"

"Well, I lived with a man who rescued me after my transport. Annabelle was working as a teacher in town, so she was acquainted with a lot more people than me. But yes, we knew people. We were in a small town, so we wouldn't go unnoticed. Annabelle transported in over two hundred miles from where I did but came in off course from her original transport site. She couldn't locate her intended drop site and was in bad shape before she could make her way to Piedmont on a wagon train. I came in about two miles from John's ranch. He found me alone in the woods after three days. I was lucky he took me in."

"Aren't you resourceful," Thomas sneers at me.

I really dislike this guy. He's already getting on what's left of my last nerve.

"Why did John take you in? Didn't he have questions about who you were? How did you and she find each other?" Estera asks.

Thomas doesn't seem interested, but the others all stare at me as if Estera's questions are the most fascinating thing they've ever heard.

"He had questions. I made up a lame story about my family getting killed and me being taken hostage by Indians, but said I'd escaped. As for Annabelle, I suspected she was a transporter right away. We had on identical dresses in different colors, I'm not clear if all countries do this, but we have what we call stock clothing, supplied by the same manufacturer for all units across the United States. I recognized the dress. She confirmed it for me when she began to cuss up a blue streak under her breath after tripping over a loose sidewalk board. No woman in 1867 would speak that way in public. I put it together from there, confronted her, and we traded stories. Don't you interact with anyone here after six months?"

I glance around the shelter at each of them and they all stare at me blankly.

Ethan shakes his head and sighs. "Too risky. The plague is in full force, not to mention leprosy and a host of things such as bedbugs, lice, and fleas that run rampant around villages. Even such minor things as fleas can cause an infection that we might not recover from if we run out of antibiotics. Besides, we're safer all around if we keep to ourselves—these people won't hesitate to kill us if they suspect that we're up to anything. They're quite distrustful. The 1800s in America is one thing, but this is medieval England."

Malcolm speaks up. "I hoped to square away the transponder by now. I don't understand why it's so wound up."

Aidan looks at Thomas and stands up. "I'm going outside." This is the first time I've heard him speak since I got here.

"It's brass monkeys outside mate, better grab a blanket." He never looks away from Aidan as he speaks.

I rest on a log set up for stools and try to warm myself at the fire as he follows Aidan outside.

"What's up with those two? Didn't you say they were traveling together when they got here? They don't seem friendly," I say.

Ethan watches Thomas go and says, "Who knows, they're tense recently."

"So, you keep to yourselves here in the forest? How far is Cotswold from here? What about food and water?"

Estera adds more wood to the fire and sits down across from me. "The main town is a couple miles north of here. We try to hunt, but all we have is one knife we've stolen. Ethan set traps set in the woods. They provide rabbits or squirrels. Malcolm constructed fish traps in the river, too, although they aren't always as successful as the forest traps. We have no means of hunting a deer or large game, like wild boars. Sometimes we have vegetables from a nearby village by sneaking over at night to steal them. They have no defense system set up, so it's easy to move in and out without being seen. There's a lake about a half a mile from here where we draw our water. We must boil it well before drinking, as the bacteria causes dysentery if we don't. Sometimes we travel into town if we need something more and try to barter or work for whatever we need."

"We depleted my survival pack, except for the antibiotics. We've saved them in case someone gets an infection or something." Malcolm holds up his backpack to show me.

"What do you speculate trapped us at our drop-off points?" I ask him.

"I reckon the entire system is still down. I think transporters across the globe are in the same situation, discouraging as that is."

His words echo what I have been apprehensive about for months.

If that's true, we're all on our own, conceivably for the rest of our lives.

The possibility overwhelms me, and I excuse myself to get some fresh air. I step outside, where the cold air feels good on my face. I wish I were in Oklahoma; at least there, I was near my drop-off point. I'm not confident I will get home from here. And if I attempt this again, would it send me somewhere else instead of back to my time? Somewhere worse than this? God only knows where I might end up. I dismiss that as an option and contemplate what else I can do. As I stand there, lost in my thoughts, I overhear a man's voice, raised and angry.

I listen a few more seconds and hear it again.

Is that Thomas?

It seems to be coming from beyond the shelter, just inside the trees. I steal my way closer and sneak about thirty feet into the forest. Hiding behind a tree, I see two figures illuminated in the moonlight. It's Thomas and Aidan.

"Thomas, we need to have the plan together and get this ball rolling. The more people we associate with, the more apt they are to find us out!"

"I understand that, don't you think I do? It's a week before Wallingford is in town. We need to bide our time here and ride it out. The system will return to working order, and then what's-his-name will transport everyone back to where they came from. The only reason we're in this mess now is because of your cock-up. We should have gotten the writings three months ago in Leeds. We could be done with this entire plot and waiting to travel home now if not for your mistake."

Whoa, what? The system will be back online?

"And if the others catch wind of something before that? I don't appreciate how that new woman looks at me."

"Well, we need to make sure they don't. And if they do somehow, then we take care of them. Simple as that. Not great timing that someone new has shown up in the mix, I'll grant you that. Either way, I'm not risking my five million for these wankers, and I need assurance you're on board with that."

"Of course I'm with you! I want my payday as much as you do. I'm not about to let these assholes stand in my way."

"Okay, good. There's a reason that Jonathan chose us for this job—he knows we'll do whatever it takes to see it done."

"Well, I don't know he'd agree with killing anyone, but I guess what he doesn't know won't hurt him. I want this done. I want to go home, claim my money, and disappear for a bit."

What the hell? Payday for what? How would they have knowledge about the system coming back online? And what does he mean 'take care of them'?

Okay, so this is a sizable development. It doesn't sound as if Ethan, Estera, or Malcolm are part of this, but how can I be sure? I don't know these people; I've been here one day.

And even though I don't particularly like Thomas, I wouldn't have guessed that he could be part of the reason we're all stranded here. I make my move back to the fire pit and perch on a log facing the direction I came from. I sure as hell don't want my back to them. I can't decide if I should try to take off alone or stay and tell the others what I overheard. After thinking about it, I decide to bed down tonight with one eye open and consider what to do tomorrow. I have no idea where I am yet, so taking off tonight would be suicide. I walk back to the shelter and find the others still inside.

"Where does everyone sleep? I don't want to intrude on anyone's space. If you have an extra blanket, I can sleep outside by the fire."

"We sleep in here. You can stay here, there's enough room." Estera spreads a blanket out for me next to the fire.

"Thank you. I'm tired, I'm going to lie down if that's okay with all of you."

"Of course. We men will sleep by the fire pit tonight. You look exhausted and must be confused, and we don't want to make you any more uncomfortable. We'll leave and let you ladies get settled," says Ethan.

"I don't need to put you out. It's fine for you all to sleep in here like you do, please. It's so cold out there, you'd freeze overnight."

"Nah, we'll be fine, at least for tonight. There's no rain out there, but if it starts, we'll come inside later," he says.

"Thank you for taking me in. I'm very grateful to be warm and have somewhere to sleep tonight."

"It's the bloody least we can do. It seems Ethan's transponder got you here, after all," says Malcolm.

Excellent point.

I fall asleep as soon as my head hits the ground, mentally and physically exhausted. I dream of running through the forest with Thomas and Aidan chasing me. I wake up with a start before dawn to the sound of myself repeating the word no. I listen to Estera stirring and I lie still, hoping not to awaken her.

"Are you all right?" she whispers. No such luck; she heard me.

"Yeah, sorry, I must have been dreaming. I talk in my sleep sometimes. I hope I wasn't doing that."

"You were. You dreamt about Thomas, I suppose, you said his name twice. Unless there's another Thomas in your life."

Oh, no.

"I did? That's weird, I don't remember what I was dreaming about."

A casual conversation where she brings up his name. This might be an opportunity to dig deeper.

"What's his deal, anyway? I sense some tension between him and Aidan."

"He's an odd one, Thomas. Aidan doesn't talk much. I can't tell you anything about him, about either of them. They got here before I did. Ethan says they stumbled into camp one day and stayed. Safety in numbers and all of that."

"Where did they come from? I wonder why they didn't settle at their transport site?"

"That's a good question. They came in from north of here, somewhere in Scotland."

"Isn't that quite a way from here? Why did they take the risk to travel so far? And they didn't meet any other transporters?"

"Apparently not. Although, they said little about their trip here, why they moved, or how they were together—at least not to me. I've never thought much about it to be honest."

"It sounds odd. What could motivate them to leave their drop-off points? When I was Oklahoma, I never strayed far because I wanted base to find me if they tried a forced transport or sent someone after me. Annabelle only traveled from her drop site because she had no other option, and stayed because we figured if they found me, they'd find her too. I just think it strange that they hooked up and left. The only reason we would consider leaving was if we were in imminent danger."

"Well, they're both odd ducks. I'm not clear why they've stayed here with all the wanderlust they seem to possess. But enough about those two. Tell me about you, Christine."

74

Where are you from? I mean before all of this. Do you have anyone at home?"

Michael.

"I live in Los Angeles with my son Michael. He's twenty. No, he's twenty-one now. I was three days away from vacation when this happened. I was taking him and his girlfriend to Aruba for his birthday."

"Oh, that's got to be tough. I'm so sorry. I have a husband back home, Jacques. We never had children—it's only the two of us. He's a professor at Sorbonne University. I worry about how he's been holding up without me. We've been together since we were seventeen years old."

"Wow, that's admirable, maintaining a relationship for that long. I couldn't do it for longer than ten years with Michael's dad. I'm not cut out for marriage, I guess."

"It's difficult to achieve, believe me. There are days when the simple fact that he's breathing enrages me."

We both giggle at that, and I feel more comfortable with her.

"Estera, I need to tell you something. I don't know that I trust anyone here yet, but I should share this with someone, and I think you're my best option."

"Okay, tell me what you need to get off your chest."

"I overheard Thomas and Aidan talking in the woods last night. They know when the system is coming online and they have to complete a job before that. I'm not convinced it's a coincidence they're here in this area. They're waiting for someone to come into town to do something. I can't be sure of what. They didn't elaborate on that. They mentioned being paid a lot of money—five million dollars—to do whatever it is, and they don't intend to let us get in the way. Also, they agreed that if we become a liability, they would take care of us. It was clear what that meant."

I see her push herself up on her elbow as I adjust my eyes to the dark.

"What? Are you positive of what they said? You may have taken it out of context."

"No, I'm certain. I listened long enough to be sure. I'm not eager to involve myself in anything even remotely threatening—I'm just trying to go home like the rest of you. But I know I heard them correctly. My son has a rather long tattoo of Chinese symbols on his back. It roughly translates to 'strength in Chinese'. Trust me when I say to you, his mistake educated me—

be sure you're clear about what you're saying before you open your mouth. I'm confident of what I heard."

She sits up straight and leans over to light the fire.

"We should tell Ethan. We can trust him."

"All right, if you think so, we'll tell him. I didn't appreciate the fact that they mentioned we could become a liability. And I don't want them to mix the rest of us up in some idiotic plan of theirs."

"Nor do I. But they said the system was coming back, and we need to find out what they know. If there's any chance of getting home, I prefer to be up to speed on it."

"So do I."

"It sounds like you were doing well in Oklahoma. This isn't a place to be for any amount of time. As women, we are very vulnerable. They accustom men here to taking whatever they choose, and females are second-class citizens to them. Plus, the disease factor is a constant worry. If those two idiots bring me a step closer by telling me when the system is coming online, I'll do anything necessary to get that information from them."

"I'm with you on that. Now that it seems the glitch is global it worries me even more. Have you tried your transponder again since you transported here?"

"No, I've been afraid to. I'm worried it will send me somewhere else if it links with another one again. Assuming that's what happened. We still aren't sure, and it took me four hundred years further into the past this time. If it did that again, who knows where I'd end up, or with whom? None of us are clear on what's safe and what isn't with the transponder."

"England is definitely a tougher road than Oklahoma was."

"Everything about this place sucks. You haven't been here long enough to relish the joys of medieval survival. By day three, you'll be tearing your hair out."

"I already am, trust me. No cut, style, or dye in six months. It must look like crap. Not that I'd know, I haven't seen myself in a mirror for this entire time. My imagination has it looking like a cross between a Q-Tip and a ball of steel wool. The glances of my reflection I've had in water did not make me feel any better, but hey, thanks for the pep talk."

"Sure, anytime. I realize I'm inspiring."

We both laugh quietly and lie back down. I can't fall back to sleep; I'm too busy wondering if Thomas and Aidan could be right about the system coming online. And hoping I've done the appropriate thing by sharing this with Estera. I pray Thomas and Aidan are correct.

TEN

Cotswold, England 1335

Thomas sits on the log next to the fire, thinking about what he should do. The other three men are sleeping, but he can't. He has too much on his mind.

I know that new bitch is trouble.

When they approached him about doing this job it seemed so simple, so easy. He would wait until they assigned him to transport a prisoner somewhere near Cotswold in 1335. Hoyt rigged the system to place him when and where he needed to be. He understood he would be here for a few months, waiting with that wanker Aidan. It was a small price for a five-million-dollar payday that would change his life. He owed people money; people who collected what was due them, no matter the means.

Thomas hadn't always gambled; only after his wife left him and took their son did he start. It began to kill time at night. He wasn't accustomed to being alone in the evening, reminding him he had lost his family. He would go to casinos and pull slots, have two or three free drinks and go home to bed. Sometimes he would play online and use a betting center, but it wasn't the same; he enjoyed going to casinos most. The sounds, the people watching, it was all part of the experience. And if someone won it big on a slot, it gave everyone else there the inspiration to keep playing. It grew into a vicious circle, hard to break free of. Before long, he started playing the tables and losing money. The rare times he won a hand seemed to buoy him to continue to play, believing a big win was just around the corner. He didn't win often, but it never stopped him from trying.

It became a financial hardship to pay his monthly expenses and still gamble, but he had gotten in so deep, he felt like he no longer had any other options. After a few months he began to borrow money from some sleazy sharks who hung around the casinos, waiting for anyone desperate enough to agree to their terms.

The first week he missed a payment they came to his house in the early morning hours to collect. He took two days off work after that visit. He told his supervisor he'd been in an automobile accident to explain the bruising and the black eyes, even renting a car to complete the facade. Soon after, he stopped paying his rent and his car payment to pay back the loans each month. His car getting repossessed was easy to explain; he had totaled it in the accident. He caught rides to work with coworkers, and the days he couldn't get a ride, he took an auto service.

Missing the rent payment was more problematic, but no one knew they had evicted him. Most just assumed he'd moved for whatever reason—and he never corrected them.

The next time he missed a payment, things escalated to an entire new level. They showed him photos of his son—at school, out with friends, and driving to work. The threat against his child was clear: they could get to him whenever they wanted to, so pay up or your son will be an easy target. Jason was seventeen and didn't speak to Thomas; he hadn't wanted to see him since the divorce. That wasn't for a lack of trying on Thomas's part. He called, emailed, and stopped by his old house, where his ex-wife and son still lived, all with no response. Jason blamed Thomas for the divorce, and he was right to.

Thomas pawned his mother's wedding ring the day he got the pictures. The ring had been the one thing he managed not to touch throughout his financial crisis, the only thing he had left of her. But he had no choice; it was that, or they'd go after his child. Thomas hoped to get his act together and reconcile with him one day and making him a target of loan sharks would not help accomplish that.

When Hoyt offered the proposition, accepting it was a way out of debt and starting over.

A path to reconciliation with his son, and perhaps even to win his wife back. But now here he was in the middle of a forest with strangers he couldn't trust and a sketchy plan at best.

Maybe Aidan and I should take a chance out on our own, it's only a week until D-Day.

Then again, the cliché about safety in numbers applied in this situation.

We've got a good thing going. With food, water and a shelter with a proper fireplace, we could be worse off.

He leaves well enough alone to see how things play out over the next few days.

* * *

Aidan stirs and sits up.

"What are you doing?"

"Nothing, just thinking. I couldn't sleep," Thomas replies.

Aidan doesn't like Thomas, and he sure as hell doesn't trust him. There is something very dark about the guy, and he fears Thomas might turn on him. Aidan lies under the stars, wondering about his family and how they are managing without him. Not telling them he would be away for a few months, he did what he could to prepare them. But knowing Claire as he did, he feared she could not stick to a budget. He'd cancelled all the credit cards before he left without telling her—that would piss her off when she found out. It's not as if they hadn't talked about her spending many times before. She didn't seem to grasp they were regularly living above their means as it was. It became Aidan who worried about how to pay for everything each month.

She bought designer clothes for her and the children and only the best furniture for the house. She had no idea whether they could afford it; if the account had capital, then it was fair game. He'd deposited cash in the bank before he took off, hoping she'd be smart enough to use it to take care of herself and the kids until he got back. She hadn't known about his plan to leave, and wouldn't know of his return either. He trusted if she needed funds her parents would run to the rescue, as they had her entire life. Working for the money would probably never cross her mind.

Claire grew up in an upper middle-class family accustomed to getting whatever she wanted—mostly. They were well-off enough to give her a new BMW on her sixteenth birthday and think nothing of it. She invariably wore the best clothes and never had to take a job for spending money as most teenagers do. Being an only child, her parents overcompensated for their guilt of working too many hours each week by giving her money.

When Aidan first met Claire in high school, he thought her the most beautiful girl he had ever seen. It shocked him when she asked him if he wanted to go to a party with her. He never thought a girl like her would even notice him, let alone want to date him. He half-expected to arrive at her house on the big night and see her friends there laughing at him, the butt of a cruel joke. But that didn't happen, and Aidan fell in love with her by the end of the night.

Aidan had grown up in a dilapidated caravan with an alcoholic mother who worked as a waitress. He never met his dad, and he wasn't sure his mother knew who his father was, although she claimed he was a lorry driver. Theirs was never a close relationship, and her drinking only widened the divide as he got older. That she brought home a string of men over the years—finding a husband being her life's goal—also hadn't helped.

None of the men proved suitable father figures, and his aunt and uncle came to get him when he turned thirteen. That's when life began to turn around for him. He started attending school, wore new clothes, and never worried about when he would eat next. They never had children of their own, so they doted over him. He loved them as if they were his parents, and they gave him a good life. When they died in a car accident when he was twenty-one, he felt as though his entire world collapsed.

Aidan wanted to marry Claire, the death of his family signaling him the time was right.

He was over the moon when she said yes to his proposal on her twenty-first birthday. They married thirteen years ago and had three children: Colin, ten; Stephen, seven; and Grace, five. He still had a hard time understanding how he'd landed a woman such as Claire, yet he thanked God every day. He knew in every relationship one person invariably loves more than the other, and he accepted in this case it was him. But he didn't care. He lived with her excessive spending; he always paid. Late on the mortgage, skip a car payment—he became skilled at juggling expenses.

The payday for this job would take care of that worry. He could take her on the trip to Switzerland she'd always wanted, and he might finally be worthy in her parents' eyes. And maybe, just maybe, he would also believe he deserved her.

He looks back up at Thomas still sitting there staring at nothing.

"Thomas, let's take a walk and have a chat, mate."

* * *

I lie there in the dark shelter worrying whether I've made the right decision by sharing what I overheard. I'm not convinced I can trust Ethan, but I decide I have no choice but to trust Estera's judgement; I don't know him any better than I do her, and I just hope it works out in my favor.

"You're sure telling Ethan is the wise thing to do?"

"I am," she says. "We need to extract more information out of them. We will need him to make that happen."

"All right then. As soon as he's up, we'll fill him in. I'll never go back to sleep now anyway, you?"

"Oh God, no. I'm up for the day. I'm far too keyed up to sleep. I wonder what those two are up to," she says.

Nothing good, that much is clear.

An hour later, the sun rises, and we venture out to join the others at the fire. Water is boiling for some much-coveted tea bought from town last week. The hot tea helps soothe my throat and warm me up. I've been nowhere so cold in my entire life, and this constant mist is enough to make anyone snap. I jump a little, spilling tea on myself when I'm startled by a loud thunderclap in the distance. When the sky lights up over the forest, I shiver.

Great, the mist will be a full-on downpour soon.

"Ethan, I thought you and I could show Christine where the lake is this morning and look at the traps while we're out," says Estera.

"Sure, we can do that. We should leave soon, looks like rain."

"I'm ready when you are," I say.

Ethan gathers up the pots for water and leads us into the forest. Once we're out of camp she grabs him by the arm and stops him.

"We need to speak to you. Christine overheard Thomas and Aidan arguing last night after they left the shelter. They claim to know when the system will be online and were talking about getting a job done in Cotswold for a lot of money."

"What? Oh bollocks, they're just spouting off the way Thomas always does. How would they learn anything about the system? And what job? They're stranded here like the rest of us."

He turns to me and frowns. "What exactly did you hear, Christine?"

"I know what they said. They said they needed to get a plan together for the operation. Some guy would be in Cotswold next week, and after that the system would be up. They talked about making it home and enjoying their payday of five million dollars each. Thomas also said if we were to become a problem, they'd take care of us. Aidan left no room to misinterpret that; he said he wasn't sure that Jonathan—whoever that is—would agree with them killing people, but he was on board if it was necessary."

"Bloody hell." He paces for a full minute before he speaks again.

"Okay, I understand why you're concerned. We'll corner them and persuade them to talk. I'll make sure Malcolm and I are ready to take them on when we return. We'll sort this out, somehow. If they have knowledge regarding the system and haven't shared it, they'll regret it. Although I don't perceive who would hire them with any confidence. Frankly, they don't give me the impression they are sharp enough to complete any job successfully."

"I agree with that; they seem like idiots to me, and I'm new here. Isn't Malcolm a prisoner? Is that a good idea? What if he's part of it?"

"Malcolm isn't a part of whatever those two wankers have gotten mixed up in. I brought him here, remember? They showed up together three months later. He's given me no reason to distrust him; in fact, he was more than cooperative—and tried diligently to repair my transponder."

"Why is he so willing to help? Why would he stay here with you and try to repair your transponder? My prisoner moved the minute he figured out I was having issues with my equipment. Annabelle's stuck around for maybe an hour and went out on his own, too. Why did Malcolm stay with you?"

He looks down at the ground and remains silent.

"Christine makes a good point. My prisoner left immediately too. She didn't want to stick with me once she figured out there was trouble with the device."

Looking up again, he sighs heavily.

"He did leave. I recaptured him because I realized I would need his help. I'm no computer expert; I don't understand the first thing about how to repair my transponder and I didn't like my odds out here alone. I live in a flat in the middle of London for Christ's sake, and I have had no military survival training in many years. I predicted I'd have a stronger chance of staying alive with him versus being alone, safety in numbers and all that bit. And again, repairing my transponder was my priority. I did not expect this turning into a seven-month sabbatical. I was only thinking about going home in the short-term."

"Okay, understood. But why has he stayed? He clearly isn't being detained by you any longer."

"Well, I think he also realized that we stood a stronger chance of survival as a team. I also promised him I would do something if he helped me get my transponder up and running. I told him I'd try to transport him somewhere more hospitable than here, than this time, when this was all over. It made sense overall we stuck together until we had this sorted."

"You did what?" Estera looks shocked. "You can't promise him that! They'll never allow you to bring him home or transport him anywhere else. They need to identify where he is at all times, you know that. The enforcement unit will see that he's moved and go after him."

"Well, they can kiss my arse for all I care. I'll work that out when I get home. We've been out here for almost seven months, fighting to stay alive on a few bits and bobs from a random rabbit or squirrel once every couple of days. They are damn well going to do as I ask, or I'll raise bloody hell and shut the godforsaken program down before I'm done with them. Whatever or whoever left us here, our employers will pay the price for that, as they're responsible for our safety when we transport. Whether it's a system glitch or whatever. Now, let's go for water and check the traps. I want to go chat with them."

We follow, neither of us speaking. We glance at each other and she shrugs her shoulders at me. As we approach a path of sorts, they crouch behind a tree and signal for me to do the same. They inspect the trail before motioning me to cross with them.

"What was that all about?" I ask.

"That's what passes as a road out here, and we've seen men ride by on horses on over one occasion. The less contact we have with outsiders, the better, you just have to trust us on that. And no offense, but it's even more of a risk with you here, as your American accent would raise questions."

We reach the river ten minutes later and fill the jugs. Ethan wades in two feet and comes out with a rudimentary trap, twigs woven into a funnel shape. He's smiling as he empties four large fish onto the grass.

"Oh wow, four fish!" Estera wraps them in the apron on her skirt and hands me another jug to fill. Four fish, six people. Great. I haven't eaten in almost two days; I could polish off two of them by myself.

"Let me go check the rabbit traps, be right back," he says, jogging off toward the water.

As soon as Ethan is out of earshot, I turn to Estera.

"Do you think it's a good idea to bring Malcolm into this?"

"We don't have a choice. Ethan will require the muscle if it comes to that. You and I can only be so much help. Thomas is built like a tank, and if it goes badly, we'll be glad Malcolm is on our side."

"All right, I guess we'll see how things play out. I can't wait to hear what they have to say for themselves."

Ethan jogs toward us holding two rabbits by the ears. Grinning, he hands them to me to tie into the apron of my skirt.

"Give me your water jugs, I'll carry all of them and you take the rabbits. We eat like kings today, ladies!"

I smile at him, the prospect of getting some food in me already making me feel stronger.

"I was wondering how we'd feed six people on four fish."

"Oh, we're only feeding four people today. Food and water deprivation work wonders when interrogating someone. Let's get to it, shall we?"

With that, he turns and starts toward the way we came in.

I stand there gawking after him with a frown on my face. Estera leans over and whispers to me, "He told us he was in the military before his segue into law enforcement. I've no idea what he did in the service. I don't ask, and he doesn't tell. But I know I want him on my side if things go bad."

We start toward camp, the rainfall drenching us as we make our way through the woods.

ELEVEN

Los Angeles, California 2070

Jonathan Hoyt takes a long drink from his beer and leans back in his chair, his gaze settling on his desk.

What a mess.

Paperwork and research notes strewn everywhere, empty food cartons from dinner and a few empty beer bottles litter the desk. It reminds him of a mad scientist's desk, which makes him chuckle to himself. He is anything but. He is a geek at heart, studying long dead astronomers and mathematicians work as a hobby in his spare time. Not that he has much spare time. His company, Hoyt Enterprises, is the largest software and IT corporation in the United States, maybe even the world at this point. He worked the last twenty years building the company at the expense of his personal relationships. He has friends and family like everyone else, but no life partner. There was someone special once—Amber—but he ruined that by focusing everything on his business and neglecting the relationship. He is one of the wealthiest men in the country and lonelier than he will admit. He's waited too long to do anything about it and now he can never be certain that a woman isn't dating him just for his money or status.

Although he regrets not nurturing his relationship with Amber, he never dwells on it. He isn't someone who let mistakes weigh him down, he uses them to become stronger and more driven.

His lack of a partner only increases his focus, and he funnels most of his energy into work.

He turns his chair to the bank of windows behind his desk to admire the view of downtown Los Angeles from his fortieth-floor penthouse. The lights of the city are beautiful at night and the sight helps him unwind.

What to do about this research?

He knows what he needs to do, but is also aware he will be hard pressed to get anyone to listen to him, let alone take him seriously. He has been sitting on this information for a few weeks while he checked and rechecked his facts. He had to be sure he was right, knowing his reputation will suffer if he goes public and is wrong. He's decided going public isn't the right way to handle things—he doesn't want or need the publicity, good or bad. He hesitates a moment before picking up the phone to dial an old friend from college. Charlotte is one of the smartest people he knows and one of the few people he trusts. They met freshman year at UCLA, striking up a friendship that endured the years. He admires her no-nonsense personality and intelligence.

The phone rings several times and he is about to hang up, when she answers.

"Hello?"

"Charlotte, you're there. It's Jonathan. Did I wake you up?"

"Jonathan, hey you. Not really, I was just dozing watching the news. What are you doing?" she says yawning.

"Nothing much, I'm sorry I interrupted your dozing."

"Nah, don't worry about it. If I fall asleep before midnight, I'll just wake up in the middle of the night and not be able to fall back to sleep, anyway."

"Charlotte, I have something I need to run by you, and I need you to keep an open mind about it."

"Well that sounds interesting," she says yawning again.

"I'm serious. Please, listen to me. I've been doing some research and I've run across something important."

"Oh God, not this again. Jonathan, there has got to be something else you can do to entertain yourself besides pouring over these old, dusty journals and conspiracy theories you find. It's not healthy. Get out, make some friends, go on a date for goodness sakes! I have a friend, Darcy, you would love her. Let me set something up. Please, for both our sanities."

Jonathan sighs and runs his hands through his hair. He knows she will not want to hear this, but he also knows he must make her listen. This time is different. This time could mean life or death.

"Charlotte, I hear you and agree, I need to get out more. Hell, I'll even agree to a date with Darcy if you'll just listen to me for three minutes."

"Now you have my attention. And by date, I mean a real date. Dinner and a concert, or a play. Not a quick bite to eat while you continue to answer your phone and pretend to be interested in the woman across the table from you. And I'm setting the stopwatch on my phone for three minutes."

"Fine, three minutes. So, here's the gist of it. I've been going over a fourteenth century astronomer's writings, Richard of Wallingford. Brilliant man, you should read up on him. He wrote a treatise he called Tractatus Albionis and created an albion which is an equatorium calculating planetary positions, eclipse calculation and ordinary astrolabe practice. Complicated stuff. His research showed a connection between planet alignments, gravitational pull and weather. He theorized that this pattern of events has a direct correlation to disease outbreaks. Although he didn't have enough pandemic information or weather history to study to establish a strong enough pattern between the two. Consequently, he got no real notoriety for his efforts. Communication and information exchange were just too limited during his time. However, he was onto something."

"Okay, what does that have to do with me, you, or life as we know it?" she asks impatiently.

"Hang in there with me Charlotte, my three minutes aren't up yet. Our present-day scientists have only accepted in the last fifty years, that planetary alignments and gravitational pull affect Earth's weather, right?"

"Yeah, so what? You aren't telling me anything I don't know. I don't believe any hard data study was ever done, what's your point?"

"Seven hundred years ago Wallingford wrote a theory and researched what our scientists now concede is a viable concept. I checked and double checked his research. Then I wrote a software program based on his theory—to organize all the information I amassed. My program tracks gravitational pull from other planets, and I also linked weather records, and uploaded information on every known pandemic in history. The program confirms that every time there was a strong gravitational pull from another planet, we experienced extreme weather. However, what I found next is the astonishing part. Just over seventy-five percent of the time after this extreme weather, a pandemic of some sort followed it. I think you'll agree that seventy-five percent is a very high percentage of reoccurrence. So, based on that pattern, I took it a step further and used my software to predict future alignments. I won't bore you with all the details, but according to my software, we are due for some very extreme weather. And a pandemic. In 2070, two years from now. The worst of that weather will concentrate here in southern California, and we aren't even close to prepared for it."

"What? Oh, come on Jonathan. A pandemic? We've seen no strain of influenza and certainly not a pandemic for almost thirty years now."

"That makes this even more dangerous. We eradicated the flu which means there is no immunity to it. No one gets flu shots anymore, and who knows how much flu vaccines the pharmaceutical companies carry on hand. I would suspect very little or even none stocked, since I'm certain the shelf life would be well out of date by now. It would take several weeks if not months to produce enough vaccine and then it would be too late. And let's take it a step further. Would we be able to meet the demand for antibiotics if it doubled or tripled in a matter of weeks? We both know the flu originates via animals or insects, but let's say you're right and the flu wasn't the pandemic this weather anomaly triggered. It could be many diseases. I can't predict the pandemic disease with certainty, but there are some frightening alternatives to the flu that come to mind. The weather will create a substantial amount of stagnant water, causing the mosquito population to explode at a rapid rate. I expect that's how it would start. You and I both realize a new strain of the flu may emerge from that easily. Or what if those mosquitoes spread encephalitis, west Nile, malaria, dengue fever, Zika virus, or any other mosquito-borne disease for example? We don't worry about those illnesses anymore, which means we are not prepared for an outbreak. It would only take a few unchecked cases to spread like wildfire. Global climate changes over the last seventy years are clear, you've seen it, and those conditions would only help improve the breeding ground for mosquitoes. Were you aware that certain types of encephalitis can spread from human to human? Mosquitos infect enough people and those people spread it to one another, we may as well throw in the towel."

"Okay, slow down Jonathan. Several things come to mind. First, the reason we no longer worry about any of those diseases is because of vector control for mosquitoes. Second, we would receive warning of a heavy rain season and adjust the vector control accordingly. We haven't seen a true pandemic in years, and I doubt we ever will again."

"Think about this, Charlotte. If the weather is anything close to my software prediction, and I assume you agree we can count on my software to be accurate, there is no way vector control will react fast enough to meet the need. Adjustments would have to be set well in advance. Do you trust the city of Los Angeles' government to react quickly enough to contain something of that magnitude? I sure don't."

"All this because of a wet winter? That's a stretch, Jonathan."

"I'm not talking about a 'wet winter'. A weather event of this magnitude would cripple Los Angeles. Unless we prepare for it now, I'm certain the weather and the resulting pest explosion could trigger a pandemic. Another thing you may have forgotten—2072 is an Olympic year and Los Angeles is the host city. People from all over the world will arrive in increased numbers. It's the perfect storm for a pandemic."

"I don't know, I'm finding it difficult to buy into this Jonathan. I find too much uncertainty in your theory. One, assuming the weather will be as bad as you foresee. Two, the vector control won't be able to keep up with the pest population. Three, pests would need to infect much of the population with influenza or an encephalitis type virus. Besides, even if I lent any credibility to some fourteenth century astronomer's theory, what are we supposed to do about it? Some scientist somewhere will notice if the gravitational pull is out of the norm which is what triggers this if I understand you."

"I understand your hesitation, Charlotte, but I'm asking you to look at the big picture here; consider all the facts not just Wallingford's theory. Remember, my software confirms his theory. And you're right, some scientist somewhere will know. Assuming they recognize the fluctuation in the gravitational pull is a problem that will affect other areas, will they share it with other scientists who study weather? Will those scientists connect the weather and disease link and pass it along? Will they send it to the Center for Disease Control or the World Health Organization?

You work for WHO, how many times has some weather scientist given any of you information to help you get ahead of a pandemic? My guess is never. What scientist will want to cut through miles of red tape and politics to look like a paranoid fear monger?"

"Oh, come on. Scientists exchange information all the time. I think *you* might be the paranoid fear monger. And seriously, Jonathan, 'fear monger'? What Victorian dictionary did you dig that one out of?" she says laughing.

"Don't you remember an incident involving the CDC way back when? I can't remember the scientists name, but he did a highly publicized tell-all interview on CNN, a whistleblower interview. He said the CDC forbid him to use phrases such as 'extreme weather' or 'climate change'. He called a summit to discuss the dangers of extreme weather and disease and the CDC pulled the plug on it. The Whitehouse and the CDC did everything in their power to debunk and humiliate him. The presidential administration at the time said that climate change was fiction and stood behind the CDC. They cancelled the guys climate study program and suspended him. He ended up working from home until he sued, and they retired him. After they suspended him, they wouldn't allow him to enter the CDC campus without prior approval. And even then, they subjected him to a body search, a car search and an armed guard escort. I can't imagine another scientist will be eager to go down that road again. I'm sure his story is legend around the CDC."

"I forgot about that, but it was so long ago."

"Maybe so, but I doubt the CDC has forgotten about it. If I can establish a real disease risk and convince just one scientist of our exposure, conceivably I can get WHO on board. I'm willing to take that gamble, but I need your help to do that. We need to get in front of this before it happens. A pandemic of this size could devastate millions of people around the globe."

"You have no proof of that! I will admit to three things; I trust your software to be accurate, but let's not lose sight of the fact that software is based on the data it's fed. Perhaps the weather won't end up as bad as you envision. I agree a string of people would need to be willing to pass along information to WHO or the CDC, and that might not happen. I also agree the CDC might not be super excited to hear about a weather-related threat. However, we don't know that for sure, it's speculation. All the circumstances would have to align to suggest a pandemic was possible. You said it yourself, the perfect storm would need to be in play. I think there's just too much doubt to consider this a viable threat. This isn't like you Jonathan, you're so analytical. You're a computer guy, you understand data and analysis. What's gotten into you?"

"I understand data, and that's why I'm so concerned. My software substantiates everything I just told you. If you saw my research and Wallingford's theory, you'd be more apt to agree, I promise you. If we could just prepare for this, inoculate people arriving for the Olympics, ready a vaccine for the general population, devise an upgraded plan for the insect surge. We might curb this before it spiraled out of control."

"I'm a biologist, not in disease control, that would be an epidemiologist. Why not contact the CDC and see what they say?"

"Do you honestly expect anyone from the CDC will listen to me? That will not happen, we both know it. They already established their stand on the issue back in 2019 or 2020, when all that mess went down with the whistleblower. This has to run through WHO for any chance of action. I only expect one slight issue that concerns me right now."

"What issue?" she says, her voice lowering.

"I don't have Wallingford's complete treatise. We lost some of it to history, unfortunately. I uploaded what I had available."

She laughs and sighs. "So, let me get this straight. You have a theory or rather an astronomer who has been dead for over seven hundred years had a theory, that you've dug up somewhere. Only the theory is incomplete, making your data incomplete or possibly even incorrect. So you only possess half a theory. This half-theory may or may not point to an upcoming pandemic, and that's only if all the pieces fall into place as you predict. Provided all that happens, it might spread the flu or encephalitis. Or some other disease you can't identify, triggered by extreme weather and a rapid explosion in the pest population? Does that about cover it? It doesn't sound so solid when I say it, does it?"

"Well, yes that's it, but hear me out. The mosquito population will balloon. What if it increases by fifty percent? That is absolutely within reason given the right circumstances. Add that to the increased population with the Olympics, well, you can imagine the results. And it would happen too fast for us to contain it unless they prepare us for it and take precautions beforehand."

"Okay, I get that. But it's a moot point as no one will ever look at this with incomplete data, you must realize that. You are basing all of this on a theory from seven hundred years ago that is incomplete. You need to track Wallingford's theories properly, and by that I mean completely. You'd have to show a pattern over the past seven hundred years, plus submit your research and software predicting upcoming planet alignments based on that theory. With that you might convince someone to take notice. Without that, considering WHO's current backlog of work, it would take years for them to complete the proper research. You would also need to defend your data with a scientist scrutinizing it at every turn to get it fast-tracked."

"What if I got the missing portion of the treatise? What if I get Wallingford's complete writings, finish uploading the theory onto my software and give you my research showing all the patterns? Would you take it to someone at WHO? Someone who would at least take it seriously? I can substantiate it, no doubt about that."

"How would you even get the complete treatise if it no longer exists?"

"I'll find a way, leave that to me. Are you willing to do that provided everything's in order? Before you answer that consider this. What if there's a chance I'm right? Don't you agree it would be too big a risk to ignore? Pandemics can kill millions of people. Would you be willing to take the chance of another one happening if we had the ability to stop it before it started? The CDC thought the weather and disease connection was explosive enough to put the kibosh on it fifty years ago."

"Or they didn't see the connection. We don't know which."

"I know which it is Charlotte. They went to a lot of trouble to discredit that whistleblower, and I have to wonder why."

She sighs heavily, and he knows she is considering it. "Only out of morbid curiosity and a healthy respect for our twenty-odd-year friendship will I agree to help you. Provided you have all the research. And that includes everything from Wallingford's treatise, which, frankly, seems very unlikely at this point. However, there is an epidemiologist I've worked with for several years who I consider a friend. I could probably convince him to look at the research."

"Thank you, Charlotte! Thank you for trusting me."

"Don't make me look like an idiot, Jonathan. I'm serious when I say I will not turn this over to my friend unless you have everything in order. I'll send you Darcy's number. Call her or our deal is off."

With that she hangs up without saying goodbye. She is blunt, but he knows she is smart, and he can count on her once she commits. For the first time in weeks, Jonathan feels as though he may do something useful with the information he's discovered. He taps his phone again and pushes the speed dial to a familiar number.

"Hey boss, what can I do for you?"

"James, hello. I'm sorry to call you so late, but I need your help with a sensitive matter."

"It's not a problem, I'm awake."

"I want you to locate and research two transporters for me. Two British transporters to be more specific. Or even Scottish would work. I need these two transporters to have financial issues. Not just late on some bills, I'm talking backed-into-a-corner type of financial problems. I need this task to be your priority, starting tomorrow morning. Everything else takes a backseat until we do this. Do you understand?"

"Of course, Mr. Hoyt. I'll get right on it tomorrow morning."

"James, it's imperative you handle this with the utmost confidentiality. I can't have a footprint on this one. You need to be extremely discreet and conduct this in a manner so it is never traced back to me, you, or Hoyt Enterprises. I want only you on this assignment, no delegating any part of it. I need this by Friday. Is that manageable?"

"You can count on me, sir."

"Thank you, James. I appreciate that I can count on you. Contact me as soon as this is complete."

He signs off the call and swivels his chair back to the view of the city. His chief of security will find the transporters he needs to pull this off. He opens another beer as he formulates a plan in his mind.

TWELVE

Los Angeles, California 2070
I sit staring at my lunch, willing myself to eat something.

Michael Stewart, prisoner control officer for the government. Twenty-one years old, my life in a vortex.

My mom is gone, missing, for almost seven months now. I remember seeing news stories in the past about lost people and thinking about how it must suck for the family. That doesn't even come close to describing the experience. The not knowing, imagining the worst— that's what comes to curl around me like a thick, suffocating blanket at night. Maddie's been great, though. She tries to ease my mind, telling me my mom can take care of herself. Who knows what's happened to the missing transporters from that day? There were fifty-two of them traveling the world, and every last one is gone—no contact at all. They traveled with no supplies and no weapons. How could they survive this long with nothing? I have a thousand questions and not one answer. To be in this situation is paralyzing.

My mom would do whatever she could to get home. She would never give up, that's not her nature. I can't help but be fearful about her being alone though; she could be an easy target for someone. I've tried to prepare myself for the worst, but I don't like to think like that—I try to stay positive. This should be the best time in my life. I have a great girlfriend, I just got a promotion and moved up a pay grade at work, which means I can finally afford my own place.

But it's hard to be happy when all I do is worry about what's happened. Thoughts of her pop into my mind at random times during the day.

Sometimes during my shift at work, I step outside alone for a minute to get my head right.

They repaired the system within two days of going down, so the time travel program resumed with no problems. But no one can figure out why we can't do a forced transport home for the missing transporters. I've heard the rumors that if they reach the one-year mark with no contact, they'll declare them dead and process insurance claims to their beneficiaries. Which is a crock of bullshit if you ask me. I won't take their goddamn insurance money—I want to know where she is. I need to understand what happened; even if she isn't alive anymore, I have to find out either way. I've got to secure a spot on the retrieval team, whatever it takes.

Frank's leading the retrieval unit based in Los Angeles, so I hope that gives me an in.

Once a team goes out, if they can't find the transporters, they can join the global co-op unit assigned to the European team. Europe had the most people out with fourteen missing from eight countries. They need all the help they can find. My unit has five lost—the most in the country for that day—spread out all over the United States.

I give up on lunch and go see Frank to plead my case to him. I won't be good at anything until I resolve this. I can't sit here and worry like I have for the last six months. I'm sure I can convince Frank to allow me on the retrieval team; he wants to find my mom as much as I do. I take the elevator up to the tenth floor and make my way to his office. He sees me coming and pretends to hide under his desk.

Hilarious, Frank.

"Hi Frank, how's it going?"

"Oh, it's going all right, kid. What's new in your neck of the woods with the grunts?"

"Same old stuff. Lots of inmates and more complaining. It never changes. So, I want to talk to you about the retrieval team recruitment."

He leans back in his chair and raises his eyebrows, his way of telling you to speak before he loses interest.

"I belong on the team, Frank. She's my mom. I should look for her, more than anyone. It's my responsibility—no one will be more dedicated to finding her than me, surely you realize that. Just tell me what to do, and I'll do it. Tell me who I should talk to, and I'll talk to them."

I sit waiting for him to respond, but he keeps staring at me, saying nothing. I stand my ground and lock eyes with him.

"Well, that's certainly one way to view it. Good God, you're as stubborn as your mother."

I sit up straighter in my chair. Now we're getting somewhere.

"Another way to look at it, maybe you're too personally involved. I could consider it a conflict of interest that may affect your performance and put the entire team at risk."

"I wouldn't do that Frank, and you know it. I only want the opportunity to prove myself. If I make the team and I'm not handling it well for whatever reason, I'll go home without a fight. I can promise you that—that's how confident I am that I'll handle this."

"Well that's a compelling argument, Michael, but it's not up to me. My supervisor has the final say on selection. I only make recommendations on candidates; the rest is above my pay grade."

"Then recommend me. All I want is a fair chance. If you do that, I'm sure I'll land the posting based on my performance merits alone. Can you do that, Frank? Please?"

Frank stares at the ceiling for a full sixty seconds before answering. "All right. I'll recommend you. But I swear to heaven Michael, if you so much as breathe wrong, I'll have your ass for it—I don't care who you are or who your mother is."

"Yes! Thank you, you won't regret this, I promise!"

"You'd better hope I don't, Mr. Stewart."

I contain my excitement until I reach the men's room. I do a fist pump in the air and smile at myself in the mirror. Once Frank recommends me, I'm a shoo-in. I knew I could talk him into it. He's the one who's always told me to fight for what I want and don't take no for an answer. All I ask is a chance to prove myself. I recognize Frank feels guilty about my mom being missing, and maybe that's why he allowed me to join the team. But it's not important why he agreed. I made it, and that's all that matters to me. Maddie isn't going to be thrilled about this, but she'll come to accept it. She'll have to.

I spend the rest of my day walking on cloud nine, although I don't dare share my good news with anyone yet, afraid I might jinx it. My good mood doesn't stop my mind from wandering though, and I obsess over whether she's hurt or dead. I'm not sure how I'd process through that, but I won't let that impede me doing my job—I can't let it distract me.

I'm on my way to the locker room to change into my street clothes when my unit supervisor motions for me to follow him.

Crap. I hope I didn't screw something up.

"Stewart, come on in and sit down."

"Yes sir."

"You know you aren't required to call me sir. Captain Aldred, or just captain, either of those will work."

"Yes, Captain Aldred. Did I do something wrong?"

"No, your performance has been outstanding, no complaints. I got a request from the top floor a few minutes ago. A request to transfer you temporarily to the transporter retrieval team. Do you know anything about that?"

Oh my God, I really made it! Damn, Frank didn't waste any time getting that done.

"Yes. I requested consideration for the team, Captain. Not that I don't like it here, I do. But you're aware my mom is a transporter who went missing, and I feel like this is what I must do sir. I mean Captain."

"Hmmm. I'm surprised they approved it for that very reason. How did it get by Vasquez?" He looks at me, waiting for a response. "That was a joke Stewart, I could give myself a promotion, and he'd sign that without even looking at it. I assume Rhoades got this pushed through for you?"

I look at him but don't answer; the last thing I want to do is get Frank pushback.

"It's all right, don't answer that, I'm sure it was him. It's fine, I'll approve it, but after this is over, I need you back here. Deal?"

"Yes captain, I give you my word on that. Thank you."

He shakes my hand and signs off the request on his computer.

Yes! It's a done deal now, no turning back.

I call Maddie to give her the good news. As expected, she's not thrilled. She's worried about me not coming home, just like the transporters we're going after. But I remind her the system works fine now and has been for six months. Whatever is keeping them stranded is just a glitch no one has figured out yet.

Right?

It's difficult to fall asleep that night, even after taking a mild sleeping pill, thinking about what's ahead. I've grown closer to Maddie through all of this, and though I've got family nearby, she's my go-to person. I never come right out and tell her how scared I am, but she seems to grasp that, anyway. I haven't been sleeping well, and my appetite isn't what it used to be. I didn't realize she'd noticed either of those things until she brought over protein powder shakes and over-the-counter sleeping pills last week.

I took my mom for granted when she was here. I thought she'd always be around, my soft place to fall, as she likes to say. She's my closest family connection, so how am I supposed to overcome something like that if she's gone forever? You expect your parents to grow old and die someday, but you usually take years to prepare for it. You don't expect to say goodbye to them one morning and never see them again, not knowing what's happened.

And if I'm being honest with myself, I'm nervous about traveling, too. I've never transported, and it freaks me out, so I'm glad Maddie is staying over to distract me. I roll over, trying to get comfortable, and she turns to face me.

"Hey, you're tossing and turning. Are you okay?" she asks.

"No, not really. I'm glad to be going, but nervous. What if we can't find her? What if we do and she's, you know? God, I can't even say the word out loud."

"She's not, Michael, she's not. They're all out there somewhere. You'll be looking for her there, and I'll be working on locating her from here. We will find her."

"I can't even remember if I told her I loved her the morning she left. How fucked up is that? She tried to hug me, and I gave her a pat on the shoulder or something lame like that. I didn't know Maddie. I didn't question that I'd never see her again."

She pulls me close and hugs me. "You're going to see her again. Don't do that to yourself. Don't let guilt overwhelm you. She knows you love her."

I pull her closer and bury my head in her hair. I want to believe her. I wish I was as certain as she is, but it's hard to do. I let myself relax, knowing that at least tomorrow I'll finally start doing something to find her. I doze on and off, and when it's time to wake up in the morning I feel like I've partied too hard the night before.

All the fizzle and none of the fun, as my grandpa says.

There's nothing worse than broken sleep.

As soon as I get to my station the next morning, Captain Aldred sends me up to report to Frank. Frank sends me to uniforms for my gear fitting. My uniform consists of a riot helmet with a built-in mask, and black lightweight all-weather vest with tons of storage pockets they assure me I will use. I get a backpack survival kit with MREs, emergency water, water purification tablets, water-proof matches, flint and antibiotics. And my weapon. The gun seems over-the-top—where we're going, there's nothing like it. It's better than an AK-47, Uzi, and M4 carbine combined. I guess it'll be good to have it; we might meet hostiles. But it makes me worry even more; my mom had no weapons with her. Maybe after this screw up the government will reconsider and arm transporters.

By lunchtime, I'm issued all my gear and instructed to meet my new supervisor in training room twelve. I ride the elevator to the fifth floor and enter the room, where Frank is sitting with four guys I've never met.

"Stewart, thanks for joining us today."

"I, uh, sorry sir, I just got my gear squared away."

"Don't look so scared, you will make your comrades here nervous."

Frank makes the introductions and we all shake hands. There are two younger guys and two about Frank's age.

They all seem decent; no one gives me a bad vibe or anything. I pay attention to intuition—my mom says that my Great-Great-Grandmother Jenelle was famous for that, and I inherited the trait.

"Let's sit down and go over the gear together before we outline our general plan. You must qualify on your firearm—we're scheduled to be at the range at two o'clock this afternoon. That shouldn't be a problem for any of you because you're there once a week, anyway. You must score a 90 percent mark to pass. If you want to try this baby out before then, that might not be a bad idea. You'll have an hour or two free after we finish here."

He hands out our weapons, and we each sign for them.

"Ammo is available at the range counter; show them your employee ID and they'll have your authorization in the system. Okay, next up, standard flex cuffs, five pair, food replacement capsules, water purifications tablets and emergency water. You have more water in your survival backpack, but we want to make sure we carry more than enough if we can't access a water source. There are five broad-spectrum antibiotics in here too. We will receive vaccinations, however, there are a lot of contagious things where we're going, and we want to prepare. If anyone gets a cut or open wound you must take an antibiotic as soon as you see it. No exceptions. You also have this standard issue Bowie knife. Your knife and firearm are both to use in extreme emergencies only. If anyone forces us to fire on them, that means we're in a situation that will require us to evacuate, or you or a teammate are in imminent danger. Any questions so far?"

We all glance around the table and shake our heads.

"Okay, on to the remaining gear. Tear gas. We'll all receive four capsules. Your helmet mask has a built-in filter, so if you engage your gas, release your mask and it won't affect you. Next, there is a sleep aid injection. This is not for your use; it is for passive retreats. They will knock someone unconscious within fifteen seconds. Our goal is to minimize our footprint while there, we want to get in and out with the least amount of disturbance. If someone breaches camp, or if we encounter hostiles, then we go to Plan B, which is to use extreme, overwhelming and deadly force. We approach all other situations passively. Last, we each have a cyanide capsule, or what the military has dubbed a suicide pill since WWI. They are about the size of an apple seed and take effect within sixty seconds. These pills put you to sleep before doing their damage. They're in the form of an edible melting container. You put the entire packet under your tongue, and within one minute you're out. Death takes place within ninety seconds after that."

I glance around the table, at a loss for words.

Shit just got real.

"This is probably not what you want to hear, but if you're captured by hostiles, or gravely injured and without help, this may be your best option. Remember, people we encounter there may not be as civilized as us. They live in a different time when something we consider barbaric may be perfectly normal to them. We don't know what we will run into. We'll be going to five different locations with five different circumstances. We may extract our transporters or ultimately look for proof of death. I realize that sounds harsh, but I need you all to prepare for whatever we encounter. We may never draw our weapons, or we may run into hostiles everywhere we go. Our main goal is to stay away from people and remove our transporters.

One other thing, there's a very good possibility the system outage has fried their trackers. Which means we must track them on our own, without the help of our transponders."

This get-together was an eye-opener.

I thought I knew what I was getting into, but until now I didn't realize how serious things could become. And my mom has been living that for six months. The reality of the situation only makes me more determined to rescue her.

The question is, am I ready?

THIRTEEN

Cotswold, England 1335

Estera and I follow Ethan back to camp in silence.

This should be interesting.

Thomas, Aidan, and Malcolm are sitting around the fire when we arrive.

Malcolm jumps up to meet us. "Rabbits and fish, brilliant mate! We still have vegetables left; we can make rabbit stew and grill the fish. I boiled some water while you were out, so we are ready to cook. I'm so hungry I could eat them minus the cooking part!"

"Thanks Malcolm, I'll go prep them and we can get it started." Ethan turns to Malcolm.

"In fact, I could use your help."

"Sure, let's do it."

I know what he is doing; he needs to see Malcolm alone to tell him what's going on.

"I can help too. I'm an expert at butchering rabbits after six months in Oklahoma."

"Perfect, you and I will take care of the rabbits and Malcolm, you can clean the fish. We'll be ready to cook in no time."

Thomas and Aidan never look at us, oblivious to anything going on.

Good.

I follow them out of earshot, to the tree stump they use as a prep table.

"Listen, we must be quick. I need your help and there isn't a lot of time to explain. Christine overheard Thomas and Aidan discussing a plan last night. The snapshot is that they're waiting for someone to arrive in Cotswold in a few days so they can complete a job. They're being paid a lot of money to do it, hired by someone named Jonathan. They say the system will be online the day after, and if we are in the way, they'll kill us."

"What the hell? Are you sure? They don't seem bright enough to work that out."

"That's just what I said," says Ethan.

I take a step closer to him. "Malcolm, trust me, there isn't time for me to give you all the details. But they're smack in the middle of something and they will drag us into it too if we don't stop them. Or find out what's going on. At the very least we need to find out about the system coming online."

He looks back and forth between Ethan and me. "Okay, if you two say they're into something then I'll bite. What's the plan, then?"

Ethan leans in closer to us. "We need to overpower and secure them for questioning. Our only advantage is that we have the element of surprise. Christine, can you tear a blanket or maybe the dress you had on when you got here into strips that I can use to tie them up with? When we finish with the rabbits, take the knife into the shelter. You'll need to hustle; hide the strips in your apron and slip them to me when I give you the signal. I'll scratch the top of my head when I want you to move next to me and hand them to me. Malcolm, when you see Christine do that, we both need to go after Thomas together. He'll be the most difficult to handle. Let's secure his hands first. Aidan won't make a move to escape because it will surprise him. Once we tie Thomas's hands and feet we go straight to Aidan, no hesitation."

"It seems like you've done this before, Ethan." Malcolm raises an eyebrow.

"Military training, a lifetime ago, I'm hoping it will all come back to me. Trust me on this, it'll all go down quickly, so I need you to be on point with me. Remember, no hesitation."

"I've got it," replies Malcolm.

We finish prepping the rabbits and Ethan slips me the knife. I hide it in my sleeve and walk straight to the shelter. I grab the dress I wore in Oklahoma and cut it into strips thick enough to be strong, and long enough to use as bindings. My hands are shaking a little. This has to go right; we'll only get one chance at restraining them. I roll the strips up into the apron of the borrowed dress and walk outside.

Malcolm is putting the fileted fish onto skewers made from sticks, and the rabbit is boiling with some vegetables. My stomach growls at the smell of it. I hear a thunderclap in the distance and I count it, an old habit. According to my count, it's five miles out, which means the torrent will be here soon. The temperature has already dropped, and the fire isn't adequate to keep anyone warm unless you're sitting right next to it. I stand behind Thomas and Aidan, ready to pass Ethan the strips.

So far, so good.

"When will the grub be ready? My stomach thinks my throat's been cut." Thomas turns around to glance at me like I'm a waitress.

"Thirty minutes, how would I know? I'm not a chef," I sneer at him.

"What's your problem? You know what, you've got a crappy attitude, and I'm sick of listening to your shite."

I walk around the fire to face him. The practical side of me thinks, they go low, you take the high road. But not this time. This guy has it coming, and I'm over him in a big way.

"What's my problem? Are you freaking serious? Oh, I don't know Thomas, let's recap; I just spent the last six months at my drop-off location in 1867, Oklahoma. And when I think I am going home, I end up here. With no prospect of ever getting home! And you want to know why my attitude isn't sunshine and lollipops? I have to believe that even someone with only half a neuron firing and a minimal grasp of human nature such as yourself could work that out. God, you're a real asshole, you know that?"

No one says anything, and Estera laughs. "Oh my God, ditto what she said. You're a complete asshole, Thomas."

I knew I liked her for a reason.

With Thomas distracted, Ethan sees his opening and scratches the top of his head. I walk behind Thomas and hand Ethan the strips of blanket, watching him and Malcolm grab Thomas from behind and tackle him.

"What the fuck?" Thomas yells.

He fights, but Ethan already has the drop on him and is securing the ties on his wrists. He moves to bind his feet, and he secures Thomas in well under a minute. Aidan stands up, and as predicted, he watches in shock with his mouth open. Ethan and Malcolm start for Aidan, and when he turns to run, he finds Estera behind him. She clocks him right in the nose and sweeps his feet out from under him, allowing Ethan to tie him up just as quickly. They struggle and curse, trying to loosen their restraints.

"Piss off Ethan, what the hell is this? You'd better explain yourself, and fast, because when I make it out of these ties, I'm gonna kick your arse!" Thomas looks like he will implode at any minute. His face is bright red and twisted into a snarl.

"Settle down chaps, we'll be back to you soon enough. We need to get dinner out of the way first. I'm starving."

Thunder booms and the sky opens as Malcolm grabs the pot of stew. Ethan takes the fish and gestures for us to follow him into the shelter.

"What about those two?" says Estera as she grabs bowls and ladles stew into them for each of us.

"They'll be fine. It's not cold enough out to kill them. They can handle a little rain; it'll do their attitude good. By the time we question them I want them ready to talk. In the meantime, let's dig in."

We eat our stew and fish, and I feel so much better after that. I didn't realize how hungry I was until I ate. After we finish, Ethan asks us all to stay inside for another thirty minutes as we ignore the yells from outside. It's clearly a power move, a way to let them know who's in charge of the situation.

"When we go outside, I need you to listen to what they say. If you hear something that makes no sense, or you have questions about it, speak up. If they don't cooperate this time 'round, we'll let them stew a bit longer. When I say I'm coming back in, I need you all to get up and follow me with no protests or questions. It may seem to you as if I'm amid getting something out of one of them, but trust me on this; I know what I'm doing with interrogations. All agreed?"

We nod our heads yes, leaving our fate in his hands. Once the rainfall stops, Ethan steps outside and motions for us to follow him. The minute we step outside, Thomas and Aidan both yell and curse, demanding that we untie them. Ethan sits on a log next to the fire and takes out the knife I used to cut the blanket strips.

When did he pick that up?

He's better than I thought. He whittles two sticks and ignores the yelling. They both finally stop, and once they do, Ethan looks up.

"All right lads, let's have a little chat, shall we? Let's start with a simple question. Who is Jonathan?"

With that he gets up and walks around the campfire to stand in front of Thomas, still holding the fully sharpened sticks.

"Fuck you, Ethan."

"Oh, that's a shame Thomas, I'd hoped you would make this easier on the both of us."

He uses his boot to knock Thomas onto his back and into the mud. He bends down and grabs his right hand, shoving a stick under his middle fingernail. Thomas screams at the top of his lungs and Estera gasps and turns away.

"I did that because you are an asshole, Thomas. Oh, and also because you irritated our new friend Christine earlier."

He walks over to Aidan next and stands looking down at him. Aidan tries to be defiant, but when Ethan moves to bend down, he flinches and screams. Ethan shakes his head in disgust and heads for the shelter as the mist starts again.

"Hey, wait, you can't leave us out here in the rain!" Aidan yells.

Ethan ignores him, and we follow him inside without acknowledging Aidan, just as he had asked.

"Aidan can think about what he wants to say for a bit. As soon as the rain breaks again, we'll see how serious he is," says Ethan.

We stay in the shelter for close to an hour until the rain finally lets up to a fine mist. Rain comes in through leaks in the roof so we spend the time repairing them with mud and moss. When we go out again, Thomas and Aidan are both shivering, looking miserable.

"All right. Let's try the same question with you, Aidan. Who is Jonathan?"

"I don't know any Jonathan."

"Right, see you in the morning, have a pleasant evening." Ethan turns toward the hut and takes two steps before Aidan shouts after him.

"Okay, okay! I'll tell you what you want, please—I'm cold, I need go inside."

"Aidan keep your damn mouth shut! Man up, it's only sodding rain, you idiot!" Thomas screams at him.

"Screw you, Thomas! You can't talk because you know nothing. You didn't ask Jonathan why he needed this done. All you're worried about is the money! Well, I asked questions, because I wanted to learn why this was important to him. I made sure I wasn't doing anything crappy. Unlike you, who couldn't give two shits about who you hurt."

Ethan grabs Aidan's arm, pulling him to his feet, and we follow them into the shelter. He pushes Aidan to the floor and kneels in front of him.

"Aidan, I will ask you one last time. Who is Jonathan?" asks Ethan.

"Jonathan is the guy who hired us."

"I know that much. Now you're wasting my time and pissing me off," Ethan says as he stands up.

"Okay, wait! He's the owner of Hoyt Enterprises—Jonathan Hoyt. He wants us to take some astronomer's book, his writings, and deliver them back to our time for him."

"What? He wants some book from a fourteenth century astronomer?"

"Well no, not the entire book. He was very specific, only a chapter, or treatise, as he called it. We only steal the whole thing if we can't figure out what section we need, but that's a last resort. He'd rather have the remaining parts intact here. All we're expected to do is take the chapter to him."

"Why? And when?"

"It's nothing; all he requires is the paperwork. He'll fix the system and we transport home the day after. We're slated to do the job on the sixteenth. On the seventeenth, we go home. If we're successful, we earn five million dollars each when we arrive home. He assured me he is not tweaking any major event in history, only he will ever be aware. I swear, that's the truth."

Ethan pulls Aidan up and walks him back outside to wait with Thomas. After returning, he sits down to address us.

"Why would Jonathan Hoyt want such an insignificant task done? He's paying a lot of money, so it's obviously not minor to him."

"There must be a good reason. Aidan didn't say he didn't know, he said it 'was nothing'." I glance to Ethan for confirmation of what I heard.

"That's true, he said that. I'll bring him inside shortly and determine what else he can tell us. Now that we understand what they're up to, I'm not sure what to do about it. It doesn't appear it would do any real harm. Although it's important enough to Hoyt to concoct this scheme to steal the chapter and shell out a huge amount of money to do so."

I look around the shelter, and Estera and Malcolm are nodding in agreement. "I'm confused why a man like Jonathan Hoyt would want a few pages from an astronomer's book. It makes no sense. It must be important."

"Perhaps he wants the formula or science or whatever is there to keep for himself?" asks Estera.

I shake my head. "No, that can't be. I mean, he only wants a small part of the book according to Aidan. Hoyt told him to leave the rest here if possible. Why would he only want a portion brought to modern day? Let's think about this. If they take the chapter to him, it's no longer part of history. Meaning no one else would have access to the it either, right? He must have archived the material down to the most minute detail to keep a record. If they deliver the writings, he'd have to have a way to access the knowledge that would be immune to changes in the timeline, some means to retrieve it later. Or somehow to remind himself why he requested the information."

"He owns and operates the largest computer and software company in the United States, possibly the world. If he wanted to stake a claim on some seven-hundred-year-old secret, he'd just take what he knows and start working on practical applications for it. His team would have whatever new technology they desired operational before anyone else had any idea it was useful," says Estera.

"Christine makes an excellent point," says Malcolm, who had been quiet until now. "If Jonathan Hoyt deems this is material he should delete from current world history or belongs in our timeline, I'd trust him on that. He's manipulating a lot to get it there. My ex-wife interned for him way back when, before he was the super conglomerate, he is now. He's brilliant, and unless he's done a complete three-sixty in terms of his moral compass, he's a decent guy. She always told me how honest he was, and the man she described wouldn't do something nefarious for his own advancement. He prides himself on the fact that he built his company from the ground up and did so screwing no one in the process. I'm as baffled as the rest of you are. It doesn't align with the businessman I've heard about—that I'm certain of."

"Well, who knows, Malcolm? People change. But I grant you he has a stellar reputation." Ethan says.

Am I the only one who thinks this whole matter is crazy?

"So what? We're overthinking this entire thing. The only information we need is if the system is coming back. Why do we care if he needs some chapter from a book? Why is that such a big deal? Let's kick them out of camp and on about their business. Us making it home, that's the priority, right?" I search their faces, one by one, looking for affirmation. "Right?"

Ethan nods. "I agree with you, Christine, but a part of me also wants to understand why Hoyt went to all this trouble. I'm not convinced we can make an informed decision without all the intelligence. Maybe it's time we bring our friend in from outside and learn what else he can tell us."

"Fair enough. But if we can't figure out the why, or it isn't significant, we agree to make them leave. Let them disappear once we confirm the system is coming back, right? I mean, what if this is only some minor data Hoyt wants to take credit for? There are many things I can live with at this point that I wouldn't have seven months ago if that means me getting home. And what about Thomas?" I ask.

Ethan sighs and grimaces before answering. "I don't agree letting them go free is an option at this stage. They'll consider us a threat to their plan. I can't imagine Thomas would let a loose end like that stand, and he doesn't strike me as the type who'll let a grudge go unchecked. I predict he'd make a move to come after us, and we need to consider that possibility. In the meantime, let him rot in the rain for all I care. He apparently didn't bother to ask Hoyt anything about the job, so he's no use to us now. If the cold weather makes him ill, he can pop an antibiotic from Malcolm's survival pack."

FOURTEEN

Cotswold, England 1335

Ethan retrieves Aidan and leads him inside to sit next to the fire.

"Thank you, thank you. I'll tell you anything you want to know. This isn't a bad thing we're doing, Ethan, just so you understand."

"Yes, well, since you've brought that up Aidan. Share with us the reason Jonathan Hoyt wants you to steal some obscure chapter from a book written by an astronomer from seven hundred years ago. And while we're getting chummy and sharing secrets, do tell why you're willing to kill us if we become a liability."

"No, no, it's not like that! I have to go along with Thomas o-o-or—well . . . you see how he is! He scares the shit out of me, Ethan. You don't know him as I do. I work with him, and I spent our first few months here on the road with him. He's as brutal as they come, trust me. If I hadn't agreed with him, he'd have gone ahead without me. I would have warned you, I swear, if he was planning to kill any of you. If you overheard me say that to him, you must've also heard me say I didn't agree Jonathan would approve of killing anyone."

"To be honest Aidan, I don't trust you even one bit, and I think you deserve whatever Thomas has in store for you. You realize now he knows you've talked, you're also a liability? We outnumber him too much to make a move on the group. You, on the other hand, should be easy pickings," says Ethan.

"What? You aren't going to let him go, are you? He'll kill me! I watched him try to strangle someone on the way here for the guy's blanket! Killing someone, anyone, was never part of the plan!"

"Really? You watched him attempt to brutally end someone's life and yet you continued on with him and brought him here? You could have stayed on your own, so don't expect any sympathy from me. Aidan, the more you talk, the less I like you. I want to know why Jonathan Hoyt wants this done. I don't want to hear anything but that. You've got one chance, Aidan, so don't botch it up."

Aidan sighs and his shoulders sag. "All right, all right. I only spoke to Hoyt one time, they did all the other communication about this through a bloke named James, one of his associates or employees I would imagine. Hoyt said this astronomer, this Richard of Wallingford guy, he's been researching some of his work. Something about gravity and planetary alignments, which I didn't grasp, to be honest. He said people typically recognize Wallingford for constructing an astronomical clock, but that's not what Hoyt's after. He's after a chapter in his book called the Tractatus Albionis, that's what he needs. In it, Wallingford describes the Albion, which Hoyt called an equatorium. I did not recognize what that is. The clock Wallingford was famous for measured tides, planetary alignments, and a bunch of other stuff I can't remember and didn't follow. The Albion calculates lunar, solar, and planetary longitudes, and predicts eclipses. I guess part of the writing disappeared over the years and he needs the missing chapter to complete some research."

"Okay so why only the writings? Why not the Albion itself? Why does he care about researching this?" Ethan asks.

"Wallingford never completed the Albion, so all he wants are the writings. Wallingford won't have time to replicate the work and distribute the leaflets before his death next year, so we have to take it now while it's still available. He told me it's integral to predicting some future planet gravitational pull. I didn't comprehend why that is important."

"And, so what? It relates to other planets gravitational pull. I don't understand why that's a big deal. Our present-day scientists would know if that were a problem," I say.

"I believe it may be more, but I can't confirm what. He was mumbling about weather patterns and pandemics and how we had to be ready before it wipes us out. He started to sound a tad bit manic to be fair, and most of what he was saying was way above my understanding, so I stopped paying attention. I wanted to verify I wasn't carrying out anything to hurt anyone, that's all I worried about. At the close of our conversation he said what we were doing is critical to all of mankind, and he was dead serious about it. All I can affirm is he's a very sharp guy and if Jonathan Hoyt believes having this chapter is crucial, who the hell am I to question it?"

"Whoa, pandemic? You're certain he used that term?" I ask.

"Yes, positive. He said it was coming, and we needed to stop it. I asked him about that as the term caught my attention, but he wouldn't say any more about it. That's when he told me this is vital to mankind. He scared me a bit to be honest. I've read about pandemics like everyone else. I'm not sure about you, but I'm not keen to see one in my lifetime, or my kid's lifetime."

"How noble of you, I'm sure you didn't agree to this just for the money," Ethan says sarcastically. "That explains the why, what about who? Why you two? No offense Aidan, but you don't exactly inspire confidence in your ability to carry out something of this magnitude. How did he have you here at the perfect time? The odds of that happening on its own would be astronomical, no pun intended," says Ethan.

"You're correct, it wasn't random. Hoyt wrote the program and built the process the government uses to transport. It was easy to hack in and tweak things to put Thomas and me here together in the correct year. As far as why us, that part was simple—we are both transporters who need money. I'm living way beyond my means, and I'm three, maybe four months from bankruptcy. If that happens, my wife might leave me and take our kids, and I couldn't live through that. Thomas gambles; he thinks no one knows, but we've all seen the signs. Hoyt came to two people he assumed would jump at the chance to rid themselves of their money problems—and we did. So now you've learned everything I have. But you can't let Thomas get to me, Ethan, he's not stable. I have a wife and kids back home! I appreciate what I did was wrong, but at least I made clear I wasn't acting in a way to hurt anyone."

"That still doesn't explain the system failure or how you have knowledge of the transponders coming online."

"That's all Hoyt. He rigged the operation to keep transporters immobilized. The system can't do a forced transport to bring anyone home until he unlocks it. He assured me what he did is untraceable. No one would find out he tampered with the procedure. No one will connect Thomas and me to any of this. He put us here several months early to pick up position, get the lie of the land and allow time to execute the plan. We understood we'd have to travel to see Wallingford. We weren't sure how long it would take or what we might run into. Besides, Hoyt could only tweak the process so much without the agency knowing someone had sabotaged it. We meant to pick up the writings from Wallingford in Leeds four months ago, but it didn't work out. So now Cotswold is the contingency plan, and our last chance to make it happen. Wallingford will be in here in five days, and the day after, the system goes online. He'll only be here for one night on his way to St. Albans. After that, Hoyt restores the operation, allowing the trapped transporters to travel home. You needn't be near your drop-off point to transport home—he knew transporters would move to safer locations. I would never have agreed to do this unless I felt certain I was getting home."

"Wait a minute," I look at Aidan, "Are you saying we got stuck here so you two won't be connected to this job?"

"Well, yeah. I mean he had to make it a complete system shutdown for one day so it would seem legit."

Oh my God. As long things appear legit, screw the rest of us, right?

I'm breathing hard and my heart feels like it will beat out of my chest.

"I watched my friend captured by Indians! I've been away from my son for almost seven months! All to protect you and that asshole outside from losing your payday and getting caught?"

I lunge for him, but Ethan catches me before I reach him. Estera takes the opportunity to step in front of Aidan and slap his face.

"You bastard. You put us all at risk. Who knows how many transporters have died because of you and Hoyt! What on God's green earth were you thinking?" She steps back and sits on a log, shaking her head.

I shake Ethan's hand from my shoulder. "Oh, my God! This situation has pissed me off for all these months, not knowing who to be angry with, wondering who dropped the ball and got us stranded here. I've seethed over whoever isn't working hard enough back at base to get us home. And the entire time, it was an egotistical billionaire who wants to play researcher and two greedy douchebags keeping us here? These are people's lives you're screwing with! People have missed time with their families, things they'll never get back; a child's first steps, maybe a parent passed. What gives you the right to decide that for us?"

I want to cry, but the tears don't come. I guess I'm just all cried out at this point. But I feel anger like I never have.

How dare they involve innocent transporters in their scheme?

Ethan stands him up and leads him back outside. He's inside again within two minutes, looking serious.

"Look everyone, I agree what they did was wrong. Hoyt had no right to strand any transporters anywhere or make us all collateral damage. But what if Hoyt's right? What if that information is something critical? He's gone to a lot of trouble, not to mention risk, to get the chapter he wants. If he's worried about it, maybe we should be."

I glance at Ethan, my brow furrowing, "Oh, come on Ethan, you aren't suggesting that we let them complete this 'job,' are you?"

"No, not them—us. I'm saying we do it. And once we're back home, we can go see Hoyt and have a proper chat about it. If we decide that it was all bollocks and his intentions are self-serving, we go to the authorities, or the press, or whoever. We out him, and the information is public, and his little plan goes up in smoke. If that happens, Thomas and Aidan will also be outed in the process. And the best part is they get no payday either way, which means they've been here for nothing, like the rest of us. What if we take the chapter as planned, but bring it back with us, intact? That would be our leverage. If Hoyt doesn't convince us it was the right thing to do, we turn it over or destroy it. Which puts him back where he is now—without the chapter. The chapter would still exist, albeit not as a part of history. What about it, guys? Are you willing to complete the job and see where it lands us?"

Malcolm stands up. "I want no part of it, sorry. I was coming here either way with no hope of going home. At the risk of sounding callous, I've got no skin in the game here."

Estera nods. "I agree with Malcolm. I just want to get home and forget the last seven months. I'm not at all convinced this is the right thing to do. I want no part of it either." With that, she turns her back on us to put more wood on the fire.

"I'll do it. I'll help you get the chapter."

Oh God, did I say that out loud?

"We can go to Hoyt together when we get back, but we agree that our plan doesn't leave this room. Until we figure out what our next move is, those two idiots can't know about this. Estera, you can't share this with anyone when you get home. Not even your husband. If it isn't successful, you'll know about it soon enough."

"Don't worry, I don't even want to know about it now, and I won't tell anyone. Do you think he's telling the truth? That the system will be back online in six days?"

Ethan looks around the room at us. "I hope so. I really hope so. I can't imagine Aidan or Thomas agreeing to do this without some guarantee they would get home when it was over. What he said makes sense, not that I agree with the strategy of stranding all the transporters, but it makes sense. I will bring them inside if it's all right with all of you. I'll tie their hands in front to give them a little relief. I'll make sure I secure the ties to their waists, so they can't attack us or something stupid. Malcolm, I will need your help to secure them."

Malcolm follows him outside while Estera and I stay in the shelter. Things feel awkward now, as if this has divided the camp. Thomas and Aidan the outcasts, Estera and Malcolm the nonparticipants, and Ethan and I, the idiots going after the chapter.

I surprised myself by answering him so quickly. It's unlike me to jump into something significant without reflecting on it, but this feels like the right thing to do. I took an oath when I hired into this position.

On my honor, I will never betray my badge, my integrity, my character, or the public trust. I will always have the courage to hold myself and others accountable for our actions.

It seems especially relevant in this situation. If that information is as critical as Hoyt seems to think, how is it *not* my responsibility to do something? The short answer is I have to follow through on the off chance he's right. I'm not willing to sacrifice even a small amount of my integrity for some government policy that says we can't alter anything from the past. I just hope I'm making the right decision, for all our sakes.

Ethan and Malcolm bring Thomas and Aidan into the shelter and retie them after allowing them to dry off. Thomas looks like he wants to kill us all and Aidan looks shell-shocked.

"You will not get away with this, Ethan. I will get the job done one way or another and get my money,"—he turns to Aidan—"and then I'm coming for you."

Aidan tries to back up farther into the corner but doesn't respond. No one speaks right away; we sit there, each lost in our own thoughts.

Thomas breaks the silence. "What the fuck is going on here? Get me out of these ties. I'll go on my way, and you'll never see me again. You must know you're all going home in six days since the narc over there sang like a canary. Stay out of sight for the next few days, after that you're home free. Don't worry Aidan, I'll catch up with you back home, mate."

"Give it a bloody rest, Thomas! It's over! We aren't going to do the job, we will not get paid, and we're lucky we've stayed alive this long to even get home. This entire thing has been such a cock-up. I should never have agreed to it. You can be as pissed off as you like, but it's over."

"Nothing's over until I say so. I've earned that money, I've been out here for months, and I didn't do all this for nothing."

"Yeah, not like the rest of us, right Thomas?" I glare at him in anger.

Ethan gets up and motions to me, so I grab a blanket and follow him outside.

After a moment, he speaks. "Looks like it might snow tonight."

"Did you bring me out here for a weather report?"

"No. You volunteered quickly. I want to make sure you're ready for what we might run into while doing this. This will be dangerous, and there's a lot to go wrong. There's always a chance we could get caught, and that could mean we might not be alive to make it home. I want you to understand that, Christine."

"I understand what it means, I do. And I want to go home as much as everyone else, so I guess we should make sure we don't get caught. You were right before, if this chapter is so important, we have to get it. It concerns me he has gone to such trouble to get it. When someone like Hoyt throws words like pandemic around, it gets my attention. We can decide what to do with the chapter later. But so help me God, if this is some ridiculous plot with no merit, I will take Hoyt down if it's the last thing I do."

"If this turns out to be nothing, I will make sure he pays, you have my word. Tomorrow we should go to Cotswold, survey the area. See where this Wallingford character will stay and get familiar with the layout. Since you've never been there, I think it's important we do that."

"I agree, and I'm up for it. I guess we should get some shut-eye. It sounds as if we've got a big day tomorrow."

"Yes, I don't know about you, but I'm knackered after all this nonsense today."

"Well, I'm not sure I know what 'knackered' means, but I'm exhausted."

Ethan laughs, muttering, "Yank," under his breath as I follow him to the hut.

The fireplace crackles, radiating welcome heat in the shelter. I think Ethan's right, it could snow tonight. I've lived nowhere where snow was a possibility, especially this time of year. Snow hits the outskirts of Los Angeles once every dozen years, but only in the San Gabriel Mountains, so I'm looking forward to seeing it snow.

After a while everyone lies down to sleep, but my mind is racing, worrying about tomorrow. I'm nervous about going into Cotswold. Ethan is right, there is a lot to go wrong, and tomorrow is only a reconnaissance day.

I hear Thomas and Aidan moving around trying to get comfortable with their ties in place. Serves them right. They're lucky one of us doesn't shank them in their sleep after what they've done. At least I understand what went wrong now and have someone to blame. If Annabelle were here, she'd try to talk me into doing something horrible to them, maybe tarring and feathering them. I think that was popular in medieval times. The memory of Annabelle makes me tear up and I cry softly to myself until the warmth of the fire finally soothes me to sleep.

I'm out like the dead for a couple of hours when I wake up with a start, hearing a noise outside. I lie back down to listen and hear a soft rustling. It must be a deer or a raccoon. We could use a deer, but I'm too tired to do anything about it. There are probably rabbits in the trap, so I tell myself we can have stew tonight. I wake up again right before dawn and the shelter is bitter cold. I put more wood on the fire and don't warm up until it blazes brightly. I scan the room and notice something looks off. Thomas's blanket is bunched up and doesn't look right. As my eyes adjust to the dark, I realize that Thomas isn't where he should be. I scan the shelter, and confirm he's not here. I crawl over to Ethan and shake him gently.

"Ethan," I whisper close to his ear. He stirs and looks up at me.

"What's the matter?"

"Thomas is gone."

Ethan sits up, almost knocking me back. He looks around and scrambles up.

"Shit."

He makes his way outside, and by this time everyone else is stirring.

Malcolm sits up, rubbing his eyes. "What's going on?"

"Thomas escaped."

"Oh, crap."

"Yep, that's the consensus."

Malcolm gets up and is rooting around his sleeping area, throwing his blanket aside.

"My backpack is missing. That fucker took my survival pack! It had all my antibiotics in there. That asshole."

By now everyone is awake, and we venture outside. Ethan jogs back into camp, shaking his head.

"He's long gone. His footprints lead north toward Cotswold, but the snow almost covers the prints. He left a few hours ago."

"He took the backpack with the antibiotics," Malcolm tells him.

Ethan kicks the snow and sits down with his head in his hands.

"I'm sorry, everyone. I can't fathom how he got out of his restraints."

"It's not your fault Ethan; he would do whatever it took to carry on as planned, he made that clear. They were ties made from a worn dress, not flex cuffs. No one is to blame, least of all you." Estera sits next to him and places her hand on his knee. "We all slept through him leaving."

Did we? I hope that was a deer I heard earlier and not Thomas escaping.

I boil water for tea and talk to Estera about using her wrap today when I go into Cotswold. Aidan is still in the shelter, so we can talk about our plans.

Ethan sits next to Malcolm and pours himself some tea. "Christine and I are going into Cotswold today to get the lie of the land. Malcolm, can you check the traps? Estera can stay here with Aidan and monitor him."

Estera stands up and stretches. "I'll go. I've got cabin fever and need to get out. I'm okay to go on my own, I'll be careful. Besides, if Aidan acts up, Malcolm is better equipped to handle him than I am."

I look at Estera and laugh. "I don't know about that—you cleaned his clock the other day when he started to run."

Ethan shrugs. "Whoever wants to go, that's fine with me. If there's anything in the traps, we need to get it before it spoils. Christine and I will be back before nightfall. We can get vegetables on our way back."

We have tea around the fire and warm up. It's not raining for once, but it looks like it might snow again. It's sure cold enough. My mind keeps wandering, going back to the day ahead. I try to focus on something less stressful and concentrate on the fact that I could go home in five days. It doesn't seem real after all this time. I can't wait to see Michael—I've missed him so much. We will take that trip to Aruba; I don't care if it puts me in the poor house for the next year. I'm sure the airlines won't honor my unused tickets, so I'll have to start over again.

Thinking about home and Michael cheers me up. I'll get through the next five days, do what we need to. I think about how strange it is, all I've focused on since being stranded has been surviving. Now I'm helping complete a task potentially critical to the entire planet. It was blind luck to end up where I am now to overhear Aidan and Thomas talking in the woods, considering all the near misses I had. Gonzalez broke his arm, putting me on the roster to transport. I ate the doughnut that made my blood sugar spike, almost preventing me from traveling. Then I ended up here. If all that hadn't happened, Ethan, Estera, and Malcolm may never have learned about Thomas and Aidan's plan, and they might have gotten away with it.

We would all have transported home never knowing what had happened or why we were stuck on that fateful day.

I watch Ethan putting wood on the fire. I've observed him before, but I take the opportunity to really look at him now. He's tall and fit, and his blonde hair curls at his neck. I suspect he wears it much shorter when he's back home, and I try to imagine that. He's a good man, doing the right thing with the Hoyt plan. He hasn't talked about his personal life. I wonder if he has a wife or a girlfriend at home.

Stop it, Christine. Remember what you always say.

Yeah, something about cupid rhyming with stupid, but it escapes me now as I watch Ethan.

"All right, there's plenty of wood. Give Aidan some tea if you don't mind so he doesn't dehydrate. We need him healthy enough to face the authorities at home. We'll be back later. Ready, Christine?"

"Will do," says Malcolm.

I nod and stand up, ready to follow Ethan into Cotswold. I step into the damp forest and for the second time in as many days, I question a decision I've made.

FIFTEEN

Los Angeles, California 2070

I wake up early. Today's the day I leave with the retrieval team and start the hunt for my mom.

If I had my way, we'd start in Oklahoma first, but that will be our last stop. There are five Los Angeles-based transporters to find, including my mom. Our route starts in New York, then down to Virginia, Wyoming, Texas, and finally Oklahoma. We're also doing a courtesy search for the Chicago division after we finish in Oklahoma. There is a missing transporter who landed over two hundred miles from my mom's drop zone but came in off course. They can't locate her in Arkansas and think there's a chance she may have traveled out of her drop area. Frank agreed to do a cursory search of the outlying areas of Piedmont while we are there.

Too keyed up to sleep, I review my plans for the morning. I need to take Max to my Aunt Kat's, so I won't have to board him. I also have to ready the house to be vacant for at least two weeks. Frank says Linda will check on the place while I'm gone, but I don't want her to walk into some mess because I forgot to turn off the water or something stupid. I never understood how much effort it takes to run a house. My mom's always taken care of all that. But I learned quickly after she went missing; nothing like getting tossed into the deep end. After all that, I'm meeting the other team members in the cafeteria for breakfast. We might only get MRE's and food replacement capsules for a while after this, so we're going to eat a decent meal before we leave.

I take a quick shower and get dressed, then chase Max down and pack up all his stuff.

How one dog can require so much is beyond me—a bed, toys, food, treats, and a blanket. He knows something's up and tries to run. Maddie has already left for work, so I'm on my own trying to bait him.

I don't need this today, Max.

I catch him by enticing him with a jerky treat and load him in the car. After dropping him off I head to work, even though I'm super early. I use the time to recheck my equipment because Frank will have my ass if I forget anything. I meet the team as planned and make small talk. No one brings up our mission. There are four other individuals on the team with me, and Frank is our unit leader. Carey is twenty-six and not married. Penn is twenty-eight and married with a new baby boy. Gray is forty-five, married and has two teenage girls, and Adams is thirty-eight and divorced with an eleven-year-old son. Carey and I have the most in common and have become friends over the past few days of training. I told him my mom is out there, and how much this means to me. I'm not sure if the other guys know or not; I don't think Frank made it common knowledge.

We're halfway through breakfast when Frank shows up. He doesn't talk about the mission either. Instead, he keeps the conversation light. He entertains us with stories about his new brother-in-law, who he doesn't seem to like very much. As we're finishing up, he gets to the business end of things.

"Guys, what we're doing is dangerous. I appreciate each of you is sacrificing time with your families to be here. I've spoken to each lost transporters' family, and they are all grateful for your willingness to travel back to look for them. No one knows what we will find in each location, or who we may run into. But I have faith in all of you to get the job done to the best of your ability. If I didn't, you wouldn't be here. That being said, let's get to the jump room and take this show on the road."

Twenty minutes later, we're all secured in pods. My heart is beating wildly. I try to hide my nervousness from my teammates, but I know my face reflects my fear. Adams gives me a thumbs up and says he'll see me on the other side. Once the countdown begins, things move fast.

I see the pinpoints of light my mom has described to me, and the next thing I'm aware of, Frank is shaking me awake. I open my eyes and peer around. Carey is out, but the others are awake and milling about.

"Welcome to 1751 New York, Stewart. Get your ass up," he says.

I sit up and shake my head, trying to clear my mind. Gray is waking Carey up and he's looking as rough as I feel.

"Okay, here's our plan, people. Gray and I will change into our period clothing and begin searching for Williams. You four will get camp squared away and stand by. If we aren't back by nightfall tomorrow, you are to transport to our next destination in Virginia. You do not wait for us; we'll catch up. If we don't show in Virginia within twelve hours of your arrival, contact base to send another commander and team member to complete the mission."

"Wait, you never told us that," Carey looks at Frank confused.

"Well, I'm telling you now, and that's an order, Carey. That's how this will go down."

I exchange a glance with Carey, but I'm trained better than to argue with Frank. He gave the directive, that's the end. They change into their clothes and conceal supplies in their clothing. They check their compasses and take off in a jog toward the city. The rest of us make camp and set up a fire. We all brought emergency blankets, although I'm not convinced they will keep us warm out here as it's friggin' freezing in these woods. The four of us settle in, one person always on watch. I bed down ready to sleep, as I'm second shift. I drift off covered in my thermal blanket, my arm wrapped around my weapon. This is camping gone wild.

* * *

Frank and Gray see a town in the distance. Smithfield isn't a big city to detect a lost transporter in with a population of under one thousand people. However, it's spread out along the edge of the water and being a port city it's a busy place. Finding him will be more difficult because Williams tracking device isn't registering. The outage disabled it, just as Frank had suspected. Frank figures he's homeless, or he got a job to survive, and it would have to be manual labor. The ships crowd the docks, coming and going all day. It would be the ideal place for a person who didn't fit in to become lost and remain anonymous. So, the first area they search is the shipyards. They spend the day roaming around the area, making small talk with as many people as they can, trying not to raise suspicion. It doesn't take them long to get a lead. Gray lucked out on their first day in town and found someone who knew him. They don't recover him that day, so they stay in a local hotel that night. They are at the dock at dawn, so they won't miss him again. Gray is unloading freight off a ship when they spot him. He doesn't resemble his employee picture a lot anymore; he has a full beard, his typically short cropped hair reaches his shoulders, and it looks like he's lost about twenty pounds.

Gray approaches him from behind. "Williams? Jim Williams?"

"Yeah, that's me. Whatever you need, I'm finished here in about thirty minutes. What dock are you at? I'll come meet you when I'm done." He never stops off-loading and never looks at Gray or Frank.

"Jim, I'm Agent Gray, here with Captain Rhoades. We're part of a retrieval team sent to take you home."

Williams stops, holding a wooden box in midair. He puts it down and turns around slowly to face them.

"Is this real? Are you for real?"

"My ID number is 78654. I'm based out of the Los Angeles unit, but I don't think we've ever met. We're out searching for all the missing transporters from April 2nd."

"Oh my God. It's about damn time, pal. There are other stranded transporters?"

"Yeah, a few. Let's send you home, Jim. I'm sure you're ready to go."

He follows them off the dock, ignoring the foreman who yells and threatens to fire him if he doesn't get back on the line.

* * *

Frank sends the message we have located Williams alive and we'll transport him after an on-site debriefing. The smile never leaves his face, thankful to be rescued, but he has lots of questions we aren't able to answer. He worries about his family, but Frank assures him they will notify them we have found him.

"Guys, I can't thank you enough for risking yourselves to come looking for me, for all of us. I had no idea the system stranded other transporters.

You do not understand what I've been through here. What a nightmare. I hope you can locate everyone. God bless all of you."

He shakes each of our hands and tells Frank he is ready to leave.

We transport Jim Williams home from camp that afternoon. The successful rescue on the first trip out boosts the whole team's spirits. Even though I didn't take part in finding him, it is encouraging to know that Frank and Gray could. Not only does it reflect well on the entire team, but it also gives me hope that we'll recover my mom.

We stay in our camp that night and transport to Charles City, Virginia, 1621 the next morning to find Philip McCarty, who transported in right outside the city. He shouldn't be too difficult to locate, as the population of Charles City was only about twelve hundred people in 1621. Frank takes Adams with him this time; he says each of us will take point with him along the trip. They leave just after noon and are back by nightfall, having had no luck. They heard about a sick colony on the outskirts of town, so they'll go there in the morning. If they don't recover him there, then they'll search for his prisoner, David Cooper, to determine if he can give them any leads.

We spend a quiet night by the fire. Penn suggests we try to bag a deer, but Frank shoots that idea down. He says we can't take the chance of getting sick by eating meat not properly prepared or cooked, and besides that, we have MREs.

What the hell have the missing transporters done for food?

We retire to bed early with Frank and Adams planning to leave at sunrise. I'm up just before dawn again; it's hard to sleep on the bare ground. I was cold even with my thermal blanket, and I spend my first few minutes awake practically sitting on top of the fire. The other guys are up not long after me, all complaining about either being stiff or having a neck ache.

At least I'm not the only one who had a rough night.

Frank and Adams leave as soon as the sun is up, taking antibiotics with them.

* * *

Adams walks into the run-down plantation house first, with Frank close behind. A nurse meets them at the door.

"Can I help you, gentlemen?"

Frank steps forward and removes his hat.

"Yes ma'am. I'm looking for my brother, Phillip McCarty. I was told he may be ill, and I am hoping to find him here."

"There are over forty men here, but I don't recognize that name."

"Can I look myself? He may use another name."

"Why would he do that? I hope he isn't here then, as we do not abide by criminals or that sort here. This is a God-fearing hospital."

"I assure you it's nothing like that. Our father disowned him over a property dispute and I'm afraid he may have taken that to heart."

"I can show you where the patients are, and if you locate him, I would be grateful if you would remove him from our hospital."

"Yes ma'am, we intend to, thank you."

They follow her into a large room with beds lining either side. Some men are up walking or sitting in chairs, but most are in beds. Adams and Frank each take a side and inspect bed to bed. About halfway through, Adams motions to Frank. McCarty looks up at them with bloodshot eyes. He shivers, and there is blood and vomit in his bedpan. Adams leans in closer and turns the mans head from side to side trying to confirm it is McCarty. The man is rail thin, his beard hiding most of his face.

"Phil? Are you Phil McCarty?"

He tries to speak but coughs violently instead, then spits blood and phlegm into the bedpan before he can gather the strength to speak.

"Who are you? Why do you want to know my name?"

"I'm Agent Adams, ID 66582 out of Los Angeles. If you're Phillip, I'm here to take you home."

A single tear rolls down his cheek as he reaches up to grasp Adams's hand.

Frank and Adams carry McCarty to camp. The nurse provided them a rudimentary stretcher of sorts made from tree branches and a blanket. He is easy to carry because he is so thin, and they make good time.

* * *

As they come into camp in the early afternoon, Frank shouts for a Med-Pac. They gave him an antibiotic when they left the hospital, but it hasn't improved his symptoms any. You can expect to see progress within two hours after a one-dose antibiotic. Frank gives him a fever reducer and covers him with a thermal blanket to stop his chills. He comes to sit down by us, out of earshot of McCarty.

"Adams suspects he may have leptospirosis. His eyes are bloodshot, and with the flu-like symptoms, coughing blood, they're all consistent signs. It's so advanced that he will need intravenous antibiotics to recover. The broad-spectrum pills we carry will not do him any good, they're more preventative or early stage effective. In his precarious condition they are useless."

"Are you sure, Boss?" Carey looks petrified.

"I'm certain, yes. Adams is the medic, and he's briefed on the diseases for the time periods we're going to. The bloodshot eyes are the most telltale sign, but everything else is consistent with it."

"Should we take the pills? Were we vaccinated against it?" Carey looks panicked now.

Adams finishes with McCarty and walks up to the group in time to answer Carey.

"It's not passed from person to person, so you don't need to worry—it's not contagious. It's spread through rat urine in fresh standing water. He probably caught it bathing, the bacteria entering his system through his eyes or nose. I hope he wasn't stupid enough to drink water without boiling it first."

Gray looks at Frank. "What do we do then? It doesn't appear he can transport home alone. Do you want one of us to escort him in a tandem transport and then meet you in Wyoming?"

"No. I'm not sure he would make it in his shape. We may be wrong about his diagnosis and he may bring something back that could start an outbreak. He's in such bad shape, I really don't think he would make it back alive. They vaccinate us; no one else back home was though. I don't know if we can help him. The best we can offer is to make him comfortable for tonight. I'll message base and see what they want us to do. Our orders are to recover proof of identity but not to transport any deceased home. I understand he's not dead yet, but he's damn close to it."

"What if he makes it through the night, Frank?" I ask.

"I'm sorry, Stewart, we can't stay any longer than tomorrow morning. It may take another day for this to run its course. We don't have that kind of time. I'm under strict orders, anyone who's deceased or terminally ill cannot transport home. I don't want to leave him in this shape either and I don't like these orders any more than the rest of you do. But for the safety of everyone, base may instruct me to terminate him."

"Terminate, Frank?" I say, thinking I didn't hear that right.

Frank lowers his eyes before answering me, his shoulders sagging.

"Yes Stewart, terminate. I have my orders. I don't have to like them, but I must follow them."

I shake my head in disbelief and walk away. Once I'm at the edge of camp, I kick a tree with my boot, trying to release my anger. A guy is sick, and base surmises killing him is the solution? And Frank will go along with it?

What the actual fuck are they thinking?

So, what, if my mom's sick, Frank will 'terminate' her and leave her in 1867 Oklahoma?

Over my dead body.

Frank walks up behind me, "Michael, I know what you're thinking."

"No, I don't imagine you do Frank." I turn to face him, my fists clenched at my sides.

"Relax kid, I do. I won't let that happen to your mom; you know that. You're both family to me."

"So, McCarty isn't family, and he's expendable, is that the deal? It's screwed up to consider this for any transporter, but yeah, my mom comes to mind." I narrow my eyes and stand up straight while jutting my chin out.

"Stand down Stewart and don't make me say that again." He takes a step toward me, never breaking eye contact.

"Termination is a last-ditch effort for a transporter who will not make it home. We cannot leave him alive. The system has determined the risk is too great to our current timeline to allow a living transporter to remain in a past timeline. I will avoid that if possible, but in this case, it may be too late for McCarty. Now get your temper in check right now officer and get your ass back to camp. I don't give a good goddamn who you are, if we need another talk like this, you'll transport home, no further discussion. Is that understood?"

I nod my head, never meeting his eyes.

"I didn't hear you, Stewart."

"Yes sir. Understood," I say, looking him in the eye.

Frank walks away, then turns back to face me.

"I bear a responsibility to your mom to bring her home. It's my fault she's out here. I can't babysit you when I need to be concentrating on getting the transporters and my team home."

"Nobody knows whose fault it is; don't try to make me feel better by taking the blame, Frank. That just pisses me off more than I already am. I'm not a kid anymore, so you can stop treating me like one."

"Then control your emotions. Stop acting like a child and start acting like you're an officer with the CCE. You know me better than that, I will sugarcoat nothing just to improve your outlook. It's a crappy situation we're in. But I shouldn't have let her travel for Gonzalez when she was up for vacation in the same week. I should have pulled her off the roster, but I didn't. She said nothing, so I let it go. And now she's missing, and if something happens to her, it falls squarely on my shoulders. So, marinate on that for a while before you suggest that I'm patronizing you. Now pull yourself together and get to camp."

Frank turns and walks away, and I kick the tree again. He's right, my anger isn't helping anything. I realized he felt guilty about my mom, but I didn't truly understand why until now.

And what about me? Am I hurting the mission being here? Am I too close to the situation to do any good? I walk back into camp embarrassed and humbled, and if the other guys suspect Frank gave me a dressing down, they don't let on. I keep my mouth shut and tell myself to man up and get my head together.

Frank sends a message to base about McCarty, and medical comes back with a list of questions for Adams, who does another exam, feeding the information to base.

Adams comes to sit with the team, looking grim. "Guys, it doesn't look good. His vitals are getting worse and his organs are failing. I can say with confidence there is no way in hell he'd ever survive a transport home at this point. It's too much for his system to tolerate. He'd arrive DOA and could risk the handlers back home."

"So, how do you terminate him? I mean, that's what you're saying, right?" Carey asks.

"Adams will give him an injection," Frank says.

Adams glances at us. "It's not ideal. It paralyzes all the muscles, including the lungs, so you can't breathe. To be honest, it's a crappy way to go out."

"What about a suicide pill? That would be more humane," I say.

Frank stares at me for a minute before speaking.

"We can offer that option to him, sure."

We follow Frank over to McCarty, who although covered in a thermal blanket, is still shivering. He's awake and attempts to sit up but collapses back down.

"Thank you for coming for me. I thought I was stuck here forever," he looks at each of us for a moment before speaking again. "I'm dying. If that's what you came to say, I already know. The antibiotics you gave me should have helped some by now, but I feel worse, not better. Are you going to send me home now?"

"I don't think so, Phil. I'm under orders that I can't transport anyone who's as sick as you are. Without modern medical technology we can't be certain about what you have. Our medic Adams thinks it may be a virus that's passed from rat urine to humans in fresh water. The problem now is that it's so far along, that he, and medical back at base, are certain you wouldn't survive the transport home. I'm sorry," Frank says.

"I went swimming with someone a week ago. We were both sick a few days after. She died two days ago."

Adams crouches down to speak to McCarty. "Phil, there isn't much else to do for you here. With your symptoms and now knowing you swam, and your friend has passed, I'm fairly certain about the virus you contracted. Even if by some miracle you were to survive the trip home, you might pose a risk to everyone there. Even if not contagious, I could be wrong, it might mutate, or you may have something different. It's all guesswork at this point without our present day testing available here in the field. Our equipment will not operate in this timeline. One thing I am sure of though is that you cannot survive a transport in your condition. I'm very sorry to tell you that.

We will keep you as comfortable as possible, but our orders say we leave tomorrow morning."

"Oh. Yeah, I get it. I'm screwed. I understand. It isn't your fault. I know I'm not going to make it. So, what happens to me now? What happens to all of you?" he asks.

"We won't be at risk. We've had vaccines and precautionary antibiotics to protect us while we're here," says Adams.

"My instructions are to terminate Phil, I'm sorry. But there are two choices," Frank says as he crouches down next to Adams.

"I don't want to die here, alone in the woods," he says, a sob escaping.

"We carry suicide pills. They induce sleep within seconds and death occurs one to two minutes later. We would all be with you Phil, you wouldn't be alone," Frank says.

"The other option is the termination injection," says Adams. "It paralyzes all your muscles. You wouldn't be able to move, and within minutes you won't be able to breathe either."

McCarty closes his eyes for a moment, then looks back up at Frank.

"Okay. I want the suicide pill. I don't want to suffocate. But I want to ask a favor. Can you please take down a letter to my wife for me? Do you have a voice recorder?"

"Voice recording won't work here. I can type something for you though."

"Okay, let's do that. And please don't tell her how I got this. Don't tell her there was another woman. This is my penance for cheating on her, I guess. But I didn't realize I was ever going home."

"I don't suppose anyone would blame you for trying to find some small amount of happiness in this situation, Phil. You couldn't have known we were coming for you. But don't worry, that detail will never leave these woods," Frank says.

Phil McCarty dictated his last will and testament to Frank after he composed a goodbye letter to his wife. Ten minutes later, he was deceased. We bury him right after Frank cuts out the tracker inserted under the skin of his upper right arm, as proof of death. I've watched no one die before, and I never want to do it again. It wasn't as peaceful to pass using the suicide pill as I'd presumed it would be. He just fell asleep at first, but a minute later, he started what Adams called Cheyne-Stokes breathing, gasping and irregular. That was hard to watch. Adams said he wasn't suffering, he was unconscious, but it was still beyond disturbing to see. I keep seeing his face as he drifted to sleep, knowing he would not wake up again. It will take me some time to get the image out of my mind. And that breathing will haunt me for even longer.

Our team leaves for Green River, Wyoming, 1868, at sunrise. We assumed this leg of the mission would be easy, as the estimated population is just over one hundred people. However, we are there for two full days with Frank and Carey searching all day on both days with no success. No one has heard of Nancy Bosch and there isn't anyone new in town. They hunt for her prisoner and find no sign of him either. We expand our search to five miles outside town, considering she might stay on her own in the woods. We go to the exact longitude and latitude of her drop-off point and search the area.

After a few hours, we find her transponder and one boot, but nothing else to identify as hers. Later that day we find human bones scattered across a quarter mile area. We can't be sure they're hers, but all evidence points toward it. Frank takes a small bone in an evidence bag for DNA testing back at base. He also saves her transponder to check the data later to prove it's hers.

Not that the data is important; how else would a modern-day transponder end up in 1868, Wyoming?

As we discuss what we've found, we conclude her prisoner killed her and took off, as he's nowhere around either. The thought makes me sick to my stomach. If it happened to this transporter, who's to say it couldn't happen to my mom too? It's a huge let down for the team, after losing McCarty in Virginia. Frank gives us a pep talk, and he glances my way more than a few times while talking. I appreciate he's just trying to make sure I'm not getting discouraged, but I don't expect any special treatment. I'll lose all credibility with the rest of the team if he does. We log her as presumed dead and camp in the rocky hills of Wyoming for the night.

I keep wondering about what may have become of Nancy Bosch. Whatever happened, it doesn't look good. She was someone's daughter, maybe someone's mother. It makes my stomach roil, imagining what she might have gone through. These last two rescues make me terrified to think what we could find in Oklahoma. I try not to show it, but I'm fidgety and nervous. Everyone is quiet during dinner, the general mood solemn. As I lie in my sleeping bag that night, I break down and cry silently to myself. I sense the weight of the world on my shoulders and more pressure than ever to locate my mom.

The next morning, we drink coffee around the fire, while everyone tries to stay positive.

We transport to Houston, Texas in 1820 during a torrential rainstorm. There's flash flooding and we stay on high ground until the storm passes the following morning. Midmorning, Frank takes Gray out again to scout for Dylan Paxton. They come back that afternoon empty-handed. The plan is to check the seedier parts of town the next day.

We enjoy a relaxing night; we need the rest, as transporting takes a lot out of you physically. I get better acquainted with the guys as we talk about our families. I tell the other guys about my mom. If they already know, none of them act surprised. I mean, we share the same last name, I guess they could work it out when someone like me with not a lot of experience makes the team. Carey doesn't let on that I had confided in him earlier. I expect they all feel bad about my mom being missing, and they try to be encouraging, telling me we'll find her no matter what.

Frank and Gray spend the better part of the day in the poor area of Houston looking for Paxton. They discover him passed out and smelling of liquor in the corner of a bar. Well, at least they think it's him—they can't ask him because he isn't able to string two words together when they find him. Once they get him to camp, we restrain him before he finally passes out. We attempt to force feed him some strong coffee and he stirs.

"Wake up." Frank kicks the bottom of maybe-Paxton's boot.

"Hey, knock it off!" The guy kicks back but misses by a mile.

"Are you Dylan Paxton?"

"Who's asking? I'm not telling you shit."

"Okay. You're free to go then."

"What? Who are you, man? What the hell do you want?"

"Nothing, you are free to go. Penn, Stewart, can you please release our guest here, so he can leave?"

Penn and I walk out from behind the rocks, and Paxton seems to sober up at the sight of us in our uniforms.

"Oh my God. Who are you? Are you guys transporters?"

"So, you are Paxton. Why wouldn't you just say that?" Frank says.

"Because I don't know who you are. I've spent the last six months just trying not to get myself killed. You cannot understand what this has been like for me; there's no way to fathom unless you've lived it. They sent me here with nothing and I've survived. So, excuse me if I'm not eager to give you my life story on a whim."

"Fair enough, Paxton. So, here's the deal. We're a retrieval team from home sent to find missing transporters. We'll transport you home as soon as you sober up," says Frank.

"I'm not the only one missing? Really? Give me more coffee. I'll be fine in an hour. And don't judge me, please. Drinking was a way to cope with being here. What else did I have?"

"No judgement here. We're just here to take you home, pal. Guys, let's get Mr. Paxton here more coffee," says Frank as he releases the flexcuffs from his hands.

SIXTEEN

Cotswold, England 1335

We start into the woods and head north toward Cotswold. It's foggy out this early, which gives the forest an eerie look. I have no conception of time; for the past seven months, I've measured it only as dawn and dusk, daylight and nighttime. We stroll in silence for a long while, each of us lost in our thoughts. I want to take my mind off what we're doing and decide that talking about something else is my best option.

"Ethan, tell me about your life back home. Is there a family waiting for you?"

"Just my daughter, Sian. She's nineteen and off at university. I'm divorced for a long time. Her mum was never keen on my military career, but we get along all right since the divorce. She's remarried to a nice bloke who treats Sian well, so I can't complain. What about you?"

"I have a son, Michael. He's twenty-one now. He works for the CCEA, in prisoner control. His dad lives on the east coast, and he doesn't see much of him. I've been split for ten years."

"Sounds like we have things in common. I've never had a friend across the pond before. I'm curious about American life, actually."

"Well, it's not that exciting, I promise. Los Angeles is a great city with tons to do. But I've lived there my entire life, so I suppose I'm immune to most of the glam and glitz it projects to the rest of the world. I lead a quiet life but living in the entertainment capital has perks. I see the occasional celebrity out and about, that's always fun. What does a guy from London do for entertainment?"

"Let's see. I pick up a double decker to Buckingham Palace to glimpse the queen. Then I grab a boat ride on the Thames while eating fish and chips,"—we both laugh at the cliché—"but seriously, I am on my boat every chance I have."

I feel less anxious about the trip into Cotswold, the conversation taking my thoughts off my worries for a bit.

"I've visited a pub or two with my mates. But my boat is my real love. She's docked in Dover, and nothing can top my time out on the sea. One day I will sail that girl around the globe. Or at least the tip of England and Wales. I don't have time to use her much, but I plan to change that once I'm home."

"That sounds lovely. I love the ocean, too. The sound of it, the smell, even the way the air feels. If I could afford it, I'd live at the beach. Beachside prices anywhere in Southern California are out of my range, that's why I live in the city and go to a beach on vacation. I had tickets to Aruba for my son, his girlfriend, and me; we were going on the trip after this transport. That ship has sailed."

"Oh, that's a shame. Although I'm sure you'll get there. Based on what I've seen of you so far, you seem like a woman who's able to have what she wants. I've never met a woman quite as direct as you are. You possess such an ease expressing your feelings, and it's refreshing. And not to mention you can cook a mean rabbit stew."

"Oh my. Direct is the nicest way anyone has ever referred to my lack of a filter, so thank you for that. But you're right, I will take my son to Aruba as planned when I get back. I don't care how much it costs—I'll blow my savings if I have to. It's a matter of principle now. Those assholes will not take that away, no matter what. Do you believe the system is coming back online? Do you think we can trust that Aidan is telling us the truth?"

"I can't be sure, you know that. However, I believe him. I don't imagine anyone agrees to stay here for months without knowing they have a way back to our time. I suppose we'll find out in five days, won't we?"

"Yes, I guess so. I hope for his sake he's not lying. I shudder to think what Estera will do to him if we don't make it home."

We both laugh at the memory of Estera punching Aidan.

"I want to show you something. Follow me."

I trail him to the brink of the forest where the trees open to a field of the greenest grass I've ever seen. When I look beyond the field, I gasp.

"Oh my God Ethan, that's beautiful!"

On a rolling hill in the distance is a stone castle. History has never been very interesting to me, but seeing this firsthand, I see the appeal. Stuck in the past for the last several months has given me a new perspective. I find myself curious about how these people live, and what their stories might be. We just don't have this kind of history in the United States, castles that are hundreds of years old, steeped in tradition. I realize I'm one of only a few people from the future who will ever see this place in its grandeur.

"Can we stay and admire it from here?"

"Sure, we can sit for a bit if you'd like to. I've seen knights in actual armor riding out of here. I've been to this castle many times, only seven hundred years from now. My daughter loves the place; I brought her almost every year when she was growing up. Beverston Castle is over a hundred years old now, but in our time, it looks much different. They added a manor in the seventeenth century and most of the castle is uninhabitable in our timeline. There are renderings of how historians picture the castle in its heyday, but they haven't quite captured the opulence. The drawings don't do it justice. I can't wait to tell them how off they are. I've spent hours here just memorizing the outline and as many details as I can. I want them to get it right when doing new renderings."

"This is really something. I can imagine what the inside of it looks like."

"Yes, I've wondered that myself. I would like to see sometime. Maybe I'll get the opportunity another time."

"How much farther is it to Cotswold?"

"Another mile at most. We'll walk at the edge of the woods until we get there. Once we arrive, I prefer to go straight to the church where Aidan says Wallingford will be staying. We might not get much time there and the less time spent in Cotswold the better. We need not bring any attention to ourselves and we don't want someone to recognize us when we go back later in the week."

"Got it. I'll follow your lead. I'm looking forward to seeing the church. I've never been to the United Kingdom, so seeing castles and old churches at their peak, it's . . . well, it's something to see. I won't ever forget this castle."

"Maybe this will persuade you to come back."

You could persuade me to come back.

"I'm sure it will."

We rise to leave, brushing the damp leaves off our clothes and continue to make our way into Cotswold.

"What do you miss most about home, Christine?"

"Hmmm. Where do I start? My son, wine, my bed, cake, my dog, cheeseburgers, family, hot showers, music, shampoo, lip gloss. The list goes on. Oh, what I wouldn't give for some lip gloss."

"We're on the same page with wine and cheeseburgers and as God is my witness, I shall never eat rabbit again."

"Neither will I! I had a lot of them in Oklahoma too."

The mention of Oklahoma pushes my thoughts to Annabelle and her fate. My face must reflect my dread as Ethan reaches over to give my hand a quick squeeze.

"I believe your friend is all right. I expect it would absolutely gut you to witness her being taken hostage by Indians."

"You have no idea, Ethan. I have never felt so helpless. She was my only friend for months back there. She's the best friend I've ever had. I don't even know if John found her, or if she's gone. It's overwhelming to think about. What if they scalped her? She has the most beautiful blond curly hair. What if they left her for dead, alone and suffering? Worse yet, what if they didn't kill her and she's living a nightmare of abuse every day? If anything's happened to her, I'll never forgive myself."

"There's nothing to forgive yourself for Christine. You couldn't take on those Indians by yourself. Sounding the alarm with John was the smartest thing to do. And the way you've described Annabelle, my money is on her. It sounds to me that if anyone could get away from Indians, it would be her. And you said that they took off with only one man guarding her while the others ran after you. That's good odds in my book."

"I've agonized over my decision to leave her. I have a tremendous amount of guilt. She pops into my mind at random times and it brings me back to that moment. You know, I used to tell her to stop being so damn happy all the time. There we were, trapped in the old west with no hope of leaving and she would find something to be cheerful about. She told me she chose happiness and joy over despair. She was never mad at me even though I got angry at her. I guess I wanted her to feel as depressed and hopeless as I was. Misery loves company and all that. I was angry at her for trying to keep me optimistic. What was I thinking?"

"You did the right thing by trying to transport home. You may have both ended up here, or even somewhere worse. Perhaps you would not have transported to the same place. We aren't certain if the transponders would have sent you anywhere together. You said yourself that Oklahoma is safer than here. At least you know where she is. If you two had transported out together but landed in different places and times, that would be a nightmare. Much like finding a needle in a haystack, as you Americans say. In Oklahoma she stands a fighting chance with people searching for her, aware of her predicament."

"You make an excellent point, thank you. She's one of the most resilient women I've ever known. The cheerfulness which used to irritate me would also push her to stay strong. I hold on to that hope now."

We continue through the forest, the fog starting to lift now. Mist covers us as usual, but no snow yet. Ethan stops and points through the trees to a cluster of thatched roof houses.

"Those are the first houses in Tetbury. The village is just beyond there. When we arrive, walk straight out of the woods as if we belong. Don't stop or talk to anyone. Your accent would, at the very least, raise some questions we don't need to deal with right now. Unless I stop, you keep walking. Cover your face as much as possible with your wrap."

"Wait, I'm confused. I thought we were going to Cotswold. Why are we stopping in Tetbury?"

"Tetbury is in Cotswold. Cotswold is an area, not an actual village. Much like your counties. Sorry, I forgot you yanks aren't familiar with our geography. Tetbury is where the chapel is. It's quite interesting as St. Mary the Virgin church sits on this site in modern times. Historians say a medieval monastery sat on the site prior to that temple being built. That monastery is where we'll be today."

"Wow, that's a lot of history."

"I agree, it's amazing. We're almost there now. Walk beside me and keep your head covered; your hair might cause some people to take notice."

"My hair? Why?"

"I know you haven't had it styled in several months, but I can still tell it has a cut and shape to it. The women's hair here is all long, as they never cut it—no salons around here. It just looks different, that's all."

"Okay, I will try my best to take that as a compliment."

"As you should. All right, here's where we cut into town. Ready?"

"Yep, my hair and I are ready to take on Tetbury."

Ethan heads out of the forest and onto a muddy path. I follow him and catch up to walk beside him. We pass a few people along the way. Most nod a greeting or say good morning.

Ethan greets them but I only nod, recalling that Ethan worried my accent might raise questions. As we draw closer to town, I see smoke rising above the tree line and smell meat cooking. As we round a bend in the path, the village comes into view. There are stalls set up for a market with animal carcasses and vegetables on display. I see a blacksmith shop and carts full of straw and small animals. The ground is muddy sludge and I feel moisture finding its way into my boots. I pull my wrap tighter around me, trying to stave off the chill. The church sits at the end of town; I can see the steeple from here. As I glance around it's hard to grasp that I'm in a medieval village, seeing it firsthand.

We continue to walk through town, stopping to browse now and again so we don't stand out. He buys a few vegetables from a booth with some coins.

Isn't he full of surprises? I wonder where he got period money.

We approach the chapel a few minutes later and Ethan opens the massive wooden doors.

The interior is much darker than it is outside, even with candles burning. The chapel is breathtaking, the woodwork exquisite. We stand in the entrance for a moment allowing our eyes to adjust. Ethan walks toward a door to the right in the main chapel and pulls it open, cringing as it squeaks loudly. We walk into a hallway lined with stone and lit with candles. There are five doors on each side along the entire sixty-foot length. He sets the vegetables wrapped in paper on the floor.

"I saw the clergy staff outside in the back as we approached, so let's make this quick. I expect we are alone for a few minutes. Just scan each room; we're trying to find where Wallingford will stay. They should have it ready for his visit. It won't be barren, but it won't appear lived in—no personal things will be out. I'll go left, you head right. If you open the door and someone is inside, pretend to faint," he says, smiling.

"If I open a door to anyone, I won't have to pretend, trust me."

I inhale a deep breath and walk to the first door, pulling it open cautiously. I determine someone must occupy the room, as there are clothes on a stone bench and the fireplace is lit. I hurry to the next room, which looks like an office. It has a desk, quill and ink bottle, and a table with a bench, but no bed. I hit what I consider pay dirt on the third door. There's a bed and a desk with a chair, and it's colder than the other rooms. I see the fireplace hasn't been lit recently; it looks ash free.

"Ethan, I think I found it," I call out softly.

He crosses the hall to the room and peeks inside.

"Brilliant. This looks like it could be it, but let's check all the rooms to be sure."

We check the rest of the rooms and decide the one I found is most likely what we're looking for. The others have signs of people occupying them, and we assume the staff lives in them.

"Okay, third door on the right. If the candles aren't lit when we come back, we'll still find it. Let's get out of here. When we get to the chapel, follow my lead; we should stop to pray in case someone saw us come in. We don't want to raise suspicion about our being here."

"I don't imagine a little praying would hurt at this point. I'm not opposed to getting all the help we can to pull this off."

"Excellent point."

He grabs our vegetables and we step into the chapel where Ethan kneels behind the second row of pews near the hall we just left. He clasps his hands in front of him and rests them on the back of the pew in front of us. He lowers his head and I can see him mouthing something to himself. I do the same and find myself really, truly praying. If someone had told me a year ago that I'd be in a medieval church praying for a successful mission, I would have laughed in their face. Yet here I am.

I pray that we get out of this alive. I pray for my son and my family, that they have the faith to believe I'm still alive and don't give up on me. I pray for Annabelle and all the other transporters stranded in time, and last, I ask that Aidan is correct about the system coming online.

I've never been one for structured religion—I don't go to church or confession. I've never embraced traditional religion in that way. I envision myself more spiritual than religious, but here and now, in the candlelight of this medieval chapel, I feel moved to pray as I never have before. I keep my head down but angled slightly to study Ethan. He is obviously more experienced than I am in church. It sounds as if he's reciting an actual prayer, unlike the random pleading I just finished. I move to sit on the pew behind me and see him make the sign of the cross, wondering if I should have done the same. He remains kneeling for a moment longer, his head on his clasped hands. When he's finished, he sits next to me, but we don't speak right away, both of us lost in the moment.

"Do you go to church at home, Ethan?"

"Most Sundays, I do, yes. It's ingrained from my childhood, I suppose."

"I envy you for that. I wish I had the faith you clearly do."

"You just knelt next to me and prayed, Christine. You have faith or you wouldn't have done that. Remember, we all find our own path in our own way, what's important is that we get there somehow. I wholly believe all paths lead to the same place; whether you call it God, Buddha, Jehovah, or whoever."

I smile at him, realizing he's right. I do have faith. He stands, offering his hand to help me up, then pulls me into a quick embrace before leading me to the door.

"Watch for Thomas; if he sees us here, he'll put it together that we're going after the chapter. He'll assume we want the payoff, and that could make him very dangerous to us," Ethan says.

"Do you foresee him attempting to complete the job?"

"Oh yes, I think he's just that stupid and desperate."

"Thomas is fast becoming my least favorite person. If the fourteenth century doesn't kill him, I just might," I say.

We stroll through town and this time I take the time to focus on the details. I soak up as much as I can, knowing I will not get an opportunity like this again. Ethan humors me and we stop at almost all the stalls to browse. He buys me a gorgeous bracelet made of blue glass beads I admire; it will become a treasured family heirloom with a stellar provenance. We reach the path that winds out of town and I'm pleased about my day so far. I can't stop grinning and I am the happiest I have been in months, almost forgetting where I am for a minute.

"Christine, I want to talk to you about something."

"Sure, what's up?"

"If we—if something goes wrong during this process, I want you to get yourself out straight away. If things get dodgy, leave me, I'll be fine. Get to camp or another safe place. Promise me? And if something happens to me, then all I ask is that you tell my daughter how much I love her. Can you do that for me?"

"Don't, Ethan. Don't even say that out loud. We are not even going to put that out into the universe. You will die an old man on your sailboat, in your sleep."

We walk along the trail in silence, but I'm thinking about what he said. What if something goes wrong? Am I willing to risk my life for this? The reality of that hits me hard, and I second-guess my decision. I ultimately decide I can't let Ethan down, I have to be all in.

Ethan slows down, inspecting the path. He puts his hand on my shoulder and leads me behind a large tree, off the trail. Seconds later, three men ride by on horses, and I see Malcolm's backpack tied to one of the man's packs. He sees it too and looks at me with raised eyebrows.

"Well, that can't be good news for Thomas," he suggests, once they pass.

We continue along the pathway and veer off to go through the rabbit traps in the hopes we'll have something for dinner. Two rabbits are in the trap, but they appear wilted. At least we have some nice carrots and potatoes from the market today.

"Hmmm, these aren't very fresh, are they? I expected Estera to be here by now; there should be a new rabbit here. I wonder why she didn't go through the traps?" he asks.

"She mentioned she had cabin fever, maybe she just went for a walk and lost track of time?" I say the words but can't shake the feeling something isn't right.

It's mid-afternoon before we turn into camp. Malcolm is sitting outside at the fire, Aidan still tied up next to him.

"Hey guys," I say.

"Hey Christine, Ethan," replies Malcolm

"Malcolm, take Aidan into the shelter for a bit," suggests Ethan.

Aidan rolls his eyes as Malcolm leads him to the hut. Malcolm returns within a minute, eager to know about the trip to town.

"Where's Estera?" I ask before he can say anything.

"I don't know. She took off early to look at the traps and I haven't seen her since. I notice you got rabbits—you didn't see her at the river?"

"No, we only stopped to check the traps for something new from this morning, but the condition of these suggest they are from yesterday. I don't like this; first we observe men with your pack, and now Estera is MIA." Ethan says.

"You saw my knapsack?"

"Yes, three men rode by on the trail and one had it tied on his horse. Ethan heard them coming, and we hid, or we would have run smack into them," I reply.

"I wonder how they got it?"

"Either Thomas lost it, ditched it, or he met someone bigger and badder than he is. My money is on the latter. That bloke is always running his mouth, and it's only a matter of time before someone shuts it for him," Ethan says.

Ethan is right; Thomas never knows when to shut up. I figured that out and I've only known him just under a week.

"I'm worried about Estera. If she said she would go through the traps, she never made it there. Should we search for her?" I ask.

"Let's give it a while, if she isn't here in two hours, we'll go find her. In the meantime, let's cook these rabbits; they aren't long before they're inedible," says Ethan

"Okay, give them to me. I can prep them."

He hands me the rabbits and I take them over to the stump table. I'm uncomfortable with Estera gone, and the backpack on that guy's horse has done nothing to ease that worry. I finish preparing the meat and chop vegetables for dinner while I consider where she might be. What I wouldn't give for a pizza and some chocolate cake right now.

With the stew boiling and my thoughts still on Estera, I sit next to Ethan.

"Thanks again for getting me the bracelet today. It is special, and I'll wear it often." I twist it around on my wrist, watching the glass catch the light from the fire. "Ethan, I think we should look for Estera after we eat. Let's not wait."

"Sure, all right. I'm not comfortable with her gone as long as we were."

Malcolm brings Aidan out and unties his hands while we eat.

"Malcolm, Christine and I are going to look for Estera after dinner."

Aidan looks back and forth between us.

"What's wrong? You didn't find her at the river?" he asks.

"No, and rabbits were still in the traps. We picked them up on our way here from town, but no sign of her there," says Ethan.

"Let me help. We can work in teams of two, Malcolm and I and you and Christine. I feel bad enough for dragging you all into this, I can help locate her."

"No way," Malcolm states, looking at Ethan.

"What am I going to do, Malcolm? Run away like that idiot Thomas? And go where? I have four days left here. I just want to stay alive until then. I'm not going anywhere, mate."

"Untie him, Malcolm. I don't even care if he takes off. He's safer here, and he knows it. Besides, I have the resources to locate him back home if I need to," says Ethan.

"Fine. The more people looking for her the better I suppose." Malcolm unties Aidan's ankles and we make a plan of sorts about where to search for Estera.

"We should each take a blanket in case she needs it when we spot her. Everyone back by dusk, with or without her. If we can't find her, we'll reconvene and figure our move from there," says Ethan.

We bring our blankets and start in opposite directions. Ethan and I move north, toward town, and Malcolm and Aidan travel south. We track a few dozen feet apart from each other to cover more ground. The woods are thick with dead logs and a layer of soggy leaves cover the forest floor. It's starting to mist again, which makes it darker than usual with the sun obscured by clouds. I feel wetness leaking through my boots again and the chill creeping into my bones. I guess after seven months in the same boots, it should be no surprise they're wearing through. I pick up a stick to poke the debris with, hoping to scare any critters out of my way. We've been out searching for about an hour when I hear him call out to me.

"Christine, over here, hurry! Bring your blanket."

I follow the sound of his voice through the trees and see him standing stock-still.

"Ethan, what's the matter?"

I rush to him, and he turns to face me.

"I found her."

I peer over the log he's standing near and see Estera curled up on the ground. She coughs and spits blood on the leaves. I move to climb over the timber, but he stops me.

"No, don't move any closer, we can't get near her. Give me your blanket, I'll throw it to her with mine."

"Why? What are you talking about?"

"Christine, he's right, you can't come near me, I'm sick," she says.

Estera lifts her head up a few inches before it collapses to the ground.

"Christine, he's right, you can't come near me, I'm sick." Her eyes are ringed in red.

She's so weak she has trouble lifting her head again and is shivering despite being covered in her blanket. Ethan throws her our blankets, and she pulls them up around her neck.

"I don't understand," I reply, frowning.

"I think she has the plague."

SEVENTEEN

Cotswold, England, 1335

Estera walks out of camp almost right after Ethan and Christine do, leaving Malcolm to deal with Aidan. She needs some time to herself to consider the past couple of days. She is certain she has made the right decision by not taking part in getting the writings from the astronomer. If the others get caught it could ruin their chances of ever seeing home. And even if they are successful, they may lose their jobs at the very least. Estera has another year, and she and Jacques are retiring to Cyprus. She's firm on not doing anything to risk that now. She's considered because the government stuck her here for seven months, they might retire her at full payout because of the trauma she has suffered. She is so near to retirement it may be possible.

It's that or take the chance of being sued by transporters they harmed not having something in place to prevent this.

She walks into the woods, searching for anything else they can eat besides rabbit. She'll check the traps later and is hoping to find some fish there to cook with mushrooms. They would all receive a boost by her making some coq au vin or a bowl of beef bourguignon. They haven't been able to catch a chicken or barter any beef since they've been here. If she could only capture a duck, she would make a decent confit de canard. Remembering Aidan told them they are going home in four days, she dreams of a hot shower and her own bed. She longs for them enough to hurt someone for them.

She sits on a log to rest for a bit, envisioning all the things she will do when she gets home. She takes longer than usual to regain her strength. She's been so weak the last couple of days, as if her body has given up in anticipation of going home. As soon as the fog lifts, she goes to check the traps but doesn't get far before she needs to rest again.

She collapses in the grass for a while, happy for some alone time and rest. So worn out she doesn't care that the grass is wet and soaking through her thin dress. She's not accustomed to being around people twenty-four seven. It's just been she and Jacques for so long, so she sneaks off by herself when possible.

She grabs a stick, scratching the back of her leg, wondering why she's had an itch there for the last day. As she pulls her dress up to inspect it, her stomach drops at the site. There are three or four small sores on the back side of her right leg. Everyone here realizes what this can mean—the plague. She tries to reason with herself that the fever and weakness she's had since yesterday is the stress of the past few days. This might be a mild flu or even a cold and bug bites.

Or maybe the sores are an irritation where she scraped herself.

But what if that's not it? What if she has the plague?

She's been sick for two days and has said nothing to anyone at camp, hoping she would feel better. Now she worries that she's exposed everyone to it, and it may be too late to do anything about it. She knows she can't go to camp now, not if there's even a slight chance she might have the plague. Or the flu. None of them have any immunity to the flu; that hasn't been around since 2050.

She needs to get as close to camp as possible without more risk of infecting the others.

They'll come looking for her when she doesn't return this afternoon, and she doesn't want them to be out after dark searching for her. Only making it about half as far as she wants to, she's just too weak to continue and can't stop shivering. She vomits before she can even lie down. She finds a soft spot of leaves to lie on, again not caring that they're soaking wet.

She falls asleep and wakes to the sound of Ethan calling her name. Her entire body hurts, and her chills have escalated to a level she's never experienced. Her blanket is not much help in keeping her warm. When she raises her head a few inches, she sees him standing about twenty feet away. His expression tells her he knows; he looks so sad. Christine jogs up behind him and starts toward her, but he stops her. She raises her head again to look at Christine.

"I found her," says Ethan.

She coughs and spits blood on the leaves.

"No, don't move any closer, we can't go near her. Give me your blanket, I'll throw it to her with mine."

"Why? What are you talking about?"

Ethan throws her the blankets, and she pulls them up around her collar, shivering.

"I don't understand," Christine says, frowning at him.

"I think she has the plague."

To hear Ethan say it out loud is a punch in the stomach to Estera. It confirms her worst fears, and she lets her head collapse back down to the pillow of leaves.

"What can we do to make you more comfortable, Estera?" Ethan asks.

"You need to go before you have more exposure to this."

"We may already be exposed, Estera. I know little about the plague, other than it's treatable with antibiotics. If we're going home in a few days, we'll take antibiotics then," Christine says.

"Antibiotics are effective only when taken at the onset. It requires more potent intravenous medication at the advanced stages. We should be careful from this point forward and minimize any further compromise of infection. We'll bring you some broth and water. We need to find Malcolm and Aidan; they're out searching for you," Ethan says as he turns to leave.

She nods her head weakly, pulling the blankets tighter around her neck. This quick conversation has taken more out of her than she wants to admit to herself.

Then it hits her like a ton of bricks.

She knows she will die here.

The reality of it is terrifying. If she could only make it until the system comes online and they go home, she'd be all right. But in her heart, she doesn't believe she can last four more days.

She thinks about Jacques and how this will destroy him. All they have is each other; both of their families gone. He will be all alone, and she's not sure he can live with that. She cries softly, alone in the woods.

What a way to go out.

She doesn't wish to suffer until the end. If it becomes undeniable that she will not last until the transponders come back online, she will eat wolfsbane flowers and end it herself. They will slow down her heartbeat and she'll just fade away.

God help me, I don't want to, but if it comes to that, it's better than the alternative.

* * *

Ethan and I hurry through the woods, heading to the area Malcolm and Aidan should be searching. What if she has exposed the rest of us? If that idiot Thomas hadn't taken Malcolm's antibiotics, we would have medication for everyone. Including Estera.

So help me, if she dies, I will make him pay.

"Should we try to find the backpack?" I ask.

"We've learned Thomas doesn't have it; whoever those men are we saw in the woods have it, and finding them could take days, if not longer. Besides, there is no guarantee the medicine is in the backpack. Thomas would keep the antibiotics if he ditched the pack, but maybe they stole it from him with the antibiotics still inside, who knows? I don't guess she has that kind of time," says Ethan.

I realize he's right, but hearing it fills me with anger and hopelessness. This is all Thomas's fault.

I hear voices and tap Ethan's shoulder. He nods and we slip behind a large tree. Thirty seconds later, Aidan walks by, oblivious to us.

He can't see us ten feet away, he had no chance of finding Estera.

"Aidan, turn around."

Aidan jumps and turns toward us. "Ethan, you scared me."

"Where's Malcolm?"

"Right behind me, or he was anyway." He looks around the forest. "Oh, here he comes."

Malcolm jogs up. "No sign of her, Ethan."

"We found her. She's sick. We think it might be the plague. We need to determine if we are sick. Has anyone had flu-like symptoms or weakness, fever, or chills? Nausea or vomiting? Sores of any type?"

"No, I have had no symptoms," I reply.

I turn to Malcolm next.

"No, nothing."

We all turn to Aidan.

"No, I'm not sick. And even if we were, we'll be home in four days and we can take antibiotics, so what does it matter?"

"We'll be all right even if we're sick and don't know it yet; the incubation period can be up to six days once infected. If no one has symptoms yet, we should have time to treat it. It may be too late for Estera though. And thanks to your partner, without antibiotics we can't help her," says Ethan.

We take turns sitting with Estera, far enough away to minimize exposure, yet close enough to talk to her. I use what's left of my old dress to make face masks as an added layer of protection. She seems to grow weaker by the hour, and after a few hours, she isn't talking much anymore and is refusing water. When Malcolm comes to sit with Estera, she lifts her head and speaks.

"Malcolm, please, I want you to bring me the flowers you showed me at the lake. It's time." Estera closes her eyes and is asleep again within minutes.

I look back and forth from Estera to Malcolm. "What is she talking about, Malcolm?"

"She wants me to bring her wolfsbane flowers. They grow at the lake. I showed them to her two months ago; they're poisonous and I didn't want her to pick them. When I was sitting with her earlier, she wanted me to promise I'd bring her some if she asked for them. She doesn't want to suffer for the next few days and then die, anyway. If she eats the flowers, they'll slow her heartbeat way down, and in her current state she won't be able to fight off the poison for long. She'll just sort of fade away."

"You won't do it though, right? What if she can make it until we're transported home? They will cure her there with a couple of antibiotics!"

"I thought of that too, and I talked to her about it. She will not make it that long, Christine. Look at her, she's going downhill. Who am I to say no, that she should suffer the next few days? It's her choice, and to be honest, I'm not convinced I wouldn't do the same myself."

"But how can we do this? How can we help her commit suicide?" I glance at Estera, to be sure she's still asleep.

"We aren't helping her commit suicide. She's dying, and she knows it. She wants to expedite it to ease her suffering. I don't see how we can deny her that; it's the humane thing to do. If we don't help her, we'll sit and watch her die an agonizing death, likely within the next twenty-four hours. We don't have a choice, but she does. And the choice is hers. I'll get the flowers for her. Give me your mask; I need something to pick and carry them in; Just touching them can expose me to the poison."

I pull my mask off and hand it to him.

"I'll go get Ethan. We'll meet you back here," I say.

As Malcolm leaves, I sit on the log. "Estera, wake up please, I need to speak to you."

She doesn't open her eyes, startling me when she speaks, "I'm awake."

"Please don't do this. I need you to fight. Hang on until we're transported home, it'll only be a few days. We'll go after the backpack and get antibiotics to keep you going. I'll make the others help me find the medicine."

"I'm too weak to transport home like this, and we both know it. Plus, you'll never find the antibiotics. Thomas is long gone or staying well out of sight. And it's likely too late for broad-spectrum antibiotics to help, anyway." She wheezes and struggles to breathe. "I need you to do something for me, and I want your word. Contact Jacques when you get back. I need him to understand how sick I am, so he knows I didn't give up on our life so easily. Tell him how much I love him. How much I've always loved him. Tell him he was my last thought on this earth. Promise me."

"Estera please, I have very few friends in this entire world, and you're one of them. I don't think I can watch you do this when there may still be some hope left to get you home!"

She tries her best to smile at me and takes a moment to control her breathing before answering.

"I'm so glad you transported here. I realize that's completely selfish of me, but it's the truth. You've made my last few days here so much more bearable, Christine. And I ask you to do this last favor for me because you are my friend. I trust only you with this most precious of requests, because I know I can count on you."

Tears run down my cheeks, and I lower my head. I nod, but don't dare speak for fear I'll break down. She smiles weakly and falls asleep again.

I run through the forest to camp to tell Ethan what's happening. I find him and Aidan by the fire and tell them what Estera plans to do.

Ethan nods when I finish. "I know it sounds harsh, but I suppose I'd do the same in her position. She's not in good shape, and she's only getting worse. She would never survive a transport home and by the time the system is up, she will be even worse."

I'm surprised to hear Ethan agree with Malcolm. I understand she's suffering, but I want her to fight until we can get her home. That said, I appreciate it's not my choice, and I must respect her wishes. I just don't want to take part. I can't help Estera end her life. Ethan and Aidan rise, taking their face masks.

"Let's go help her by at least being there with her." Aidan steps closer to me. "She needs you right now; be there for her even if you don't agree with the way she's handling it."

Who ever thought Aidan could possess such empathy?

I make myself a new mask and set out with Ethan and Aidan. When we reach Estera, she's sweating and has pulled the blankets off. I see she's vomited several times, and her cough seems worse. Malcolm is right, she will not recover from this without modern medical aid, and the realization makes me ill. I can't stand to see her like this; she's in such pain. Malcolm jogs to the log we're sitting on, holding the wolfsbane wrapped in my old face mask. He crushes the flowers with a rock, using the mask as a bowl. He walks over to Estera when Aidan speaks up.

"Don't go near her, Malcolm. We can wrap it up and toss it to her."

"I'll be fine. I'll keep my mask on, and I'll give it to her and back off. I'm probably already exposed to it anyway, so what's the difference?"

Malcolm leans over and opens the cloth with the crushed flowers.

"Here you go, Estera. Put them in your mouth and let the petals become soft and break down a bit, then swallow them. There's root in there too, that's where most of the toxin is."

Malcolm puts the crushed flowers down next to Estera with a cup of water and comes to stand with us again. We watch Estera swallow the wolfsbane and she turns to me, her eyes full of tears.

"You can trust me, Estera. I'll do what you ask," I say, my tears flowing now.

She falls asleep two hours later and doesn't wake up again. Ethan and Malcolm cover her with rocks as a burial. None of us know if we risk infection to bury her in a traditional grave. We can't chance a large fire drawing attention to our camp, so we do what we can out of respect for her.

We all gather around the fire at camp and I say what I'm certain is on all of our minds.

"Let's talk about the obvious. What if we're sick and not showing symptoms yet? Sharing camp with her may expose us," I say.

"Would antibiotics help?" Malcolm asks.

"Yes, if we take them within the first couple of days after symptoms present, we'd be fine," Ethan says.

"We're going home in a few days, perhaps you're not sure whether to believe that, but I'm positive of it. Trust me, we'll be back in plenty of time for antibiotics if we need them," Aidan says.

I glance at Malcolm and he hangs his head. He knows he won't be going home and if he is infected, he will likely die here. Thomas will be responsible for his death as well.

I go to the shelter to grieve on my own. I haven't known Estera long, but we speed relationships here. It's ironic that it took me being stranded here and in Oklahoma to form the best friendships I've had in years with her and Annabelle. I liked Estera, and I'm angry that we couldn't do anything to save her. I'll keep my promise to her and make sure that Jacques knows how she cared about him. How even at the end, she worried about him.

I lie on the floor of the shelter and cry.

I want this to be over. I want to go home.

I want to give up and let someone else save the world and get the stupid chapter. I've kept myself together throughout this entire journey, stuck in Oklahoma, coming here, learning about Thomas and Aidan's plan. But in this moment, I feel defeated. I miss my son and my life and if we don't transport home soon, well, I doubt that I can keep it together much longer. I don't know if I'd have the strength to keep going after that if we didn't get home. I mean, what for? So I can scrape along for the next year living in a hut in the woods of medieval England? A year is generous because there's no doubt in my mind something would get me soon enough; either disease or other people. That would be a foregone conclusion, and who wants to wait for that to happen? Not me, it would be like living on eggshells. I would do what Estera did. I'd give up if there was nothing but a brutal, painful end in sight. I could have stayed alive in Oklahoma, but this place does not instill the same confidence in me.

Malcolm makes soup for dinner, and we eat in silence, the reality of today's event driving our mood. Ethan finally breaks the silence.

"I want to make spears tomorrow, to have weapons on hand. Malcolm, can you gather some sticks thick enough for me to use, and I'll carve them? Aidan, you can help him?"

"Sure. We can do that, right Aidan?"

"Of course."

"What do you want me to do?" I ask.

"Nothing Christine, you can stick around camp with me."

"Why? I'm capable of helping. Don't treat me differently because I'm a woman, Ethan. Good God, have I not proven I can be useful?"

Ethan looks at me with raised eyebrows.

"I didn't mean that at all, there's just nothing else to do but check the traps and I planned to do that myself."

I hang my head for a minute and sigh. I feel like an idiot for snapping at him.

"I'm sorry, I'm just a little on edge."

"We all are, nothing to be sorry about."

We spend the rest of the evening in the shelter around the fire, as the snow has started up again. The guys chat about guns and weapons and it bores me, putting me to sleep. I'm exhausted, and don't wake until after they're up the following morning. By the time I get outside, Ethan is working on his first spear.

"Good morning. Malcolm and Aidan are out gathering more sticks. I want you and I to carry weapons at the church, in case we need them."

"Yeah, that makes me more secure, for sure."

"You're still up for the plan then?"

"Yes. I'm ready to do this and go home. I'm not sure about you, but I'm over this bullshit."

"Yeah, I'm with you on that."

"Did you hear there is some idiotic company in Miami trying to get rights to send people back in time as adventure vacations? Yep, they want to send regular people, with no training and no supplies, into the past to survive. They can send a distress signal if they want to come home. Damn morons do not understand what they're talking about. This would be the worst vacation they would ever go on! And those dipshits are going to charge people—who have no clue what they're getting into—for it. What a bunch of assholes."

Ethan laughs and puts down the spear he's working on.

"Well, that was a colorful description. Why don't you tell me how you really feel? But you're right, those morons have no clue."

"Well, some people call them cuss words, I call them sentence enhancers."

"Sentence enhancers, I must remember that. You certainly have a unique way of expressing yourself. I've never met a woman as bold and outspoken as you."

"And you don't want to gag me yet?" I say, laughing.

"Not at all. It's nice to talk to someone who's comfortable saying what's on their mind."

"Well, I've never been one to mince words, and I am blunt sometimes, I know. I'm accepting donations to remove the foot from my mouth. But I will say it's refreshing to meet someone who doesn't take offense to my directness."

"On the contrary, I like it. You mentioned you are divorced. How is it possible that you're single, Christine? You seem to be quite the catch."

I feel myself blush.

I didn't see that coming.

"Oh, I don't know, I've been waiting to get down to my fighting weight, I guess. This journey has taken that last twenty pounds off I think, so watch out world when I get home. I guess the idiots in Miami could market this as a weight loss program if nothing else."

He laughs again and works on the second spear.

"Eating nothing but rabbit and vegetables will do that. I'm down myself, so let's try to think of that as a positive. Maybe not the only positive thing to come of this," he says, smiling.

Is he flirting with me? It's been so long since a man has flirted with me, I'm not sure I'd recognize it.

"Right, maybe not the only positive thing. Now that I've lost some weight, I can afford to splurge a little. When I get home, I'm having pizza and ice cream, and ice in everything I drink. Oh, and steak and chocolate cake too. And that's just for lunch."

Malcolm and Aidan walk out of the forest, each carrying an armful of sticks.

"Who's having chocolate cake?" asks Malcolm.

"We are, in our dreams," I say.

"I can't even think about food or I might cry like a baby," says Aidan, sighing.

Malcolm drops the stick at Ethan's feet. "This enough?"

"Yep, that'll do for now."

"We saw some men riding through the woods toward town. They didn't see us, but it was sure close. I'm glad we will have weapons again," says Aidan.

I see Malcolm give Ethan a strange look, and a slight nod of the head.

"Ethan, got a minute to chat? Let's go for a walk, yes?" Malcolm says.

Aidan sits down next to Ethan. "Should I break these twigs off of the sticks for you?"

"Sure, Malcolm. And yes Aidan, that'll help, thank you," says Ethan as he gets up.

"What do you mean 'have weapons again'?" I gaze at Ethan, waiting for an answer.

Aidan shrugs. "We had spears, but used them all before you got here, and haven't made any more of them until now."

"What did you use them on? Did you hunt with them?"

Malcolm looks at Ethan again, who refuses to look me in the eye.

"Take that walk now, Ethan?" asks Malcolm.

"Hold on a minute. Since when do we have private conversations around here? I asked you about having weapons again, and no one has answered me. What's going on? Somebody had better talk," I say.

Malcolm and Ethan exchange a glance again, and now I see they're keeping something from me. Ethan nods to Malcolm.

"We should tell her, she needs to prepare if they show up," says Ethan.

"Well, *someone* had better tell me *something*," I say.

"They attacked our camp. Five men came in to rob us and they tried to take Estera. We took care of all of them but one. He got on his horse, and we couldn't catch him, but we wounded him so badly we assumed there was no way he'd recover from his injuries. So we didn't worry about him. Ethan, he was one man I saw today. He's alive, and they may be out there looking for us again. They were close to camp," says Malcolm.

"I didn't notice that it was him," says Aidan.

"Well you weren't looking then, because it was him," says Malcolm.

"How many?" asks Ethan.

"Five. With arrows," he says.

I'm watching them both and get a sick sensation in my stomach.

They tried to take Estera?

"Christine, you need to stay out of sight. Don't leave camp for anything, not even with one of us with you. Do you understand? If they find us and see you, they will come for you."

I wrap my arms around my waist and stay silent. I understand what they're saying. Those men get ahold of me and it'll be game over.

"Don't worry," Ethan says. "We didn't let them take Estera and we won't let them take you either."

"You're also down one man now. Make sure I have spears for myself. I'll be damned if some medieval asshole will take me. Not when we're so close to getting home. I'll do whatever it takes to survive at this point."

EIGHTEEN

Piedmont, Oklahoma 1867

Finally. We're on the move to Oklahoma to locate my mom. We transported Paxton to base this morning after sobering him up enough to make the trip. I see where he was coming from; he thought he was never going home and starting over. There's a tough road ahead of him when he gets back, for sure. He had been clean and sober for a few years before being here. I guess that's over. Frank transports him as the rest of the team prepare to take off for Oklahoma.

We transport to the outskirts of Piedmont in the middle of some woods, late morning. I look around, realizing this is where she came in. I wonder what she thought of it. The weather is cold now, but it was spring when she arrived. Maybe the wildflowers were in bloom and the tree branches were full of leaves.

We set up camp and plan to start out the next day, as our transponders show heavy rain today. We spend the day doing recon on the surrounding area. There's a river nearby, just outside the trees, and beyond that the landscape thins out until it eventually opens to grassy plains. I have my period clothing on, and I feel ridiculous, although the hat's okay.

I get a fitful night's sleep and wake up before everyone else. I walk to the edge of the tree line and sit on a boulder with my coffee to watch the sun rise. Yesterday's rain glistens on the grass and the air smells fresh. Under different circumstances this would be a beautiful place. But I struggle to enjoy the scenery; I feel my mom's presence here and I'm eager to start the search for her.

"You okay, Michael?"

I turn to see Frank there, coffee cup in hand. He sits down next to me, spilling some of his drink as he does.

"These damn collapsible cups are for shit."

"Yeah, they are, and I'm fine. Just eager to get out there and find my mom."

"I see that. But we have to work this the right way; we can't raise suspicion or cause anyone to follow us back to camp."

"I understand. You don't have to worry about me. I'm not gonna cause any trouble. I'll be cool. I only want to find her however we need to get that done."

"All right then, I'll finish my coffee and we'll get moving."

Frank changes into his clothes, and I can't help but laugh at him. The pants are too short for his tall frame, showing way too much of his boot. The clothing he wore on our other rescues fit okay, but wardrobe went wrong somewhere with this outfit. We leave clothing behind once we leave a search area to lighten our load, which is unfortunate; Frank could really use some of those pants at this point. His hair is always super short and cropped so uniforms made him a hairpiece with a longer, more period-friendly style. It looks ridiculous on him. When he wore the toupee in New York and Virginia it didn't look so bad. Now that he's worn it and it's not combed or anything, it's a mess, with hair sticking up every which way. It's so weird to see him like this, as he is always so dialed in as far as his uniform and grooming goes. He's former military, he shines his boots and has creases in his pants every day. Seeing him in dirty clothes with his hair in that shape is too much. Even the other guys get on board and make fun of him, and he threatens to shoot all of us unless we shut up. That makes us laugh even harder which angers him more. He puts his hat on, and that helps the hair situation, but not by much. The team approach me before we go to wish me luck and let me know that they're pulling for me to find her. Their gesture makes me a little emotional and motivates me.

We leave camp early, as it's a three-mile walk into town, and hit the saloon first. Our story is that Frank is my mom's brother trying to locate her. We walk in and no one pays us any attention. I was expecting it to be as it is in the old movies, where a stranger comes in and everyone stops what they're doing and stares.

Nope.

No one seems to care who we are or why we're there. Frank orders us each a drink and we sit at the bar making small talk with the bartender. He asks if we're passing through and we tell him we're trying to find Frank's sister, and the last he'd heard she was in the area. The bartender says he's never heard of her, but suggests we talk to the doctor, as he knows everyone.

We finish our drinks and set off in search of him. As we stand on the wooden sidewalk outside the saloon trying to make up our minds on which way to go, a man follows us out.

"I heard you in there. Who are you looking for?"

"My sister. Christine Stewart."

"I'm sure you're not her brother. So, who are you?"

I step closer to him, bracing to take him down if he starts anything.

"Whoa, back up asshole. I'm certain he isn't her brother because I know her; she brought me here. I'm Marcus Simpson."

"You're her prisoner? Good, you'll do just fine. Come with us," Frank grabs him by the collar and yanks him off the sidewalk.

"Hey, let go of me. I don't have to go anywhere with you!"

"You do unless you want us to taser you and take you to camp for questioning. Trust me pal, if you think I'm bad, you'll prefer not to meet the other fellows," he replies, still walking him away from the saloon.

"Okay, okay, what do you want?"

"What do we want? You've got to be kidding me. How can one person be so stupid?" I glance at Frank when asking, and he shakes his head and shrugs his shoulders.

"Hard to fathom, but we've found him. Come on asshole, keep walking," he says.

We lead him to the end of the street out of earshot. Frank looks at him with his eyebrows raised, waiting for him to talk.

"Listen, I don't know anything. I saw her last where we dropped in. Her thing, that transponder thing wasn't working, so I left to come to town. That was almost seven months ago."

"You left her behind alone, with no weapon or supplies? Just took off to have her fend for herself? You couldn't have helped her a little?" I ask.

I can't believe what I'm hearing.

"Well, yeah, what was I supposed to do for her? Besides, that bitch got what she deserved. She was going to leave me, what's the difference?"

"Please let me kill him, Frank. She's my mother, asshole!" I stand up straight, fists clenched at my sides, ready to go after him.

"Stand down, Stewart," he orders.

"Oh shit, sorry man, I didn't realize. Don't let him hurt me!" He turns to Frank, looking terrified.

Frank shakes his head again. "And you haven't seen her since then? How is that even possible? If you did anything to her, I'll allow him to kill you— that's a promise."

"No, I didn't do anything! I haven't noticed her around for a few days. She was here before; she hung out with that schoolteacher a lot. I never spoke to her and never let her see me. I figured it would piss her off that I left her alone, and no offense, but she's kinda mean, so I avoided her. It's not like we run in the same circle of people. I play poker for a living man. These assholes don't know how to count cards yet, so I make a damn killing at it!"

"I don't give a shit what you do here. You said you saw her before, was she all right? Where's the schoolteacher? What's her name?" I ask, ready to beat it out of him if I must.

"Dude, do I seem like I know where the schoolteacher lives? Go to the school, I'm sure you can find her there. It's at the other end of town. You can't miss it, a red building with a big bell outside."

"If something has happened to her, or you're bullshitting me, I swear I'll be back for you," I say, meaning it.

He throws his hands up in frustration while he walks down the sidewalk to the saloon.

What a moron. He cheats people at cards, and that's his claim to fame here?

"So, she was okay. He saw her here, Frank!"

But he hasn't seen her for a few days. What does that mean? Did she go somewhere else?

Why would she do that?

"So he claims. Let's find the teacher, see what she knows."

We arrive at the schoolhouse, but they've locked the front door. We wander to the rear of the building and find an old man raking leaves.

"School's closed today. It's Sunday, everyone's at church," he states.

"Can you help us find the schoolteacher?"

"Ms. Harris? I don't reckon she's at church. No sir, I don't imagine she's a churchgoer, that one. I suppose she's out at John Harding's place, or at home. I help around here, try to keep it picked up for the kids, that's all."

"And where would those places be?" I can see Frank is losing his patience.

"How would I know where the schoolteacher lives? I'm an old man, I got no business with that information." He stops working and leans on the handle of his rake. "But I can tell you where John Harding lives if you want to go see him."

"That would be helpful, please," says Frank.

"Head north outta town, and once you're out of town, head west. You'll run right into his ranch in about a mile, a mile and a half. Unless you're blind. You don't look blind, so I reckon you'll find it."

With that, he goes back to work and ignores us.

We start on our way and go west once we pass the last building in town. We walk about a mile, and I see a house on the horizon. As we get closer, I notice it's a small ranch with a garden.

There are chickens, horses, and goats in a fenced pen and a large dog roaming free. It appears deserted, other than the animals. We knock on the front door and call out. After a few minutes, we hear someone inside yelling at us to go away.

"John Harding, my name is Frank Rhoades. I'm Christine Stewart's brother. Open the door, we're looking for Christine."

The door opens to a disheveled-looking man about forty or fifty years old holding a whiskey bottle. I smell the alcohol on him from four feet away. He looks us up and down.

"You're not Christine's brother."

"Yes, I am. My name's Frank. Do you know where she is?"

"Indians killed her brother on their way here from New York, along with the rest of her family. Unless you believe her other story, which is that she's from California and her son is there waiting for her to get home. Who knows?" he says, swinging his arm in the air, spilling whiskey from the bottle.

"I'll tell you what *is* true, though; she isn't here anymore. She left. Go away and leave me alone."

He's slurring his words, and I can see he's been drinking for a while.

"She's gone, and she's not coming back."

His eyes well up and then I understand. Did my mom have a relationship with this guy?

No way, not her type. Why is he so emotional then? Maybe it's the liquor. *C'mon man, take it down a notch, jeez.*

I step closer to him. "So, where did she go?"

"Home. Back to her life, I suppose. Back to her son and whoever else is there."

He takes a long swig from the whiskey bottle and staggers back inside. He moves to close the door, but Frank puts his boot inside the threshold, blocking it. John reaches behind the door and a moment later points a rifle at us.

"Get off my property right now before I blow a hole in your gut."

We raise our hands in surrender and back away.

"We're leaving, take it easy," Frank says as we back off the porch.

He slams the door and we walk away, off the property.

"We need to find the schoolteacher. She's the key here. Let's go back to camp for now, and tomorrow we'll be able to talk to her at school."

"Frank, we need to locate her now!"

"Michael, we've done our investigation for today. If we continue to do more, we'll blow any chance of finding her. We're going back, that's an order. We head out again tomorrow."

I reluctantly follow his orders and we head to camp. I don't dare step out of line again like I did in Virginia for fear he'll send me home. I realize he's right, but I'm so anxious. I've waited so long to find out what happened to my mom, and now we're so close, but so far at the same time. It's frustrating, waiting to resume our search. If we could find the teacher today, we'd be on schedule. The delay is killing me, we're wasting time doing nothing. What if she's in trouble right this minute, and I'm back at camp, chilling? I get how poking around town more might raise some suspicions, but I don't give one damn about what these locals think of me. I just want to find her.

Gray brought a deck of cards, so we play poker for the rest of the afternoon to stave off the intermittent boredom and anxiety. We use pebbles as money, and Frank ends up with most of them at the end of the game. I'm getting to know the guys well, and I feel like we're a team now, like we'd have each other's backs if needed. I try to relax and play it cool, but inside I'm so keyed up I'll never be able to sleep. We eat our MREs, so we can save our food replacement capsules for when we're out of everything else. The night progresses, and I get more impatient with each passing hour. I must have fallen asleep at some point, because I dream about Maddie.

I'm up again before dawn and drinking coffee on the rocks above the river, watching the sun come up when Carey comes to sit with me.

"Hey man. It'll be all right in the end, and if it's not, then it's not the end. My mom says that to me all the time. I used to think it was stupid, but now I look at it as solid logic."

"I appreciate the support, Carey. I'm hopeful about how things will go today. Once we talk to the teacher, we'll find her, or at least where she's gone to."

I listen to myself say the words, but I don't believe them, and my anxiety level spirals out of control. I almost lost it yesterday with Marcus. My emotions have been boiling right under the surface for months now, and I sense I might lose it any minute. I'm not sure how much more I can pile on and still maintain my reserve. I'm trying my best to practice self-control, but seriously, I have never felt this close to going to pieces before.

Frank walks up and sits next to Carey. He sips his coffee and stays silent.

"Okay bud, I'll see you when you get back." Carey shakes my hand and walks back to camp.

"Let's get some chow and get moving, yes?" says Frank. He looks over at me, eyebrows raised. "Keep a cool head today and we'll get it handled."

"Yes sir, I understand. I'll be all right, and I'll follow your lead. You can count on me."

"Good. Let's get boots on the ground."

We go toward town, following the same route we did yesterday. The monotony of walking helps calm my nerves, the rhythm soothing me. As we approach the main road, I see Marcus on a horse outside the saloon.

Jeez, not this idiot again.

"Hey guys, I was hoping I'd see you again. I have a proposal for you. If you can get a message to my family back home, I'll put you in touch with the guy your mom was living with."

He rides his horse beside us and holds up an envelope, presumably the note to his family.

Frank stops walking and looks up at him. He sighs and puts his hand on the horse's neck.

"Listen, Marcus, is it? You're getting on my last nerve here, pal. We've already spoken to John Harding, so you're a little late with that message. But now that I realize you had that knowledge yesterday and didn't share it with us, well, that pisses me off. And if you're not out of my sight in ten seconds, I will reach into my vest pocket, take out my Bowie knife, and stick it clean through your thigh. I will watch you bleed out right here in the street. You'll just be another asshole who pissed someone off and paid for it. And Stewart and I, well, we'll transport home tomorrow without a care in the world, never giving you another thought."

Marcus pulls the reins on his horse and turns back toward the saloon.

"Assholes. Nice wig," he calls out over his shoulder as he rides away.

Frank glowers at him and it takes all my self-restraint not to laugh at the wig jab.

We trudge on and reach the schoolhouse within ten minutes. Kids are playing outside and the door is open. A woman sits at the desk at the front of the room. I see her before we get inside.

Her curly blonde hair is tied in a ponytail, and she is concentrating on the papers in front of her.

She looks up as she sees us enter.

"Gentlemen? I think you may be in the wrong building. This is the schoolhouse. Unless you're here to pick up your child, you've taken an incorrect turn somewhere."

With that, she goes back to grading papers.

"Hi, I'm Frank and this is Michael. We're looking for the schoolteacher, and I assume that's you?"

She doesn't glance up. "It is. What can I do for you?"

"We're searching for Christine Stewart, and I hear you might know her."

She stops what she's doing but doesn't look up yet. She takes a minute and inhales a deep breath before she speaks.

"And who's asking?"

"I'm her brother. Our family heard she was in these parts, and we're searching for her."

She smiles and nods her head.

"Really? Christine doesn't have a brother. She has a sister named Kat. So, would you like to explain to me who you really are before I grab the gun under my desk and shoot your ass?"

I step forward and clear my throat.

"I'm her son, Michael. I just want to find my mom, ma'am. Can you help us? Please?"

Her mouth drops open, and she stares at me for a long time before speaking.

"Michael, tell me your dog's name. And your girlfriend's name. And where you were planning to go for vacation seven months ago."

"Huh? Um, okay. Well, let's see, our dog's name is Max, my girlfriend is Maddie, and we were going to Aruba. You've probably never heard of it, it's an island in the Caribbean Sea."

She laughs and stands up. "I know where Aruba is. I'm from Chicago. I'm a transporter from Chicago. It's about time Christine sent you to take me home! I mean sheesh, she's been home long enough!"

Frank and I look at each other, confused. She's a transporter?

"We should have a chat. Christine isn't home, and she didn't send us to pick you up. Are you Annabelle Harris by any chance? We're assigned to conduct a courtesy search for you in the surrounding area for the Chicago division once we've found Christine," says Frank.

"What? What do you mean she isn't there? She transported out of here a week ago."

"How do you know that? Why didn't you go? Why would you think she came home and sent us to come back for you?"

"Okay, let's sit down guys," Annabelle says as she leads us to a table in the room's corner.

"So, first, yes, I am Annabelle Harris. Christine and I met after we were stranded here for about a month. I came to Piedmont after my transport landed me off course in Arkansas and I couldn't get my transponder to work. Our transponders flashed on about a week ago, so we thought we would get home. But Indians took me before we tried. She told John—that's who she was staying with—that if she wasn't here when he got back, to tell me she got home, and I should keep trying. If it didn't work, she'd send someone to get me."

"She never made it back, Annabelle. She's been missing for seven months."

"Where did she go, then? She'd left without a trace by the time we got back. John and the search party found me—I'd gotten away while the Indians were chasing her. She made it back after running from the Indians and found John. Then she sent him to find me so she could transport home. That's the last time he saw her. So . . . if she didn't get there, then where is she? I mean, it makes no sense!"

I can't comprehend what I'm hearing. She was transporting home. Where the hell is she then and is she still alive? Since she didn't make it home, she could be anywhere. The enormity of that hits me hard. My breathing becomes rapid and I feel my stomach turn. All at once I feel underqualified for this mission. What the hell do I know about finding transporters? I babysit prisoners at work. I concentrate on slowing my breathing down; I need to get my head together and focus.

"What about John? He was the last one to see her. We need to find out what happened to her!" I say.

I stand up, ready to run out of the building and straight back to that ranch.

"No way. You're on the wrong path there Michael, trust me. John was in love with your mom. Still is. He's been a mess since she left. He would do anything for her, and would give anything to have her back now."

"Was she, did she love him too?"

"Oh God no. Not in that way. He's a kind and decent man who helped your mom when she was alone here. He took her in and kept her safe. It's hard to tell now, he's drinking and not himself the past few days, but he helped her. He did. She tried to repay that kindness, but they were never together like that." She gets up and paces back and forth a few times before speaking again, her worry written all over her face. "Where did she go? We need to get her!"

Frank tries to calm everyone down. "I agree, and we can work on that from home. We'll get you home and then work on finding out where Christine is."

"Frank, what if John knows something? What if he did something to her? What if Annabelle is wrong?"

"Michael, she isn't here. Annabelle makes sense. The guy we saw yesterday cried when he talked about her; he's not doing well. Her transponder took her somewhere else, and we have to figure out where that is, but we should do that from the mainframe at base."

"I want a minute to say goodbye to the kids, please. I don't want to just disappear on them."

Annabelle walks outside to the yard to tell the twelve children goodbye. I watch her hug each child and stoop down to their level to talk to them. Some of them cry, and she spends a few extra minutes with them. She walks across the street and comes back with a woman from the general store.

"Mary, this is Frank and Michael. These are my friends from home. There's been a family emergency and I must leave town. Can you please tell Mr. Tyler I won't be coming back to the boarding house, and he'll need another teacher? Can I ask you to lock up the school please?"

She hands Mary the keys to the school and rings the bell in the yard. The kids gather up their books and leave, waving goodbye to Annabelle on their way out. I notice a tear fall, though she wipes it away quickly.

"These kids are the only thing I will miss. Let's go, I'm more than ready to leave. I only have a horse which I'd like to leave with John. Do you mind if we bring her to the ranch? I assume you camped in the walnut grove where Christine came in?"

"Sure, that's no problem. You can ride, and we'll walk beside you," says Frank.

She comes over to stand in front of me and give me a hug.

"You look like her. I love your mom, Michael. She's my best friend. Don't worry, we'll find her. I don't care what it takes, we'll find her."

Somehow, I trust she means that, and I believe her.

NINETEEN

Piedmont, Oklahoma 1867 / Los Angeles, CA 2070 / Cotswold, England 1335

Annabelle ties the horse to the fence and knocks on the door. John swings it open looking angry, but as soon as he sees her standing there, he relaxes.

"Annabelle."

He looks past her at Frank and me and then back to Annabelle.

"What are you doing here with them?"

"John, I'm leaving with them, and I won't be back. I'm giving my horse to you; she's tied at the railing, so you'll need to get her squared away later. I just wanted to say goodbye."

"Going where with them?"

"Home, John. They're taking me to see my girls and my husband Joe. Thank you for helping Christine and me while we were here. I don't think we would have survived without you."

"Will you see her?"

"Yes, I'll see her. Not right away, but yes."

"Tell her I, well I . . . I'm sorry I didn't say goodbye properly."

"I will. I promise." She gives him a quick hug and walks off the porch. John is shutting the door when I jog up to him.

"Wait, please. Thank you for rescuing my mom."

"Your mom?"

He glances at Annabelle and frowns.

"My mother, Christine."

I put my hand out, and he shakes it, his mouth open in surprise. I walk to Frank and Annabelle. John stands in the cabin's door until we disappear over the horizon.

As we approach camp, I hear the guys cheer. They think Annabelle is my mom. I step forward and introduce her. They look confused until Frank explains that she was our next and final rescue here. He tells them the story of what we've found out and they all seem disappointed.

I know the feeling.

But now that we know she has transported elsewhere, we can concentrate on that angle. But I can't let myself wonder where she might be, or I'll lose it. I force myself to focus on getting back and working with IT support to find out what we can.

Frank sends a message to base we've recovered Annabelle and will transport back today. Base confirms contact with her family and the team's families, who will be there when we get home. I have Maddie down as my new in case of emergency, so she'll be there. My Aunt Kat and grandparents will expect a call to say come in, she is home. Instead, they'll get a visit to tell them we have not recovered her. That will be such a letdown for them, like *I've* let them down.

We transport that afternoon to a full house of people waiting for us. Straight out of the jump pods we pass through a decontamination room. We drop our clothes into hazardous waste bins and continue to a sanitizing shower before we change into fresh uniforms. We're scanned to make sure we aren't sick and given antibiotics anyway as a precaution. From there, they usher us into a two-hour debriefing where they question us about the details of our mission. I guess that we located some transporters makes us minor celebrities. We're told not to speak to the press; they'll release a statement later that day. Which is fine by me, I don't want to talk to them, anyway. Why would I tell the world I couldn't find her and we're worse off than before?

When they release us to the lobby, Maddie is there waiting for me. She runs to me and we hug, happy to see each other. In some ways, she's all I have now.

I honestly didn't expect to be back without my mom. I had thought about the possibility, but I always assumed we'd find her. Now that we've confirmed she isn't in Oklahoma, the possibilities are infinite, and it's overwhelming to consider.

I watch Annabelle run to a man and two little girls, who I assume are her family. She is crying and scoops the children up in her arms. As I walk by, she grabs my arm.

"Michael, I meant what I said. I will stay here for as long as it takes, so I can be here for you and help bring your mom back."

"Annabelle, I can't ask you to uproot your whole life and your family's life; that wouldn't be fair. I appreciate that you want to help, but you can do that from home."

"Sorry kid, not your call. Your mom and I went through something together that I cannot ever explain to you. The uncertainty we lived with was indescribable. All we had to make it through was each other, and because of that, we have a bond. One that I don't expect anyone to understand. She's my closest friend, there is no way I will leave her twisting in the wind. No way. That's not how I'm built. So, like it or not, you're stuck with me until she gets home. Now go take care of business and I'll see you soon."

With that she hugs me, and her husband shrugs at me. "Trust me, if she says we're not leaving, then we're not."

"Yay, we're going to the beach, Daddy!" One of the little blonde girls squeals and hugs her dad around his knee.

I suppose that commits Annabelle to staying. It causes me to worry knowing she is concerned enough to stay here until she's found.

My mom has never been big on close friends. She has a lot of what I'd call a step above acquaintances. She goes out for drinks with people from work, and there are other women she's known for years, but not that one best friend.

Annabelle really seems to care about her, and it makes me happy that my mom has found such a good friend. I have so many questions for her about her time with my mom, but they must wait. I need to go home and regroup before I go to IT with Frank tomorrow. I'm hoping Maddie can give me some advice about where to start our search.

Later that day I'm finally released. Frank has ordered the team to grab some sleep and reconvene in the morning at eight o'clock. Maddie has been staying at the house to look after Max, who had not been behaving at Aunt Kat's house. After he chewed up a third pair of her shoes, she called Maddie to come get him. He goes berserk when he sees me, jumping and crying, running around me as I step into the house. I flop onto the couch and he takes a running leap into my arms, licking my face and crying the entire time. He runs to Maddie next, repeating the process. We both laugh as he moves between us, then runs to his bed to drag toys to the couch. My mom being gone has traumatized him and with me away for a week, he might have thought I had abandoned him.

I sink further into the couch, savoring the way it feels to be home.

"Wanna order some food and chill with a movie?" I ask.

"Okay sure, but first give me the highlights of the mission."

I tell her about finding Williams, McCarty, and Paxton, and what we suspect are the remains of Bosch. I recount everything about Oklahoma, and she looks concerned.

"So, your mom left before Annabelle got back, and she said their transponders were showing signs of coming on?"

"Yeah, that's what she mentioned."

She bites her bottom lip the way she does when she's worried, her brow furrowing. "Michael, I need to go to the office. I want to look at something."

"Now? We just left and you're off for the day. Plus, I just got home."

"Trust me, I really need to check some stuff out."

"About my mom? What?"

"Maybe. I don't want to say yet until I'm sure of what I'm talking about. I need to review some things."

"Let's go." I grab the car fob and stand.

"No, no you stay here, eat, and get some sleep,"—she's already on her phone ordering a car—"you can't go in there without clearance, anyway. I should run before I lose this thought. I'll call you later when I'm done and I'm on my way back."

"Okay, I guess so, I'll be here." She gives me a quick kiss and heads for the door.

"It's just us, Max." Max trots after Maddie and stands looking at the door whining for a minute after she goes.

I know the feeling Max.

I shower and change, then eat dinner and try to watch a movie, but I feel restless and can't concentrate enough to get into the plot. My phone rings and Maddie's face pops up.

"Hey, you on your way over?" I ask.

"Hey there. No, I'll be here all night. I think I'm onto something, and I can't leave until I see it through to the end. Can you bring me some clothes in the morning when you come in? You said you're meeting the team, right? I have some stuff in your closet, bring me a pair of jeans and a sweater, comfortable clothes."

"Um, all right, but are you sure you need to stay all night? I mean, do you know something about where my mom is?"

"Maybe. I think so. I'm running the final analysis and I'll know more in the morning."

"Oh my God, what? Tell me."

"I can't, not yet anyway. But if I'm right, my supervisor will bring Frank in and explain everything."

I try the treadmill to burn some restlessness off, but it does no good. To be honest, I can't wait until morning to work with IT to locate my mom. If Maddie knows something, maybe they're close to getting useful intel. If I sleep at all, it will be a miracle.

I meet the guys in the briefing room the next morning, and we sit around and talk until Frank gets there right after eight o'clock.

"Okay guys, everyone can have a free day today. Go to the range, restock your equipment, anything you need to get done. I want to take Stewart with me to IT, since we worked on the Oklahoma rescue together. Does anyone have any objections to that?"

All the guys say no problem, so I follow Frank to IT. I've never been in here; they allow no one in except IT personnel without special passes. I look around the office and see Maddie at a desk studying the screen in front of her. She looks up and sees me, and I hold up the backpack I brought her clothes in. She walks over, smiles, and squeezes my hand discreetly before taking it from me.

Once she leaves to change, I survey the place. It's a massive operation with at least two dozen people working on computers. There's a large screen on one end of the room that lists transporters names, destinations, return times, etcetera. As transporters depart and arrive, it updates their status.

There's a separate area that houses the enforcement team. They assign each member of the team prisoners to track. If a prisoner's tracker places them in a restricted area, it notifies the enforcement team immediately. The enforcement agent will transport the prisoner, with no warning, to another time and place. The system configures the new destination and off they go. If their trackers no longer detect signals of life on the prisoner—and this part is creepy—it highlights their information on the scan as expired. They are declared expired as casually as we declare a carton of milk perished. No one knows how they died, only that they are gone.

Once the agent confirms death via the prisoner's tracker data, they send the records to archives and it removes them from the active files. Archiving the records generates a letter to the family telling them that the prisoner is deceased. That's coldhearted if you ask me.

It reminds me of a hospital waiting room, when someone goes in for surgery and they show their status on the screen: in pre-op, in surgery, in recovery. This must have been a logistical nightmare when the system was down.

I glance at the top of the screen, and the missing transporters' names are all there, highlighted in red and showing MIA status. The sight of that screen is jarring—it looks so final, somehow.

A guy who looks like he slept in his clothes motions for Frank and me to come into his office. He's sipping coffee with one hand and typing with the other.

"Hey Rhoades, how's it going? You must be Stewart. So, after you told Thomas yesterday what the rescued transporter stated about their transponders cuing on, she went to work on it. Sorry, I don't remember any transporters names. Anyway, she had the idea that perhaps someone else somewhere had the same phenomenon with their transponder. So, she checked worldwide and guess what? She found out that our girl's transponder and another transponder in England show trace signs of activity at the same time. Then she traced back further, and the system shows one other transponder in France who had the same hit a few months earlier. It shows that somehow the magnetic fields crossed, and they connected. How, I haven't figured out yet, but it reads like there was a short time when they linked as one signal. We had no reason to analyze for that before now; we couldn't even make a forced transport work, the system kept showing everything as inoperable. So, until now, no one had reviewed registered activity on the transponders since the outage."

This IT dude needs to consider decaf; he's talking so fast and not making sense, and he's looking at us as if we should understand what all this means.

"Okay, so what?" Frank looks like he's losing patience, and we've only been here for five minutes.

"So what? The 'so what' is the common denominator. The transponder in England. Don't you see? If the British transporter isn't in France and isn't in Oklahoma, then France and Oklahoma must be in England. I suppose our girl could be in France, but I'd say there's a lower chance of that. I believe these three transporters are together—England, France, and Oklahoma. You know they aren't in Oklahoma, so that leaves France in 1710 or England in 1335."

"1710 or 1335? Are you serious? We transported her to 1867 when she left here. You're saying they could send her back over five-hundred years further, and to another country?"

Frank's face mimics what I'm thinking.

"Yep, those are the areas and time periods the signals originated from. I'd bet my next paycheck she's in one of those places. I'd try England first, because that's the common denominator in all this. If you allow me a while, I can call my contacts over in Europe and share my information with them. I'll tell them we want to enter their timeline to search for our transporter, and if I offer a courtesy search for theirs that will improve our chances of authorization. I'm confident they'll go for that. Their hands are full right now with a lot of missing transporters in Europe. They've assembled a general European retrieval team to help expedite the process, but it's still slow going. I'm positive they'd welcome the offer of you searching for two of theirs."

"Do it, please. Set that up and I'll advise the rest of the team of what we're planning. You have my number, report to me once you have a go on the mission."

"I'm on it, sir. Give me an hour."

We head down to the meeting room. Frank has already sent a message out to the team, so they are all waiting for us there. I don't understand all of what the guy upstairs told us, but I got the general idea of it. The snapshot is he thinks my mom is in France or England, most likely England. In 1335.

Holy crap.

The good news is that it sounds as if she's with two other transporters. So at least she isn't alone. But medieval England? We need to get to her soon. That time and place is no joke.

Disease, lack of food, knights, a dozen other things run through my mind.

Frank briefs the other guys and makes sure they are all on board to make the trip. The retrieval team is a voluntary assignment; you can opt out anytime, so I'm relieved when they all agree. We work smoothly together and I trust them.

"We will put this trip on the fast track men, which means you will get vaccines in the next hour. As soon as they have them ready in medical, I'll receive notification. Right after, we go to the history lab for a crash course on the time and place. We need to equip ourselves as much as possible to best handle whatever comes our way. This will be like nothing you've ever seen before, I guarantee it, so forget everything you think you learned on our last excursion," he says.

"Okay guys, our plan is to drop into England in 1335, to the same point the British transporter went to. Our primary goal is to recover our transporter Stewart, however, we'll also search for the British transporter, Ethan Grant, and the French transporter, Estera Bargeron. With any luck they'll all be together and make our job easy. We leave in the morning, so inspect your equipment tonight. Go home and get a proper night's sleep, and we'll meet in the jump area tomorrow at seven o'clock sharp."

We file out and go our separate ways. Maddie meets me in the cafeteria before I go to receive vaccines, and she's worried about me traveling to England.

"Michael, do you have to go? Maybe Frank should take senior transporters? I mean, it's medieval England for God's sake."

"I'll be fine. I won't withdraw now. Besides, we're a team, and we all perform well together. Frank knows what he's doing, and he's our supervisor. I won't do anything stupid. If I follow his orders, I'll be safe."

As worried as she is, there is no way I will bow out now, I have to follow through. I'm so proud of her; she figured out where my mom is. Or at least pointed us in the right direction. I was so overwhelmed and hopeless when I got home, thinking it would be nearly impossible to figure that out. Maddie has given me hope when I had lost all faith in ever finding her again.

I finally get a decent night's sleep, but only because my body can't continue without it any longer. We wake up and head into work, where I give Maddie the car fob so she can take it home later. We decide she should stay at the house, so Max doesn't think I'm abandoning him again, as I don't know how long I'll be on assignment. Besides, it'll be awhile before he'll be welcome at Aunt Kat's again, thanks to his shoe fetish.

I check my equipment one last time before going inside. I'm the first one in the jump room, so I run down to the cafeteria to grab coffee. By the time I'm back, Carey and Gray are there.

"What's up?" I say as I fist bump them and sit, waiting for the rest of them to arrive.

"Not much. Ready to fly, you?" says Carey.

"You know it."

"I've got a good feeling about this, Stewart. We will find all three of them." Gray squeezes my shoulder and slaps me on the back. That's a monumental show of affection for him.

Penn and Adams come through the door, followed by Frank.

"Let's do this, team," says Frank.

We arrive in Cotswold, England late morning. It's raining, and the temperature is well below respectable. We're layered up, but I'm still cold, and I didn't bring any extra cold weather gear. Each of us has on a T-shirt, a long-sleeved uniform polo shirt, a lined jacket, and a tactical gear vest. We carry thermal coats rolled up in our backpacks, but it seems like so much trouble to struggle into it over all this gear. We suck it up and tolerate the cold instead. Our equipment weighs close to twenty-five pounds, and it's difficult to move around with all of it on. We bring more supplies this time as we can't be sure how long we will be away. We have supplies in every Velcro pocket of our vests, and we stock the backpacks with even more.

Frank estimates we came in a little off course and need to head two miles north, straight through the forest. We skirt around a small settlement of mud huts with thatched roofs and come upon an incredible castle. We pause for a minute, as none of us can walk by without stopping to stare at it. It impresses even Frank. We don't have this in America, so seeing something like this is a once-in-a-lifetime experience. I wish we could bring our phones so I could take a picture for Maddie. I don't think I'll be able to describe it to her.

As we move on, the forest becomes denser. The wet leaves stick to our pants as our boots unsettle them. It is eerily quiet here, the only sound our footfall on the leaves. The entire place feels damp and smells of wet wood and vegetation. At this pace we'll be there in an hour. We keep moving in near silence, passing a lake where we watch a man checking fish traps. We crouch and wait for him to leave so we don't risk him seeing us. The quiet is foreign but helps avoid an incident when we intersect a path and five men ride by. As we drop to our bellies, they ride right past without seeing us, our camouflaged uniforms concealing us.

After walking for another thirty minutes we hear voices. Frank gives the stop signal, and he and Gray move ahead to do recon. We see three men sitting at a fire pit talking.

Frank decides that since this is so close to the British transporter's drop-off point, we should stake it out and watch them for a while. We all hold positions inside the tree line to wait and watch. Thirty minutes go by with nothing happening but them cooking a rabbit in a pot, and I'm eager to get moving again.

I'm about to ask Frank about moving on when a woman walks out of the tree line on the opposite side of the clearing. Her hair is longer and messier than it normally is, and she's in some weird dress with an apron, but it's her.

It's my mom.

Frank looks at me and then gives the other guys the thumbs up. I walk into the clearing, the other five behind me. The men jump to their feet and hold out spears made of sticks. They stand there staring at us, maybe in shock. If they're from this time, then we will look like aliens to them with our helmets and uniforms. If they're transporters, then they'll recognize our uniforms and know we're here for them. My mom freezes in place, looking confused. I step forward and reach to lift off my helmet. I let it drop to the ground at my feet. She bursts into tears and drops to a crouch, balancing on her heels. Her face in her hands, she cannot stand yet.

"Michael! Oh my God, Michael!"

She springs up and runs to me where she throws her arms around my neck, crying the entire time.

"What are you doing here? Oh my God, how did you get here? How did you locate me?"

Frank takes his helmet off and she cries even harder. She pulls back and cups my face with her hands. Now I'm tearing up, and I glance over and see Frank wiping his cheeks. The other guys have all taken their helmets off and are wiping their eyes.

"Mom, I'm so glad you're okay. You're okay, aren't you? Are you hurt?"

"No, I'm fine honey. I'm just so happy to see you, I've missed you so much. I love you so much."

"I love you too, Mom. I was so worried about you. No one knew what happened to you. And then we left for Oklahoma and couldn't find you and that John guy said you went home."

"You talked to John? How on earth did you guys find out about him?"

"It's a long story. But then Annabelle confirmed that you'd been staying with him and told us that your transponders had been on, sort of, for that one day. IT worked on it from there. Maddie worked it out."

"Wait, you saw Annabelle? She's alive?"

"Yeah, she's fine, she's home now. Well, she's in L.A.—she said she's not going back to Chicago until I bring you home."

"Oh my God, she's alive! Ethan, she's alive! Oh my God, I'm so happy!"

We hug again, and Ethan steps up to shake Frank's hand.

"Hi, I'm Ethan Grant. I'm a British transporter. This is Aidan, he transported in at Scotland, and this is Malcolm. I escorted him here seven months ago."

Ethan turns to my mom, smiling, and hugs her.

"I'm happy Annabelle's safe, and I'm so pleased your son is here. I told you everything would work out."

* * *

Michael is here, it doesn't seem real.

I gaze at Frank and tear up. He holds his arms out and I fall into them, crying. I knew he wouldn't give up on me, that he'd keep searching no matter what. Michael introduces me to the rest of the team, and we all thank them for their sacrifice in searching for us. We sit at the fire and I hold Michael's hand and refuse to let go while Frank tells us about the transporters missing across the globe. So, Malcolm was right; it was a global interruption.

"We'll be here for a day or so. Ethan, you're one transporter we are searching for as part of our co-op retrieval agreement. There's also a woman from France we are searching for. Based on her transponder activity, she may also be near here. The French retrieval team could not find her in Versailles, which was her drop-off point."

Estera. They've come looking for her too.

I shake my head at Frank. "Her name is Estera Bargeron. She died two days ago, after she got the plague. We buried her under a rock grave in the woods about a mile from here. She was my friend," I say, hanging my head.

I wipe a few tears from my eyes as I tell them about her, and Michael moves closer to me to put his arm around my shoulder. Frank closes his eyes for a minute before he speaks.

"I'm sorry we couldn't get here soon enough to save her. This entire thing is such a tragedy. This mess will affect hundreds of lives for years."

Ethan speaks, but I catch his eye and shake my head. I don't want to say anything about Jonathan or our plan. Ethan and I should figure out how much we choose to say before we talk to anyone else. It's enough that Aidan and Malcolm know. And God only knows where Thomas is; he's a loose end in all of this.

"We can transport everyone home in the morning. Tonight, we'll camp out here with you." Frank looks around the fire as Ethan and I exchange glances.

Well, I guess I will tell them everything.

"Yeah, about that. There are two things I need to tell you. Michael say nothing until I finish, please," I say.

Michael looks at Frank and then at me. "Mom, what the hell is there to talk about? We go home tomorrow. Someone can show us where the French transporter is at first light, or even today before dark, and we'll take her tracker for proof of death. In the meantime, we have antibiotics that each of you needs to take in case she exposed you to the plague."

"Okay, just listen to me, all of you."

I explain how Thomas and Aidan knew of the outage, how they planned it, and the mission to steal the chapter. Ethan and I explain how we plan to complete the job and then decide what to do with the chapter after we get home and confront Hoyt.

"Transport us home the day after tomorrow. We'll be fine, we've been here this long, what's another couple of days?" I say.

Frank and Michael both laugh. "The difference is you will be in danger, Mom! This is ridiculous."

One guy on the team shakes his head and looks at me as if I were crazy. "Hi, Ms. Stewart, my name's Carey, and seriously, that is the stupidest idea I've ever heard."

Gray slaps the back of Carey's head. "Carey, you will be respectful."

I turn to Michael and grasp both of his hands. "Michael, this is my way to make a mark, to do something because it's the right thing. I can't walk away now, I just can't. Please try to understand."

"Mom, no one will ever know you did this. You can't even confirm why this guy wants the book, or whatever it is."

"True, but that doesn't matter. If there's a chance this is as important as Hoyt thinks it is, I need to help. I really hope you'll understand and support me in that decision."

"Mom, I don't get it, but I can't tell you what to do. So, if you're staying then so am I. There's no way I'm leaving you here. What if the system isn't online in two days? We can't take that chance. You'd still be here, and we'd have to return for you. What if we couldn't find you again? How would we explain we need to come back? No way, it won't work."

"Absolutely not! You're not staying here, Michael. If things aren't back to normal, you do a forced transport on us," I say.

Frank speaks up now, looking serious. "That won't work if the system's still down, Christine or we would have done that months ago. I can't leave Michael here and take the rest of the unit back. It's out of the question. He's right, we couldn't explain to base why we had to come back for you. Either we all go back now, or we all stay."

"Christine, I think we should reconsider your involvement in the job. We made this plan before we realized your son would be here. That changes things, doesn't it? I can't let you risk not getting home. Go with your son. I can handle this alone and we will still meet in Los Angeles after and confront Hoyt."

"Never, Ethan! One person cannot do this—it's way too dangerous. I've committed to you and I'm sticking to the plan."

Gray chimes in. "Then we all stay. We all remain with Stewart, and we all carry out the plan. More people will mean a quick in and out. Then we transport out that night. None of us will ever speak of it again. It never happened. We're a team, and we stay together."

Gray looks at Frank for confirmation of his plan. The others—Carey, Penn, and Adams— all nod.

Frank looks at each one of them and gestures to Michael. "Michael? Are we all in agreement?"

I look at Frank and answer before Michael has a chance to. "No way Frank! I'm not okay with that at all. What the hell is wrong with you? Michael goes home, and if you all need to go together, then fine, go with him."

Frank sighs, "Christine, I've known you for a long time, and I realize it's hard for you to see Michael as anything other than your son. But he's a grown man and a valuable member of this unit, and our team has agreed to stay, and well, that's what we're going to do. And you can protest all you'd like, but the decision is made and that's it. I am still your immediate supervisor, let's not forget that."

I try to stare him down, but he doesn't blink even once, and I know I will not win this battle. I've known him long enough to understand that once he's decided, it's over.

"Fine. We'll all go together after we complete the job." I don't break eye contact with Frank for a minute to let him know I'm not happy about this development.

"Yes sir! We stay and all transport together when we're done," Michael says.

Ethan clears his throat. "There's one more thing. Sorry lads, but I should mention it. I made Malcolm a promise and I want to keep it. He stayed with me and tried to repair the transponder. I owe him for that. I told him I'd do my best to transfer him somewhere else, to a more hospitable time. Can you help me with that? I don't want to put anyone's career on the line, but I'd like to keep my promise, if I can."

Frank nods to Malcolm. "Got anything in mind?"

"Actually, I quite like the thought of America. More specifically, Oklahoma in 1867. Christine's told us all about it, and it sounds brilliant to me."

TWENTY

Cotswold, England 1335

"Are you planning to share your MREs, at least? I see some in your pack, and if I eat rabbit or fish one more time, I will lose it. And if someone doesn't find me something with sugar in it, I will hurt one of you," I say, still angry about Frank's decision.

The guys laugh and display their supply of MREs while we sort through them and pick what we want. I choose spaghetti with meat sauce and peach cobbler for dessert. As I eat, I feel like I've died and gone to heaven. I never imagined a crappy MRE could taste so wonderful.

Even Aidan is in excellent spirits as we eat and get caught up on what's been happening around the world in our timeline since we were missing. Frank gives everyone an antibiotic because we were in contact with Estera and may still be in the incubation period.

Throughout the night, I can't bring myself to leave Michael's side. I'm so relieved to see him, the weight of the last seven months lifted off my shoulders.

"Michael, are Grandma and Grandpa all good? And Aunt Kat? This had to worry them sick."

"Yeah, they're all fine. Aunt Kat's been spending a lot of time with them to keep them busy. I've been doing stuff with Grandpa too when I have time."

"Good, I miss them all so much. What about Max?"

"Max is great, Maddie is staying at the house with him. He misses you and slept on your bed for a long while when you were first gone. He wouldn't sleep with me and dragged one of your T-shirts into his bed. So I let him keep it."

"Oh, my poor baby. He misses me. How was John when you saw him in Oklahoma?"

"I have nothing to compare to, but he didn't seem that great to be honest. He was drinking and seemed pretty broken up that you left. Were you and him, I mean, did you, ya know, like him?"

"No, not *like* him, like him. He saved me, Michael. If not for him, I can't say where or how I would be. He was kind and very respectful. I'm alive today because of him. I hope he'll be all right. I worry about him."

"I think he'll be okay, I told him I was your son. He seemed surprised to learn that, but Annabelle talked to him too."

"Annabelle is really okay too? Are you sure she wasn't hurt?"

"She's fine, I promise. She misses you and is worried sick, but other than that she's good. Her husband and little girls were at base when we got there."

"I have tons to ask you about, but it can wait. I'm so glad you're okay and Annabelle got home. There wasn't a day that went by I didn't worry about you. I'll breathe easy now, knowing you're safe."

"*You* worried? How do you think I felt? Not knowing what happened or where you were? Especially after leaving Oklahoma. That was tough. But Maddie worked it out, and I'm just so glad we found you, Mom."

"What about your promotions test? How did you score?"

"Aced it. I moved up a paygrade and I test for lead in two months. I can afford to move out. Maddie and I want a place together."

"Oh honey, that's terrific!"

"Mom, you're fake smiling at me right now."

I sigh and remove the forced grin from my face.

"Maybe, sorry. I'm so thrilled they promoted you, and you know I love Maddie. I couldn't be happier that you two are getting serious. I guess reuniting and finding out I will be an empty nester in the same day is a lot to take in, that's all."

He gives me a hug, and overcome with emotion I tear up, yet again.

"I've got to be on my own some time, Mom. I'll still be close and only a phone call away. Maybe I shouldn't have said anything. It kinda slipped out. I'm excited about it and didn't think about how you'd cope, sorry."

"No, no, it's great, I promise. It's been a big day, and after all these months I'm overwhelmed with relief to see you is all. I'm proud of you, and will be the first person to buy you a housewarming gift."

He smiles at me, and I squeeze his hand before we join the others at the fire pit.

Ethan and I review the plan to get Wallingford's chapter with the team in more detail.

Aidan doesn't protest even though his payday is circling the drain. I suspect he's happy to be going home like the rest of us. We stay up later than usual, glad for the company, and I'm ecstatic my son is here. This will be the only point in seven months I won't go to sleep worrying about him.

We're getting fixed to wrap things up for the night when Ethan sits up straight and turns to look at the forest behind him. I see he's tense and on alert, but no one else has noticed.

He picks up the spear at his feet and grips it in his hand. I walk over to him and sit down.

"What's up? What's got you spooked?"

"Nothing, it's nothing. I thought I heard something, but it was probably just an animal."

I turn to look in the direction he's staring but see nothing. Clouds cover the moon, making it too dark to recognize anything but the outline of trees. I let it pass, wondering if maybe all the excitement has him on edge. Then I pick up something too, leaves crunching as if someone's stepping on them. Frank hears it too because he's on his feet in an instant. The rest of the team spot Frank's uneasiness and grab their guns.

Michael pushes me down to the ground and stands over me, weapon drawn. I'm struggling to rise when an arrow hits Adams in the thigh and men spill into the camp from all directions. The retrieval team already have their weapons pointed at them. Adams is down and bleeding, but he leaves his weapon trained on one man. I'm still down behind Michael when Ethan steps in front of both of us. Frank has his gun shouldered, and his voice is steady and strong when he speaks.

"Put your weapons down and we won't kill you. If you fire again, every one of you will die where you stand. We consider you a hostile enemy and will use lethal force to contain you."

One man laughs and glances at the other intruders.

"Right, then. You going to throw that strange contraption at me, are you? My arrow will pierce your heart faster than you will have whatever that is in the air."

He draws his bowstring back and is bracing to let go when Frank fires. The shot is so quiet you wouldn't have been able to detect it a hundred feet away. A hissing sound is the only noise as it exits the barrel. The bullet hits him in the arm, and he drops the bow. The other men stare in shock. One by one, they put their bows and arrows down while Frank barks out orders.

"Gray, confiscate their weapons. Stewart and Penn secure them. Carey, grab the Med-Pac and take care of Adams, then the prisoner. Everyone else okay? Is anyone else hit? Christine?"

We all give him the okay, but he doesn't lower his gun until the other four men are secure.

"Gentlemen, that was a mistake you can prevent from happening again. Your friend should have listened to me. You will all receive your weapons when we leave, and you'll never see us again. Until then, you are prisoners of the United States government and will stay here until further notice."

None of them dare to speak; they gawk at Frank, frozen in place.

"In the meantime, let's get this idiot bandaged up and squared away before the blood attracts wild animals we don't want in camp. Carey, give me an update on Adams please," Frank says.

"Adams is stable, boss. Superficial wound only," Carey shouts back to Frank.

I check on Adams, and Carey already has him patched up. The arrow only penetrated deep enough to make it stick. I listen to Ethan tell Frank this is the same group who attacked camp before and attempted to kidnap Estera.

Assholes. Got what you deserved this time.

Michael rushes over to make sure I'm okay then returns to his unit. He seems so much older and more mature, though it's only been seven months. I know this was hard on him.

Families across the world suffered at the hands of Jonathon Hoyt, and it will forever change them. My family is one of those. When everyone transports home, the families of those transporters who didn't make it will have to deal with the reality that they're gone forever. I thank God my son is not one of those who must learn to live without his family member.

I can't wait to get my hands on Jonathan Hoyt.

I watch the intruders, and they seem half fascinated, half petrified by the guys, watching their every move. Then I realize; their clothing, weapons, medical supplies, and MREs are all things they have never seen. I had paid little attention because they're all normal to me.

However, they stand out here in a big way, and none of our new guests have uttered so much as a word since being secured in the flex-cuffs. I walk over to Frank and Ethan.

"Can anyone get in on this conversation, or is the boy's club closed?"

"Ha! You're the president of that club, doll. How are you holding up after the excitement?"

"I'm fine. I can take you to Estera tomorrow. It'll offer us a chance to get caught up. Hey, do you suppose we should allow our detainees some of those MREs? It appears malnutrition might be an upgrade for them, and I'm certain you brought enough. I think they're scared shitless of you boys. It must be a lot for them, the weapons and clothes."

"Well, look who's gone soft. Sure, we can throw some meals their way. I'll issue a guy to stand guard while they eat so they don't cause any trouble."

Ethan laughs. "I imagine we'd see more trouble out of a two-legged squirrel Frank."

Ethan and Malcolm volunteer to sleep by the fire with the prisoners, but the retrieval unit insists that these are their captives and they'll keep them under their surveillance. Ethan, Malcolm, Aidan, and I move to the shelter for the night. Before I leave, I give Michael another hug and a kiss on his cheek. The other guys rib him a little and I threaten to tell all their moms about it when we get home.

The next morning, I'm the last one up for the day. By the time I come out of the shelter, everyone is having breakfast, and the camp feels alive with the sound of the group laughing and talking. Even the prisoners join the conversation. I overhear Adams asking one of them about where he lives and what he does for a living. He seems fascinated with whatever he hears, and then they both laugh loudly and continue eating.

"Morning Ethan. Where's Michael?"

"Morning. Malcolm took him and Frank to Estera's grave. They need to take her tracker for proof of death. They were hoping to finish before you got up to spare you having to do it. Let's get together after you eat and go over our plan for tomorrow one more time, yes?"

"Sure. First, I demand some of that coffee Frank brought with. My caffeine withdrawal is in full bloom this morning."

Gray overhears me and hands me a cup. "Here you go, Ms. Stewart. You must have freaked out without coffee. I know I would. There is cream and sugar if you need it," he says, handing me a steaming cup. "Also, one guy we detained just mentioned something that might pertain to the job tomorrow. He was going on about an abbot who's coming to Cotswold on a church stopover trip. But now he can't stay at the church because they flooded it, damaging the sleeping quarters. So, I guess he's staying at some castle instead. Two of these individuals are working at the castle tomorrow, preparing for a big dinner tomorrow tonight. They're worried they won't make it there. He said the people at the castle hired a good deal of the townspeople for extra help and he doesn't want to miss his chance at getting paid. It sounds like it could be the Wallingford guy you're going after. Maybe ask him about it?"

"What? Oh hell. That may be a problem. Ethan, what do you think?"

Ethan walks over to the raiders. "You have knowledge about an abbot coming to this area? Is his name Wallingford?" One of them nods yes and Ethan walks back to sit with us again.

"Well, maybe not. There are people willing to help now, and weapons. We also have people no one will pay attention to. They're supposed to be there to set up, right? So, what if we cut a deal? Since we're all leaving tomorrow after we pick up the paperwork, let's give them the MREs. I'm certain Frank would be okay with that. We also gained antibiotics. With the plague sweeping the area, those are more valuable than gold."

Michael comes up from behind me. "But they don't even realize what antibiotics are, and they do not understand what they're capable of."

I nearly jump out of my seat. "Jeez, you scared me. When did you get back?" I stand up and stretch, trying to ease my restlessness.

"About sixty seconds ago, just in time to hear Gray tell you what the local said," he replies.

"You make a good point, Michael. But what if they know someone who's sick now? What if we supply them one pill to try out? That person will show signs of improvement within hours. Then they'd realize—and appreciate—

what the antibiotics can do for the Plague." Ethan looks at each of us, waiting for someone to answer.

"He's right, Michael. Let's tell Frank and see what we can have done. There's not much time," I say.

We bring Frank up to date on what Gray overheard, and he agrees to relinquish any remaining MREs and antibiotics when we leave.

"I'll report we lost the supplies crossing a river. What can they do, fire me?"

Frank brings the rest of the team up to speed, and they lead the prisoners over to the fire pit. Ethan starts right in, wasting no time.

"I understand you are to work a dinner in honor of Sir Richard Wallingford tomorrow night?"

None of them answer Ethan, so Frank tries next.

"Listen up gentlemen. I want to go home. I am getting cranky the longer I stay here. I cannot go home until I help my friends here finish something. That project involves one Sir Richard of Wallingford. Now, please understand that this will happen. I'm being friendly because I've had breakfast and coffee, and I know I'm going home tomorrow. Should that change, I will be very unhappy. Life will not go well for you if I am unhappy. At this moment, I will grant you valuables in return for your cooperation. If I become unhappy, those commodities will be off the table and I will no longer be asking you to cooperate. If that's too vague for you, let me say this; My weapon will ensure you do what I choose."

He peers at them with raised eyebrows, his signature expression that means he's waiting for you to respond.

One man shifts position a bit and studies Frank.

"What, what treasures? The valuables you promise to bid us. What are they?"

Ethan jumps in before Frank can answer. "All the food we carry. After we eat tomorrow, whatever's left is yours. You may take it home to your families. There's also something even more worthwhile. They're called antibiotics. It's a medicinal pill that will cure you if you catch the Black Death."

They all scoff and laugh at him, like he's just told them he intends to sprout a second head or something. "Nothing can cure the Black Death. Once you are ill, you will die."

"That's not true. These will cure it, I guarantee it. There are enough for four or five capsules each. If you have a family member now who's beginning to grow sick, you can take one today. You give them to the sick person at the onset of the illness. Go to them and try it. They will recover within two hours, and you'll know to trust us."

One man seems to sit up straighter at hearing that. He looks at the others and clears his throat.

"I'll do it. My son is ill. He woke weak with fever yesterday and likely does not fare better this morning. I am working at the castle tomorrow to buy herbs to relieve his fever. He is near, on the other side of the church. We have horses tied in the forest. We can be there quickly. Let me go to him with the medicine, please."

"All right. I'll go with you," Ethan stands up, ready to go.

"Bring Adams, he's a medic. Take the Med-Pac with him too," says Frank.

Frank motions for Adams to get ready and he gathers up his pack.

"How many people in your family?" Adams asks. "I want to bring enough for all of them. If your son's sick, your family will get it. Here, you take this one now."

"Same for you, Adams. I know we vaccinate everyone, but until you are certain what they're sick with, you need to protect yourself. I can't risk you bringing anything back to camp to the rest of the unit."

"Yes sir, I'm on it."

Adams swallows a pill and hands another one to the man next to him. The man hesitates, looking at it.

"Dude, I just took one, it's fine."

"My name is Charles, not dude."

Adams laughs and slaps him on the back. "Okay, Charles, take the pill and let's get on the road. The sooner we get to your kid, the better. I mean your child, your son."

Frank stares at Adams's leg. "Are you okay to ride with that?"

"Yeah, surface wound, it didn't penetrate very much, superficial wound only. I took a pain reliever and can't even feel it. They aren't very good with their arrows. Whichever one of them shot me could use some time at the archery range."

The three of them take off and are out of sight in a few seconds.

And now we wait.

The other men sit silently until Michael goes to them, and after a few minutes they're all talking. My son can make friends anywhere, anytime. It's a gift he has. I straighten camp and search for something else to do once I'm finished. I join Michael and the locals and decide I should get all the information I can from them about the dinner tomorrow. I question them about the floor plan of the castle, but they know little about it. They are familiar with the general layout of the dining room and kitchen, but that's all. I think it would be best for them to sneak us in as the help. Now that the retrieval team is here, we have sleep aid injections. We can put Wallingford out to reduce the risk of being caught.

According to Aidan, Jonathan was certain Wallingford would stay at the church.

Something changed history, and that worries me. We're the only thing different this time around, so our being here was the catalyst to propel the change. Could Thomas have done something to sabotage the church and change the location? Michael taps my arm and frowns at me.

"Mom? What's wrong? You look worried."

"Nothing, just thinking is all."

"Where do you live? I've not heard your accents," one local asks.

Michael looks at me, then at the man. "We're from America. It's across the Atlantic Ocean, it would take months to go there by ship."

"That is a very long journey. I have been told it takes many months to cross the sea. Did you run into any pirates? Or any French?" This makes all the locals laugh.

"Well, that's a long story, and it's very, very complicated. It's a long way off and I can't wait to go back. No offense to your rainy little island here, but I miss home," says Michael.

I spend the rest of the day catching up with Michael. The lost transporters have been huge national news for months. He never gave an interview, but all the news stations and talk shows tried to get him to. He tells me the government has paid my mortgage while I've been missing. They told Michael they would continue to do so for up to one year, or until I get home, whichever comes first. At least I don't need to worry about that. I'll have so many things to deal with. He also tells me they plan to pay out life insurance to relatives at the one-year mark. So that was it, then. After a year, if they couldn't recover us, they would write us off and move on it seems.

Maybe when I get home, I'll do an interview. Tell everyone what we experienced here and how the government planned to abandon us.

No, I won't.

I cherish my privacy and I prefer to get back to my old life. I'm certain one of the other missing transporters will go public with their stories. I'm also sure their experience has been as terrible—or worse—than mine.

The government will pay far more than life insurance before this is over. And rightfully so.

A few hours later, Ethan, Adams, and the detainee ride into camp on horses. The local talks excitedly to the other intruders, and they whisper and glance over at the rest of us.

The local with Ethan and Adams speaks up, now the spokesperson for the group.

"We will help you. We will get you into the castle as banquet servers or groundskeepers. They have hired only two of us, you will need to release the others. We want the food and the medicine, all of it. After we provide you safe passage, we cannot assist you any further. They will kill us too if they discover you are intruders. We will give you all the information we have today, but that will be all we can do for you. Do we agree gentlemen?"

Ethan looks at me and shrugs. I nod my head and glance at Frank, who nods in agreement.

"Fine. We agree. You need to be sure you can get us in. Once we're in, we will handle everything else. We need at least three of us inside. Also, I cannot agree to release the rest of your group until after we are out. They can stay hidden outside with our men. If things go wrong, they will extract us, but we may not help you. Once inside, we do not know each other. You must find your own way out. After tonight you will never see us again. You cannot tell anyone where you got the medicine. If you must, put it in their food, it will work the same. You cannot let anyone see the MR—I mean, the food. Remove the wrapping before you share it. Agreed?" says Frank.

They nod in agreement, and we seal the arrangement with a handshake between Ethan, Frank, and the spokesperson.

Ethan motions me over to where he and Frank are standing.

"Listen, we got some information on our outing today. The damage at the church, it was intentional. The reason Wallingford's plans changed is that someone damaged the church and made it uninhabitable. I will assume it was our friend Thomas."

"Of course it was, I figured as much. That makes sense. I kept wondering what had changed history, since we're the sole variable here. So, he knows we're going after the book and he's trying to save his payday, and now we must worry about him in the mix tomorrow. Great," I say as I sigh.

"Don't worry about him, Christine. My team will take care of him. Ethan's already given me a good physical description, so I'll brief the guys," says Frank.

Malcolm approaches with Aidan close behind.

"Aidan and I can help. We'll go with the team tomorrow and help them keep watch at the perimeter; we know what Thomas looks like. It'll be far easier for us to pinpoint him. He's rather generic looking and may blend in more than you think."

Ethan looks surprised by the offer. "Malcolm, I thought you weren't interested in getting involved. And Aidan, you realize there's nothing in it for you. No payday even if you help."

"I'm not interested, but I wouldn't feel good about letting the other guys go out there without my help. My willingness to help isn't about the job, it's about the people. You asked Frank to send me to America, and I appreciate that more than I can express. Think of this as a thank you," Malcolm says.

Aidan sighs and runs his hands through his hair. "I understand there's no payout. I'm sorry I ever got mixed up in all of this." He lifts his hands and lets them collapse back onto his thighs. "Maybe me assisting will help my case when I get home. As for Thomas, no love lost; he deserves whatever he gets."

Frank gives Malcolm a nod. "I appreciate the help, Malcolm. As soon as we're out tomorrow, I'll transport you to Oklahoma, to the same coordinates Christine went to."

"Malcolm, when you get there, I'm sure you'll run into my prisoner Marcus. Try to straighten that kid out, will you? He comes from a very nice family, and I think he could use a little guidance," I say.

Malcolm nods and walks off toward the shelter.

TWENTY-ONE

Cotswold, England 1335

We spend the next day relaxing and reviewing the plan again and again, preparing for the mission. There are so many variables it's difficult to create any specific plans, so we work with a general outline instead. Our basic game plan is to bring Ethan, Frank, and me inside with the men who are already hired. Michael tries his best to talk me into letting him take my place, but I shoot that idea down. Aidan and Ethan will be on the perimeter lines with the rest of the retrieval unit, watching for Thomas and waiting to extract us if necessary. Now that we know the church damage was deliberate, we're certain Thomas had something to do with it. We're taking tear gas pills, sleep aid injections, and knives in with us for protection. Frank switches clothes with Malcolm, as he can't go into the castle in his uniform. Frank's period clothing is too elaborate and we all agree Malcolm's clothing will draw less attention.

Once we have the chapter, we will return to camp. We'll leave the MREs and antibiotics in the shelter for the men, then Frank will send Malcolm to Oklahoma. Ethan will transport to present day England, then Aidan will travel to Scotland, with me, Frank, and the team leaving last. It seems a solid strategy in theory, but we know there are a hundred things that could go wrong.

The retrieval team all nap, they expect no sleep tonight. I struggle to sleep, too wound up to relax and I notice Ethan doesn't even try. As the day wears on, I become more anxious. I question myself for agreeing to stay and carry out this idea, and worse yet, involving Michael in this scheme. I think I should have stood my ground, or better yet, agreed to go home yesterday.

However, I know that Ethan and Malcolm can't pull this off alone, and it's too late now to change my mind. We eat an early dinner and make small talk to keep our minds off the upcoming job, but everyone is quieter than normal. I suppose we're all running over the agenda, getting mentally prepared.

Ethan and Frank gather up supplies, and the retrieval team checks and rechecks equipment. As the sun lowers in late afternoon, Frank gives the go signal. We walk single file through the woods until we arrive at the edge of the forest, where it opens to the grassy hill. The castle is even more majestic than I remember it when lit up with torches, and I can't believe I will be inside there soon. I only wish it were under different circumstances. My thoughts flash to when Ethan and I were here a few days ago and commented that we would like to see the inside.

Careful what you wish for.

"Okay people, here we go. Ethan, Christine, and I will move in with these two," he nods to the two men. "Everyone else establish a perimeter on either side of the castle. Stay alert for Thomas. If you see him, extract him with the least buzz possible. If we need to evacuate, then open fire without your silencers on. We'll recognize the sound right away, and it'll create a distraction. If any of the locals give you any trouble, sedate them."

I hug Michael and tell him to be careful before the team takes off to skirt the edge of the woodland and stand position. I inhale a deep breath and we follow the two locals up the hill.

Ethan talks the entire way there, reviewing last-minute details. "Christine and Frank, try not to talk; only one-word answers so your accents don't raise questions."

"Yeah, I know, don't stress. I was covert in Oklahoma for six months, I can make it through two hours here."

"Not to worry Ethan, I will speak as little as possible. I don't want to deal with anything more than we already have to," says Frank.

"Let's do one last equipment check, confirm your flex cuffs, tear gas pills, sleep aid injections, and knife are secure."

I watch them check their waist bands and I touch the pockets of my apron. Everything intact. I have the knife in my waistband. It keeps poking me, reminding me it's there.

We approach the castle within ten minutes, and the local leads us around to what looks like a service entrance to the kitchen.

A stout, middle-aged woman wearing a dirty apron comes out to meet us.

"Well it's about time, aye! I needed you here hours ago. Who are they?" She eyes us up and down, not trying to hide her displeasure.

The taller local speaks up. "This is my sister. She can cook, and these two will work wherever you desire them. They only want a little food at the end of service."

"Can she cook? I do not need any skinny bird underfoot, gettin' in my way all night."

"Yes, she cooks and cleans, whatever you require."

Cook? This will be interesting.

"Well, does she talk?"

"She's shy, she doesn't do well around strangers, but she's a good worker."

I lower my eyes, staring at the ground. She stands with her hands on her hips, eyeing me.

"Ahh, fine. I need all the help I can get. Get in here and chop the potatoes. Can you skin a rabbit?"

I nod my head and do a little curtsy, my improvisational skills spiraling out of control.

"Well, don't just stand there, woman, in you go! You, take the others with you to the grand dining chamber and help get the tables dressed," she gestures to the local.

She grabs my arm and yanks me in where she leads me to a long butcher-block table with six other women in various stages of food preparation. I turn to see Frank and Ethan looking after me with shock on their faces. She places a sack of potatoes and a small knife on the table.

Thank God I did this in Oklahoma.

After I finish what feels like two hundred potatoes, she drops a dozen rabbits on the counter in front of me. I butcher those expertly and she nods, impressed. She gives me carrots next, and I cut them the same way the girl next to me does. I glimpse Ethan in the doorway, and he motions for me to follow him.

I look at the woman to my right, "I have to use the restroom. Where is it?"

She studies me, confused. "There's no rest room, we work until we're done. No one rests until dinner is over."

Oh, duh, they wouldn't use the term restroom. That was stupid of me. "I mean I have to urinate."

She stares at me blankly. "I have to pee."

"Why didn't you say so, eh? The chamber pot is just 'round the corner. Empty it when you're done, mistress wants it clean for tonight."

I nod and walk toward the doorway I saw Ethan go through a moment before. He is waiting for me as soon as I enter and takes my arm to guide me into a dark hallway.

"How's it going in there? Any problems? She seemed aggressive."

"She's a wretch, but it's going okay. I think I impressed her with my butchering skills. What's happening with you two?"

"Nothing much yet. More servers are arriving to set up. With more people, it will be easier to sneak off without being noticed. I wanted to check on you. One of us will come to get you when we're ready. Watch for us."

"I'll be counting the minutes, believe me. Be careful."

With that, he's off and I'm back in the kitchen. The galley manager tosses a dozen chickens onto the table and walks off without a word.

Crap.

I've never plucked or butchered fowl before, John always did that in Oklahoma. Our fair division of labor, even though we didn't get many there. He did the rare chicken we got, and I did rabbits. I stall for a minute to watch the cook across from me start her chickens and follow her lead. I have a good grasp on it by the time I'm working on my third bird. I smile to myself, remembering something my grandmother always used to say; chicken one month, feathers the next. She would laugh if she could see me now. I fall into a rhythm doing the work, but I feel like I'm wasting my time in here; I should look for Wallingford and the book. It is smarter to wait for a full house when they won't miss us so much, but I'm itching to get done and get out.

The kitchen manager walks by and slaps the back of my head, wrenching me out of the daydream, "Get to work! Don't stand there wasting time!"

My first instinct is to turn around and clock her, but instead I manage an incredible amount of self-restraint and pick up another chicken. I fear she is about to make me snap, so I take a deep breath and count to ten in my head. The new kinder, more patient me somehow prevails.

Within the hour, the place is bustling. Cooked meats and vegetables are being brought out to the banquet room. I see boar, deer, chicken, rabbits, and fish all pass by on elaborately laid out platters. Roast vegetables and candied fruits are being plated, and I'm instructed to carry one. I pick up the heavy platter and follow the others out, resisting the urge to sample the food.

The dining area fills with women in beautiful gowns and men in military style jackets. There is an enormous amount of food and wine being served. I set my platter down and Frank is across the table clearing room for more trays. He nods his head to the right, and I see Thomas there, busy serving wine. Ethan is behind him, and we establish eye contact. Thomas walks away, and Frank follows. We continue to work on the table, glancing at each other. After a minute, he nods for me to follow him. I tell the woman I'm working with I will get more food but follow Ethan out of the dining chamber. We catch Frank, who is approaching a side door that exits outside.

"We need to get to him, and fast," Ethan says.

"He went out here, let's go with shock and awe. Quick and dirty, just get him incapacitated. Christine, stay here and keep watch."

I want to flip him the bird, but I curb the instinct and go with a verbal assault instead.

"No, I'm not keeping watch, I'm going with you. That's ridiculous Frank, I'm not helpless."

He turns to look at me and I curl my lip at him. He shakes his head and gives me his best disappointed scowl but says nothing. We step through the exit but find no one in sight. Frank leads, and we start around the corner of the castle when Thomas jumps in front of him with a rock in hand, swinging for his head. Ethan steps forward and I don't think, I just react—I rush past Ethan and lunge for Thomas, pushing him back with all my weight. He stumbles backward and releases the rock. Ethan moves in and tackles him. Frank grabs flex cuffs he has hidden in his waistband and binds Thomas's hands behind his back. He continues to struggle until Frank plants a boot on his back.

"Okay, okay, you got me, now what? We're all going home tomorrow, anyway. All I want is the book. You'll never see me again."

Frank flips Thomas over, so he is lying on his back looking up at us. I pick up the rock and raise my arm, but Ethan grabs my wrist, stopping me. He takes it from me and shakes his head.

"Thomas, you're a world-class asshole, and if it's the last thing I do, I'll make you pay for what you did to Estera," I say.

"What are you going on about? I have done nothing to Estera. And who the hell are you?" he asks, looking at Frank.

"You stole Malcom's backpack with the antibiotics, and she died when she got the plague. You may as well have killed her with your own hands!" I reply angrily.

His face pales for a minute, but he recovers swiftly.

"Well, that's not my fault. Malcolm is a prisoner, something all of you seem to have forgotten. Those antibiotics were accessible, I was just the only one sharp enough to get them. And it's Ethan's fault anyway. I needed them for the infection starting on my finger thanks to the stick he shoved under my nail."

Ethan takes a step closer to Thomas. "Fuck it, you deserve this," he states as he lifts the rock and hits Thomas on the head.

I stiffen when he hits him because it's unexpected.

"Don't worry, it's only a little love tap, enough to knock him unconscious for a while is all," he adds as he drops the rock.

They drag Thomas inside a small stable, out of sight.

"The prick deserved it. Let's get back in there before someone misses us. He'll be okay here for a while," Frank says as he starts around the corner, then stops and turns to me. "And Christine, whatever that was, don't let that happen again. That's how people get hurt."

"He intended to crack your skull with that rock Frank, I didn't think, I reacted. You said shock and awe, I only followed your order," I say.

Ethan laughs, "Well, she's got you there, Frank. She shocked us, and I for one am in awe."

Frank grunts and walks toward the door. We stand just inside the threshold, making sure there is no one in the hallway and it's clear to sneak back to our stations in the dining room. I feel a sense of relief that Thomas is out of the mix, at least for now.

200

I grab a platter of meat on my way back, so I don't raise suspicion. People file into the banquet hall, and I get caught up in the moment. It's all so excessive, and the dresses are phenomenal. What an opportunity to experience this firsthand, and I can't help but marvel at the grandness of it all. They announce the duke and duchess and they enter with trumpets and fanfare, followed by their guest of honor, Sir Richard of Wallingford. Dinner begins, and I'm told to keep the wine flowing by my new labor dictator, the kitchen manager.

Ethan comes to stand next to me as I wait in the corner for someone to signal they need more alcohol.

I know I could use some.

"We think it's time, while everyone is busy with dinner and we know where Wallingford is. Plus, we don't have to bother with Thomas for a bit. Meet us in the room left of the kitchen—we think those stairs lead to the chambers."

"All right, be there in a minute. I have to leave when the warden isn't looking, or she'll drag me back."

He walks off without a word and I watch him go to Frank and whisper something. As Ethan moves toward the hallway near the kitchen, I see Frank put down his platter and sneak off.

I glance around the room and see the old woman fussing with the meat, so I move quickly to the hall. It is dark, even with the torches lit on the wall sconces. I find Ethan and Frank and hurry toward them.

"Okay, these stairs should lead to the bedrooms. There may be guards up there. Use your tear gas capsules first if you need to incapacitate someone, as they are the least invasive; break it in two and flee if you use one," says Frank.

We start down the hall to the stairs. The walls are stone and the steps spiral up two floors.

At the top of the landing, it opens to a massive corridor with four high wooden doors on each side. A guard steps in front of us to block our way. Before he can say anything, Ethan puts the sleep aid injector to his neck. It's difficult to do, as he's wearing armor, but he gets the injection in where his helmet and chest guard leave a small area exposed. The armor is noisy, and it takes both Ethan and Frank to guide him to the floor without creating too much clamor. I crouch next to the guard to touch the armor plate and chainmail. I can't help myself, I will never see anything like this again.

"Christine please, focus. Let's make this quick. He'll be out for a while, but no telling if anyone else is here. As soon as one of us finds the book, signal the rest of us and let's get the hell out of here. I suspect it won't take long for them to notice we're missing, and that we came here together will make them realize something is going on," says Frank.

I rise and touch the pocket of my apron as reassurance, confirming my tear gas and flex cuffs are there. No need to check the knife, it continues to dig into my side every time I move. I open the heavy wooden door to the first room. It's occupied, I can tell, bed unmade and water still in the freestanding tub. I notice a dress hung over a chair and quickly decide this isn't the right room. I move on to the next, and it's empty except for a bed. I re-enter the hall to see Frank exit a room holding a leather satchel.

"I found the book. Let's find the correct part and we're out. Find Ethan to help us go through this."

"That was fast."

"I'm motivated. I don't want to meet any of that guys pals," he motions to the guard at the end of the hall.

"Okay, go into this room. It's empty, so we won't have a concern about anyone coming in," I motion to the door behind me.

Frank crosses the hall and enters the room I just left, while I walk down the hall calling Ethan's name softly. A door opens to my right and Ethan peers out.

"Frank found it, he's in an empty room waiting for us, let's go."

He follows me to the room where Frank has the contents of the satchel laid out on the bed.

Frank looks up as we enter the room. "I can't read this crap; I can't even discern most of the words. The writing is bizarre."

Ethan looks at the sheets strewn on the bed. "It is medieval calligraphy, it's hard to read. We need to find the heading with 'Albion' on it, that's the section we take."

We continue to search, each taking a part of the writings. It takes a lot of time because it's so difficult to understand. I'm about to give up when I see it. "Got it! 'Tractatus Albionis,' right? Here it is."

Ethan double checks to make sure we have the entire chapter and hands it to Frank, who tucks it into his vest for safekeeping.

Ethan opens the door and peers out. "Let's get the hell out of here. Christine, stay between Frank and me when we pass. If the kitchen woman sees you, she will attempt to bring you back to duty, and I don't want her to draw attention to us."

As we gather up the rest of the writings to return the satchel, the sound of gunfire in the distance makes us all freeze. We stare at one another as Ethan sets the pouch on the bed.

"Let's move, people. We need to get out that's our signal to evacuate," Frank replies.

I scan the papers scattered across the bed, knowing there's no time to return them to the satchel. We move to the hall and down the stairs. No one in the banquet hall seems to know anything is amiss; the dinner is in full swing with musicians playing and people eating and drinking. They wouldn't hear the shots over the noise. We make it to the hallway that leads outside and Ethan runs smack into the kitchen manager. She looks past him at me and steps forward to grab my arm.

"What are you doing in here? You have no business here. Get to work before I have the guards lock you up. You'll be lucky to have anything at night's end. Get back out there!" She strengthens her grasp on my arm and tries to pull me toward her.

Ethan pulls me behind him. "She's ill and we're taking her home, get out of my way."

"You'll do no such thing! She is working this dinner by order of the duke. Now let her pass or I'll call the guards to remove you."

As soon as she speaks, Frank stabs the sleep aid injection in her neck, and she crumples to the floor.

"Screw you lady, we're out of here," Frank replies, as we step over her.

I grab her shoes before they drag her out of sight. Ethan and Frank look at me like I'm crazy.

"I owe her one, trust me," I say, recalling her slap on the back of my head.

The two locals see us come around the corner and rush toward us. We tell them we need to go now, and they follow us.

"Did you hear that noise a moment ago? What was that? What's happening?" one of them asks.

"No time to explain, keep moving," Ethan replies.

We stride through the kitchen and out the door. I realize we have no flashlights as we step into the darkness. We stand there trying to adjust our eyes to the dark, when Carey appears out of nowhere.

I throw the kitchen managers shoes as far as I can toward the tree line. "That's for the slap on the head, you shrew."

"Follow me everyone, all hell is about to break loose. Thomas wound up outside somehow and was making his way to the castle when they captured him. They're searching the grounds and making their move to the edge of the forest," Carey reports, out of breath.

We run, following Carey, when a guard about a hundred yards out yells for us to stop.

Carey turns, and using his night vision, drops him by shooting him in the leg. Now it's on; other guards are running toward the downed man and looking in our direction. We trail Carey and reach the woodland and the others in minutes. Gray leads the group into the woods when we pick up someone yelling from behind.

"Wait! Don't leave me! I'm a transporter! Wait! Don't leave me behind!"

I recognize Thomas's voice. Penn looks at Gray and nods. I want to tell them to leave his ass here. But if we do, they may kill him before the system transports him tomorrow. And the only reason that bothers me is because I want to make certain he pays for Estera's death. Him dying here would be too easy.

"I've got this. Cover me and I'll get him," he states.

Penn races off across the grassy hill and we hear shots. My eyes have adjusted to the dark and I see two figures on the hill drop. I see Gray with night vision on, and he fires again. Penn reaches Thomas and pulls him along. Arrows fly around them, some landing in the grass mere feet from them, but somehow Penn gets him back to the group.

"What the hell dude, How did you escape those guards? Get moving, asshole," Penn pushes Thomas forward.

Thomas is breathing heavily, struggling to catch his breath. His hands are still in the flex cuffs behind his back and he stumbles and falls. Penn grabs him by the shirt and yanks him up.

"They are trying to kill me," he says, still gasping for breath.

"You're a train wreck man, get going. I won't go back for you again," Penn declares, pushing him forward again.

Gray starts off through the forest and we all follow, using the lights on the retrieval team's helmets to guide us. We arrive at camp and Frank gets right to work gathering the antibiotics and MREs.

"Okay guys, here's the food and the medicine we promised you. I suggest you take off now; the guards might not find us tonight, but they'll be here by first light."

"Where will you go? How shall you stay hidden from them?" They study Frank and seem concerned.

"Don't worry about us, pal. We'll be on our way home shortly. We will be just fine. Don't forget what we told you about the medicine; you only need one tablet per person. You can grind it up in their food if you think they won't want to take it. Remember, food out of the wrapping or it will mean trouble for you. Fill the packets with rocks and sink them in the lake. Good luck guys."

Frank cuts the flex cuffs on the locals who we held as detainees during the mission. He shakes hands with all of them. They mount their horses and ride off south, away from town and the castle, their food and medicine packed on their horses.

Ethan pours water on the fire and leaves the spears propped against the log bench. The retrieval team already have their gear on, so they're ready to travel.

"Malcolm are you ready to leave? You're firm on Oklahoma?"

"Yes, America it is. Thank you all for agreeing to send me there. I am eternally grateful for being allowed to leave this place."

He moves through the group shaking hands and wishing us all luck. When he gets to Thomas, he pauses.

"Estera would be alive today if you hadn't stolen my backpack with the antibiotics."

He punches him in the face, and Thomas goes down like a sack of potatoes. He struggles to get up, but Ethan pushes him back down with his boot. Malcolm smiles at Ethan and he and Frank go to the shelter to switch back into their own clothes again.

Frank sends Malcolm to the same coordinates I transported to seven months ago, but not before handing him several antibiotics.

"I put these aside for you since that asshole over there stole yours."

Malcolm embraces Frank and pockets the pills.

I say a little prayer to myself that he'll be okay in Oklahoma. I've given him as much information as I can about how to make it there, and I expect it will help him. I ask him to give a message to John for me. To tell him how thankful I am for what he did for me, and I'm doing well and reunited with my son back home. I hope that will give him some sense of closure.

Based on what Michael told me, it doesn't sound as if John has been handling my departure well.

Frank is ready to send Aidan home next, then Thomas. But not before Ethan warns them that if Hoyt proves they were lying when we meet with him, he'll find them no matter where they hide. Ethan makes sure they both understand they are not to talk about the mission or anything the retrieval team did.

"One other thing, Thomas. Estera's death directly results from your decision to steal Malcolm's antibiotics. I'm certain that's actionable in the eyes of the government. If you say one word about anything tonight or the retrieval team's involvement, that will be the first offense I inform them of. In fact, I may tell them anyway. You deserve to pay for that, and I'm not sure I can let it go," says Ethan.

"If anyone comes down on me about Estera, I'll tell the government everything I know about what you all have done, count on that," says Thomas.

"Take your best shot. It will be your word against all of ours. And if you think Jonathan Hoyt will corroborate your story you'd best guess again. No one will believe anything you say," says Ethan.

I step up and get right in Thomas's face. "Thomas, make no mistake, I *will* tell the authorities you went rogue. That you struck out on your own, taking the only antibiotics we had, resulting in Estera's death. That's the truth, and I promise you, if it's the last thing I do, I'll make sure you're punished for that. I'd kill you here and now, but that would only lower me to your level. More to the point, it would be too good a death for you. I want you to suffer. As much as Estera did," I say.

"I'll tell them the same story," says Ethan.

"As will I," says Aidan.

"You can all get screwed. No way will I let you take me down. Hoyt owes me, and I intend to get payment from him."

"I guess we'll see about that, won't we?" I say.

"Goodbye, asshole, have fun explaining why you're in flex cuffs when you get home," says Frank, as he transports Thomas before he can say another word.

Aidan is the next to go home, which leaves Ethan, me and the retrieval unit.

When it's time for Ethan to leave, I'm conflicted. I want him to reach home, but part of me will miss him more than I wish to admit to myself. He asks Frank for a moment and pulls me aside. The rest of the group pretend to be busy to give us privacy.

"So, I'll skip across the pond in a week and meet you in Los Angeles. I'll call you when I arrive and we can visit Hoyt together. I realize my timing may be not be ideal, but I'd fancy taking you to dinner when I'm there."

"Like a date?"

"If you remove that incredulous expression from your face, then yes, just like a date."

"I'm sorry, I didn't realize I did that, it just surprised me."

"Well, it shouldn't surprise you. You're one of a kind, Christine, and I recognize that. You're bold, compassionate, and just the right amount of salty. Yet you have a gentle air about you. It's an intriguing combination that I find quite charming. So, I'll say cheers and see you in a week. Think about dinner."

"Don't you need my number to get in touch with me?"

"I don't imagine you are difficult to find Christine; I know where you work, remember? If I can't find your number, I don't deserve to have dinner with you. I'll be in touch."

He winks and leans over to kiss me on the cheek. I sense myself blushing and turn to look over at the guys. I see Frank and Michael turn away quickly, pretending they haven't been watching.

It doesn't seem to bother me when Ethan winks at me, not like it did when Miller the med aide did.

Ethan walks over to Frank and tells him he's ready to go. He turns to face me and maintains eye contact with me until he's gone. Well, the guy knows how to leave an impression, I'll give him that. I stand staring at the spot where Ethan stood a moment before.

"Mom, are you okay?"

"I'm fine, honey. I'm glad Ethan got to go back."

"Well tell that to your face because I don't think it knows yet."

I smile to convince him I'm fine.

Or maybe I'm trying to persuade myself.

Frank calls us over and prepares to do a group transport. I'm so excited it's difficult to contain myself. He scans each of us, and soon I'm dizzy and feel the familiar sensation begin to take over.

Please God, let the transport take me home this time.

TWENTY-TWO

Los Angeles, California 2070

We arrive home early on a Thursday afternoon to what I can only describe as mayhem. We go to the decontamination room, as we always do, and dump our clothes in the hazardous waste container. I take off the bracelet Ethan bought me and curl it up in my hand, not willing to release that to the bin. As I let my dress and apron drop, I feel strangely melancholy. This dress represents some of what I've been through the past several months. It almost seems to trivialize that by just tossing them aside like this. We're tested for toxins and then sent through a second decontaminant shower for safe measure. As soon as we're changed into fresh uniforms, we're vaccinated before being released. They scan us to establish we aren't sick or carried back any diseases with us. I test negative for the plague. The antibiotics Frank gave us prevented it from developing.

I stop by my locker and grab my phone, watch and employee identification, pulling the lanyard over my head. I gaze at the employee picture on my ID. It seems like so long ago and I look like a different person now. I bag the uniform that I stored there the day I left for Oklahoma.

I don't turn my phone on, not wanting to deal with messages or emails yet.

As I walk out of the locker room and make my way to the main lobby, I notice the top brass is there, plus my parents and sister. My mom and dad both cry when they see me, which causes me to burst into tears for what feels like the hundredth time this year. I cried a lot during my first couple of days in Oklahoma, and that continued throughout the time the government stranded me. I don't remember the last time I wept before then. I realize that

I've shed more tears in these months than I have in the last several years. Honestly, it's been cathartic to get it all out.

My sister Kat hugs me so long I tell her I can't breathe to convince her to let go.

"I thought I lost my sister. I'm so happy you're home," Kat says, tearing up.

"I missed you, too."

We hug again, and as I pull away, I see Annabelle. She's standing in the room's corner, tears in her eyes, watching me. I tell Kat I'll be back and run to Annabelle. She holds her arms open and I fall into them, crying again.

"Annabelle, I'm just so sorry I couldn't get home to send someone for you. I didn't realize I would transport anywhere else. Are you all right? How did you escape the Indians?"

"Don't worry about all that; none of that is your fault. You did nothing wrong, and besides, Michael and Frank came and rescued me. I'll tell you all about how I got away this weekend. You need to continue home, shower, eat, and sleep. I can call you tomorrow."

"Okay, thank you. Let me sync my number to your phone."

"I already have it. I got it from Kat."

"You met Kat?"

Girl, we've been out for drinks. I love that woman!"

"Of course you have," I say laughing as I wipe my eyes with the back of my hand.

"I should have guessed, knowing you both as I do. How long are you here for? When do you fly home?"

"I wanted to make sure you got home. The agency gave me some extra time off. I guess they think that will compensate me for seven months in hell," she says rolling her eyes.

"What? Michael was serious, you've been here for a week waiting for me?"

"Of course I have! You're my best friend, and I realized you would need to vent to someone who gets it. We both need that. So, I'm here for selfish reasons. Besides, the girls think they've hit the vacation lottery; we've been to Disneyland and Joe thinks he's died and gone to heaven with the beaches here."

"Oh, Annabelle, I'm so glad you're here. There's so much to tell you. Call me tomorrow. Right now, I'm going home to eat, sleep, and bathe. Not in that order."

"I cleaned your house for you, it's all squared away. I also got you some fabulous bubble bath bombs and that jasmine shampoo you love. I changed your bed and laid out new pajamas and slippers. I wasn't sure what you'd want to eat, so I programmed the Chef-Aid with a filet mignon, baked potato, and garden salad. But I remember how much you love Mexican food, so I also ordered a taco, enchilada, beans, and rice plate. And a molten chocolate cake for dessert."

"Oh my God. Thank you. You don't know what that means to me."

"Trust me, I do! I appreciate how it feels to miss the conveniences of home. Besides, all I did was wave a dust cloth here and there, undock the vacuum and program the shower cleaner. No big deal. I just wanted you to come home and relax."

She hugs me again and two of the cutest little girls I have ever seen run up to her and hug her legs. They smile up at me and I can see they look just like her. Their curly, wild blonde hair is adorable. I turn to find Michael and see him talking to our facility director. I stride over to him, just as Frank steps up. I watch the chief study my employee badge.

"Michael, let's go, I'm exhausted."

"Hello, you must be Christine Stewart. I'm Commander Watkins. Nice to meet you. I've heard many great things about you. We'll see you're finished with debriefing in two hours and on your way home. In the meantime, I'm sure we can scare you up something from the cafeteria if you're hungry."

He extends his hand and smiles his fake, practiced grin at me. I shake hands as the anger of the past months comes to a head inside me.

"With all due respect sir, I'm going home, and you can take that debriefing and stuff it where the sun doesn't shine. I haven't enjoyed a shower, a decent meal, or a real bed in seven months. While you slept soundly, ate dinner every night in your warm house, and got to take a hot shower every day, I was trying to stay alive. I didn't know if I would see my son again, or ever get back. I've earned the right to go home, and if you want to debrief me, you can send Internal Affairs to my house tomorrow afternoon and meet with me. Sir."

It seems the new me is no longer on board.

Frank sighs and steps between me and the commander to do damage control.

"Sir, I'll go through debriefing for my team today. Transporter Stewart and the rest of the team went through a difficult time. They should get some much-needed rest before interviews. They've gone through decontamination and vaccines, so they're safe to leave. I accept full responsibility for them. I also need to speak to you about a prisoner I transported to Oklahoma from England. I made a field decision and I want to make certain my decision isn't reversed once the enforcement team here and in England learn of it."

Watkins presses his lips together in a tight line, not speaking for a moment, before nodding his head.

"All right Rhoades. Stewart, we'll be in touch tomorrow. In the meantime, be careful out there. I'd leave the back way, through the secure tunnel. It's a shit show out there with the press. I must remind you not to speak to them until after debriefing. Every news station from Los Angeles is waiting to meet to you."

"Sir, the last thing I want is to talk to the press. Today or ever. I just want to go home. If you'll excuse me, I will get my son and do that."

I walk away, not bothering to wait for him to respond. I couldn't care less if they fire me for insubordination or any other reason they may come up with. My parents offer to take Michael, Maddie, and I home. We drive out the back and duck in the back of my dad's SUV to avoid the press. I gaze out the window on the trip home. The once familiar sights and sounds of the city now an assault on my senses. The sound of horse hoofs and carts replaced with the steady drone of cars and mass transit. The unspoiled countryside lost to a landscape of skyscrapers and neon signs. I sigh to myself and wonder if other rescued transporters have made the same parallels. When we pull up to my house, there are more news vans parked there. My dad and Michael push their way through them with me, Maddie and my mom right behind. As soon as I walk through the door, Max hops around trying to jump up on me. I think if a dog could faint, he probably would at this point.

My dad makes sure we are secure and that no news crews have gotten into the backyard.

They leave after that, giving me some much-needed time to myself. Michael heads to his bedroom and I go straight to mine. I take the bracelet out of my pants pocket and set it on the dresser. The sunlight coming through the window makes the beads sparkle and I smile, remembering the day Ethan got it for me.

I study myself in the mirror for the first time in months and can't believe how rough my hair looks. I weigh myself and find that I have dropped twenty pounds. I guess I should expect that when all I've had to eat is meat, vegetables, and the occasional fruit for seven months. Bread is an unnecessary luxury when you make it from scratch yourself.

I soak in a hot bubble bath for an hour with the bath bombs Annabelle left me and then take a shower. I didn't realize how much I needed that. It's incredible how shaving my legs has improved my mood. Annabelle has my new pajamas laid out on the bed and a chocolate candy bar on my pillow. After I change, I head to the kitchen for food. The smell of my taco plate reminds me how long it's been since I've eaten a decent meal. Michael and Maddie join me, and when we eat together, it almost feels like it's a normal day.

Almost.

Only the trove of reporters on my lawn cautions me otherwise.

I turn on the news and the transporters coming home is the top news story. I'm glad none of them caught me on camera in my current state, looking like a refugee from a third world country. The London news crews film Ethan on his way to a waiting car outside the building where he's based. He tries to cover his face, but I'd recognize him anywhere.

My cell rings and a local number I don't know comes up on the screen. Jeez, I only charged my phone maybe an hour ago. My first thought is that it's a reporter, but I answer anyway, knowing I can always block them if it is.

"Ms. Stewart? Is this Christine Stewart?"

"Who's calling?"

"This is Neil from Chase Bank's Credit Card Division. I'm calling about your past due Visa card account."

"Neil, can you please send my statement to my phone? I've been out of town for the last seven months. I'm happy to pay it, and I apologize for the delay, but I think once I've spoken to your financial department, I can get all of this settled."

"Ma'am, we've tried to call you for months and got your voice mail every time. You never returned our calls, so I doubt you will talk your way out of this. Unless you died, and you don't sound dead, you will owe a ton of late charges."

"Uh, huh. Well, I've been as close to dead as a person can get without dying. Listen Neil, I've been away—in 1867 Oklahoma and 1335 England—for seven months, this is my first day back. I'm too tired to do this right now. Please forward the outstanding balance so I can pay it off."

"Ms. Stewart, it doesn't matter—wait, what? Oh my God, are you a transporter who came home today? Really?"

"Yes, Neil, really. And I would appreciate it if you wouldn't share that with anyone else in your office. I'd prefer to maintain my privacy right now."

"Oh, I won't Ms. Stewart, I promise. You're a national hero! I'll waive the late fees and send you just the principle balance. I'm glad you made it home, Ms. Stewart."

"Thank you, Neil. I appreciate that."

I receive two similar calls throughout the day. Because we are the highlight of the news cycle, this has transitioned easier than I expected. It had worried me I'd have to fight to resolve this crap.

Michael and I spend the rest of the day relaxing in our pajamas, both of us exhausted. We watch a movie and snack on the chocolate cake Annabelle ordered in the Chef-Aid. My parents call to check on us, and I take a while to convince them we're both all right, just tired.

I realize I can no longer stay awake, so I give up and go to bed. Lying down on a real mattress is amazing and I fall asleep within minutes. I remember seeing a movie where someone returned from a shipwreck. When he went home, he couldn't sleep in a bed anymore and would make a bed on the floor each night. Not this girl. I sleep through the night and wake up at seven o'clock restless.

I decide I need to go for a run, remembering how quickly I tired when I was fleeing from the Indians in Oklahoma. I put my hair up in a baseball cap, put on sunglasses and realize I could be anyone, just another anonymous somebody out for a jog. Satisfied with my disguise, I head to the kitchen to make a piece of toast using the old counter toaster Michael loves so much.

"I caught you. You like the old toaster better!"

I spin around to catch Michael smiling.

"Well, I admit the toast beats the stuff out of the Chef-Aid."

"Why are you wearing sunglasses, Mom?"

"Oh, I forgot I had them on. I'm going for a run."

"The reporters will just follow you."

"I don't think so; I have a plan. See you soon."

I finish my toast and exit the back door. I climb the fence and cut through the common area before I reach the street. I put my ear buds in and sync my watch to them. The music fills my ears, and I could run for miles. I missed music and my runs, and it feels so great when my feet hit the pavement. Once I turn the corner to jog past my house, my rhythm is perfect. I stare straight ahead and don't break stride, and not one reporter pays the slightest bit of attention to me.

Yes!

I pass my house on the way back an hour later. I kick my shoes off, take a shower, and Annabelle calls as I'm changing into jeans and a T-shirt. We make plans for her to come over in thirty minutes. She arrives right on time. I see her through the window as she flings her car door shut and holds up her hands to ward off the reporters. I open the front door for her, leaving the security screen closed. The reporters are so hungry for an article all their focus is on her and they don't notice me. I hear Annabelle shouting over the crowd.

"Jesus people, can you give us a break? I haven't seen my friend since she got home. Can you please just allow her some privacy to become re-acclimated to her life? I'll throw ya'll an interview, but only if you leave her alone. You need to leave now, and I'll give a formal statement next week. But please, I'm asking nicely, allow us transporters some time to get back to normal. You do not understand what we've been through, and we'll never tell you about it unless you back off. None of us will want to do a press conference if you keep this crap up."

With that, she starts up the path where I pull the screen open. She slams it shut behind her, blocking a reporter who followed her up the walkway.

"Girl, I don't know how you take it, all of them camped out in front of your house. I didn't deal with that as I haven't been home yet."

"I've been hoping that by ignoring them, they'd lose interest and go away."

"Ha! No such luck, sister. We're the biggest news out there right now. Everyone loves an exceptional human-interest story with a happy ending. How are you? Are you holding up all right?"

"Feeling better with each passing hour. Just showering and sleeping in my bed improved my attitude tenfold. How are you? Are the girls adjusting to having you back?"

"Yep, it's all positive on my end."

Michael and Maddie walk out and come over to hug Annabelle. "I thought I heard your voice," says Michael.

"Hey there, you two. How's things with you?"

"Good, glad my mom's home. Maddie and I are going to lunch and a movie. See ya both later. Love you, Mom."

"Love you too. Have fun."

Oh, to be young again. They walk to the door laughing and talking and seem unaffected by all this. I've been through the wringer and can't imagine feeling normal again for at least a few days.

"Come sit down, Annabelle. Is it too early for wine?"

"Hell no, it's eleven thirty. That's close enough to noon for me. Besides, we didn't drink any alcohol the entire time we were in Oklahoma except that one night. I can't believe we downed that disgusting whiskey of John's."

"How was John doing?"

"He'll be okay. He started drinking, but he was on the mend."

"I suppose he's gone for years now since we are back in our timeline. I asked Malcolm to check on him for me as he will be in 1867."

"Who's Malcolm?"

"Oh God, there is so much to tell you. You're the only person in this entire world who will understand, Annabelle. I was in England for about a week, but it seemed like months; a lot happened."

"I'm ready, girlfriend. Grab the wine, let's catch up."

I tell her everything. Hiding from the Indians, meeting up with John, and waking up in England. I continue with finding out about Thomas and Aidan's plans, Estera dying, my day in Tetbury with Ethan, the castle dinner, and getting the chapter. I conclude by explaining how Ethan and I propose to confront Hoyt. She never interrupts me, just listens to all of it.

"Wow. Is that the bracelet he bought you, the one you're wearing?"

"Seriously? You listen to that whole narrative and that's your first question?"

"Well, yeah. That and the dinner date are the best parts. I'm happy you found someone!"

"I didn't 'find someone'. I'm not even sure I'll go to dinner with him."

"Yes, you are! Stop being so antisocial, Christine. Despite your best efforts to push me aside, I'm still here and I'm not going anywhere. So, if you can manage it with me, you can do it with him, too. You're very likable, you know—when you're not trying to drive people away."

She sips her wine, as if she's just given me a weather report, not insulted my personality.

She's not the first to tell me that, but she might be the first I listen to. So, I ignore the jab, trying not to be a little hurt.

I ask her about how she got away from the Indians while they were chasing me. She escaped when something distracted the lone Indian left to guard her and she took off into the walnut grove. Somehow, she made it far enough away to hide from him. He went after her, but she climbed to the top of a tree and hid in the branches and leaves. She says she had the idea remembering that I had spent my first couple of nights in Oklahoma in a walnut tree. She stayed there until the search party found her the following afternoon, still hiding in the tree. It's a harrowing tale, and I'm so amazed—but not surprised—she pulled it off.

We chat until my cell rings. It's base to schedule my debriefing; they set it for six o'clock. I putter around the house the rest of the day with not much to do since Annabelle cleaned it from top to bottom. I monitor the news while I deal with my bills. I draft a generic paragraph to each of them outlining my extenuating circumstances and ask that they remove any delinquent charges from my balance and adjust my credit report. My paychecks accumulated in my account for seven months, so I have the means to pay everything off. I'll still have a respectable chunk of change because the government paid my mortgage too. I complete that with an hour remaining before the debriefing team arrives. I take Max outside and play fetch with him to his delight, when I get another incoming call and see a series of random numbers pop up on the screen.

"Hello?"

"Well, hello there yourself."

I recognize his voice right away. The British accent helps.

"Ethan, how are you?"

"Finer than a fiddle, how are you?"

"I, I uh, I'm okay. Just getting accustomed to being home. How is that going for you?"

"Oh, you know, it's strange, but I'm adjusting. I thought I'd come over to Los Angeles in a few days so we can see Hoyt together. I'm spending the weekend with my daughter, but plan to fly out late Monday. I can pick you up around two o'clock on Tuesday if you're free?"

"Yes, that'll work. Do you have a pen? I can give you my address."

"Yes, I'm ready, go on."

I recite my address for him, providing him some quick directions from the airport hotel where he'll be staying.

"See you Tuesday then. Cheers."

"Um, okay then. Cheers to you too, I think."

I hear him laugh as he says goodbye and hangs up. I recline on my patio chair and stare at my phone. Three days until he's here.

Good God, I need the salon.

I make an appointment for Monday for a manicure, pedicure, cut, and color. I know I shouldn't be nervous about seeing him; I spent a week camping with him. Anything he sees after that will be a hundred times better.

I sigh and scan my hundreds of emails, working to get current before the debriefing team arrives. They arrive right on time, four of them. They spend an hour and a half listening to my report and asking me questions. I tell them about what Thomas did, and that Aidan and Ethan will corroborate the information. They cannot contact Malcolm, but I don't think that will matter. It gives me more satisfaction than I could imagine. They waste the next thirty minutes telling me what I can't talk about, which includes most of my experience. I assure them I have no intention of speaking to the press, but they make me sign a confidentiality agreement anyway. I wonder to myself if I should have had legal representation here and if anybody else had an attorney present for debriefing. I would never consider that necessary under normal circumstances, but this is anything but routine.

When they issue me a new identification badge, they deactivate my old one. They ask if I'd like to use any personal days before returning to work, as they're adding three weeks paid courtesy time to my benefits bank. The same extra time Annabelle referred to the day I got back, I guess. I opt to take the time off. I need a break and I've more than earned it after the last several months.

Michael gets home soon after they leave and we eat dinner together, deciding to stay in and watch a movie. I go to bed early again, still struggling to catch up on sleep; transporting is a brutal version of jet lag.

I devote the rest of the weekend to visiting with my family. It's good to spend the time with everyone and just unwind. We barbeque and play board games, and I laugh more than I have in months. Annabelle joins us with Joe and the girls. I like Joe, and he and my dad seem to hit it off. The kids dote over Max and he soaks it all up. Michael and Maddie play hide and seek with the girls and they giggle every time the dog barks, giving away their hiding spot. I relax on the deck and look around at the people in my life. I feel like the luckiest woman alive.

And for a moment, my entire world is right.

TWENTY-THREE

Los Angeles, California 2070

I go to the salon the following morning and emerge a new woman. I catch myself looking at my fingernails throughout the day; I haven't seen them painted in so long. All the little things I hadn't done for months make a difference and I'm feeling like myself again.

Tuesday comes quickly, and although apprehensive about confronting Hoyt, I'm excited to see Ethan. I change clothes three times and finally settle on jeans, wedge sandals, and a semi-sheer lavender blouse.

And the glass bead bracelet.

Ready an hour early, I wander the house trying to distract myself. Michael worries and wants to come with me to meet Hoyt, but I convince him it will be fine because I'll be with Ethan. I promise to call him if something goes wrong, and he only agrees to leave and spend the day with Maddie after I insist.

At noon, I see a car pull up to the house. Only a few reporters remain out front, but they recognize Ethan right away and swarm him. I open the door for him, inhaling his cologne as he steps past me. His hair is short, his jeans are new, and his button-down shirt fits him like a glove.

"Oh my. You clean up nicely, Ms. Stewart."

I feel my cheeks flush and glimpse at my feet, around the room, anywhere but at him.

"So do you—thank you—I mean, thanks for the compliment," I stammer, still unable to meet his gaze.

"Christine, it's me. Look at me. It's me. Why are you acting as if you're nervous? There's absolutely no reason for you to be uneasy with me, ever."

"I'm not nervous, well, okay, maybe I am a little. I just don't do compliments well. Annabelle called me antisocial, and I think she might be right," I say, finally looking him in the eye.

He laughs and leans against the wall, relaxed.

"Does she, now? Well, I think your social skills are outstanding. And I shall count on them today when we talk to Jonathan Hoyt, so don't go shy on me."

He crosses the entryway and wraps me in a hug, giving me a kiss on the cheek. I settle into his embrace and let out the breath I've been holding, my anxiety leaving with it. We pull apart and smile at each other, the awkwardness of the moment gone.

"Did you bring the chapter from Frank?"

"Yes, right here in my purse. Don't worry, I'll be civil with Hoyt. I can't wait to see what he says."

"All right, let's get to it, yes?"

We battle our way past the reporters, who possess a renewed enthusiasm after Ethan's appearance. We make small talk on the way to Hoyt Enterprises and I point out local landmarks to him. This is his first time in California, so he's fascinated by all the famous sites in Los Angeles. It doesn't take long to arrive to the fifty-story building with ceiling to floor glass windows that reflect the city skyline. It's a busy company with people coming and going. We find a spot in the parking garage and walk to the main entrance. There's a huge receptionist station with four receptionists greeting visitors, answering phones, and directing people to various places. We approach the first available receptionist, and Ethan rests his arms on the counter.

"Good afternoon. We're here to see Jonathan Hoyt, please."

"Your name, sir? What time is your appointment?"

"Well, that's the sticking point. We don't have an appointment."

"Oh, without an appointment, you won't be able to meet with Mr. Hoyt. His schedule books months in advance, and he only takes appointments that are pre-approved and relate to current projects."

She beams at Ethan and hands him a business card.

"You can go onto our website and request a consultation through his digital calendar coordinator. You should be able to set up a date sometime within the next few months, provided security approves the meeting content."

"I appreciate that you must follow protocol. But I expect if you advise Mr. Hoyt that Ethan Ward and Christine Stewart are here to meet with him, that might motivate him to create time for us. We're transporters just back from England. Tell him we bring a message from Richard of Wallingford."

"Sir, I'm willing to call his personal assistant on your behalf, but the chances of you seeing him today are zero. Trust me."

"Understood, but I'd appreciate it if you'd at least try."

He smiles at her, and she bats her eyelashes and speaks into the small speaker built into her earpiece.

Oh, brother.

"Hi Steph, it's Candice. I have Ethan Ward and Christine,"—she looks at me with raised eyebrows, and I repeat my last name—"Stewart here to see Mr. Hoyt. They say they are here from England and have a message for him from a Richard Wallingford. Okay, will do."

I consider correcting her, to inform her I am not British. But I decide it's not worth the effort and resolve to keep my mouth shut. The new me is irritatingly tolerant.

She smiles up at Ethan, never acknowledging me. My mind flashes to the snippy med aide who did my physical the day I left for Oklahoma, and I'm convinced they're besties.

"Grab a seat in the lobby, Mr. Ward, and I'll let you know as soon as there is word from upstairs."

"Thank you so much, Candice."

I struggle not to roll my eyes at him.

We sit in the lounge area where Candice ignores us until she glances up, frowning. She talks for a minute then waves us over.

"I must admit I'm shocked, but he will see you. Security will arrive in a minute to escort you up."

We wait in the lobby until a man in a blue blazer with Hoyt Enterprises emblazoned on it approaches and instructs us to follow him. He pushes the button for the penthouse, never making eye contact with us. It only takes thirty seconds to reach the top, where it opens to a large reception area. A woman sits behind an enormous desk and rises when we exit the lift.

"Mr. Ward, Ms. Stewart, Mr. Hoyt will be with you soon. Please, have a seat. Can I bring you something to drink? Coffee, tea, water?"

We both decline and sit on a couch I'm sure cost more than my car. After several minutes, she whispers into her headset. Standing, she smiles, saying he'll see us now. She opens the double doors and motions us in, where we step into a large office with stunning artwork hung on every wall. Jonathan Hoyt walks from behind his desk to shake our hands before motioning us to a group of chairs.

"Well, I must admit, your message has me very curious. Why don't you explain what this is all about?"

Ethan speaks first. "Mr. Hoyt, we were with Thomas and Aidan in England before they transported home. We know of your plan to retrieve Wallingford's writings. In fact, we stopped them from completing the scheme."

"Well, you are direct, Mr. Ward. But I'm not familiar with what you're talking about. I'm afraid I don't recognize those names."

I decide I'm not willing to skirt around the issue; patience has never been my strong suit.

I lean forward in my chair, elbows on my knees.

"Jonathan, we can dance all day, but I have better things to do. And to be honest, I'm still cranky after being stranded in the past for the last seven months. So, let me lay this out. They told us about the plan to take the chapter and the five-million-dollar payout. I realize I've left out the minutia, but I think that should sufficiently snapshot it for you. If you keep denying it, then I guess we're through here. We'll go to the press and tell them everything. Otherwise, you can get real with us right now and stop wasting our time. While we prevented Thomas and Aidan from getting the writing, we never said we didn't complete the job. We're holding the chapter. We want to know why you need it and what you intend to do."

"Christine's right, Hoyt. Either start talking, or we can just walk and get on with our lives. If we don't like your answer, we will expose you. And you'd best brace for the onslaught of public disapproval when people find out you're responsible for all of us being abandoned. And the deaths of the transporters who didn't make it home. Prepare to kiss your enterprise goodbye, and I won't lose a moment of sleep over it."

Hoyt continues to look at us but says nothing. Ethan grasps my hand, and we stand up to leave. We take three steps toward the door before he stops us.

"Wait, please. Sit down and let's talk."

We turn around but remain standing. Ethan looks impatient, and I can see he's irritated when he speaks.

"So far, we've done all the talking, so explain yourself or we walk."

Jonathan takes a long sip from a glass water bottle and sits up straight in his chair.

"What is this, a blackmail attempt? You came in here to demand the money they were to receive, is that it?"

"What? No, nothing like that, we aren't after money," I reply.

"When Aidan mentioned preventing a pandemic, we became concerned. He didn't know much else, and we couldn't take a chance there may be some truth to what you were saying," says Ethan.

"You only want to comprehend why it was critical to get the chapter?"

"Yes! We can't determine what the proper move is unless we figure out why you put this whole thing together. You went to a lot of trouble to buy it and we need answers."

"Please, sit down. First, allow me to apologize for accusing you of trying to blackmail me just now but understand that it wouldn't be the first time someone has tried. A man in my position must be careful. Besides that, Thomas and Aidan both swore their confidentiality concerning this. So you can imagine how this has thrown me, you coming here unannounced with intel on the project. I want you to understand why I did this, why I *had* to do this. Please, sit back down and I'll start at the beginning. It's essential that you realize who I am to grasp the why of all of this."

He hits a button on the side table phone.

"Stephanie, please cancel my one o'clock with the recruitment department. I will need about an hour with Mr. Ward and Ms. Stewart. Have you two eaten? I can have my assistant order lunch."

"We didn't come here for lunch," I answer, resisting the urge to roll my eyes yet again.

Hoyt nods and begins speaking. "I was thirteen years old when I built my original computer from salvaged parts. It came naturally to me. By the following year, I was writing code and could hack into my school's database and change grades for anyone willing to pay for it. After I graduated high school, I attended UCLA to study computer science, but it bored me. They could teach me nothing there; I was years in front of my professors. So, I enrolled in astronomy classes and that kept me interested enough to continue attending school. It hooked me from the start. But even that couldn't stem my restlessness after a year. At twenty, I dropped out of college and started my business. It took off almost immediately. Within two years they selected me to submit a plan and bid to the government for a new time travel program. Obviously I won the contract because here I am today."

"Maybe you can fast track us to the part about why we're here," Ethan says, losing patience.

"I'm getting there, indulge me a minute longer. So, because of the contract I landed, my company expanded to meet the demands of drafting such an extraordinary and complicated program. I formed my enterprise with the culture that transparency breeds trust, and trust breeds loyalty. It's worked well for me. I pride myself on the fact that I employ loyal staff and I kept my ethics and integrity intact throughout my rise to success."

He reaches for the water bottle again, then changes his mind. "I'm going to pour a drink. I hope that doesn't bother you. Would either of you like a scotch?"

Ethan and I both decline the offer, as Hoyt fills a tumbler from the bar in the room's corner. He takes a slow drink before rejoining us.

"I've always been interested in astrophysics, the vastness of the surrounding galaxies, the possibility of alien life—it's been something I've loved learning about my entire life. I've also studied writings and theories from ancient astronomers, I find them fascinating. Did you realize many of them were mathematicians? They had so much knowledge, with no way to use it. Most recently I've been studying Richard of Wallingford. He was one of the most forward-thinking mathematicians and astronomers in history. His astronomical clock impressed me, it's the most intricate ever made. I ran across his Albion invention and it floored me. For something constructed in the fourteenth century, it was way ahead of its day."

Ethan leans forward, "The book you wanted brought back?"

"Yes, the book, or treatise as they called it then, is his invention in written form. I have most of it but was missing a chapter. We lost it to history, so the only solution was to go back in time and retrieve it. I confirmed Wallingford would carry it with him when he gave a speech in Leeds and then again when he traveled to St. Albans. That was a matter of historical record."

"And why was that important enough for you to coordinate this scheme of yours?" I ask, my voice rising.

"I studied his work that measures planet alignment. There is a definite correlation between other planets alignment and earth's gravitational pull. That affects our weather, and extreme weather causes disease and pandemics."

"I'm not clear what you're getting at Hoyt. All of this happened because you want to continue studying this theory?" says Ethan.

"No, because I uncovered something in the research I've already completed. Wallingford already had a good base laid, but I took it a step further. I created a software program that established a pattern over the last seven hundred years between the planet alignments, weather, and pandemics. The model was solid enough to convince me to continue my research. I formulated the near future alignments, just to see what I would find. And what I found scared the hell out of me. My analysis shows we are due for another strong gravitational pull and some very extreme weather two years from now, which will concentrate here on the west coast."

"I agree with Ethan, I still don't get it. Maybe I'm slow, but how does some weather prediction motivate you to screw with the CCEA's time travel program?" I lean back in my chair, crossing my arms.

"The probability of a global pandemic motivated me Ms. Stewart. We aren't prepared for that and it would be catastrophic if it were to happen."

He explains everything to us. The parallels between the weather and pandemics throughout history, the probable lack of preparedness by our health system, and finally the need to have complete research before presenting it to WHO. When he finishes, I am overwhelmed and frightened.

"Okay, so I understand why this information would lead you to conclude this might have disastrous results in two years. That doesn't explain why you stranded transporters around the globe? Do you have any sense what you've caused? People have died because of your decision," I proclaim.

"I'm not convinced you fully conceive what you've done, Hoyt," Ethan says angrily.

"Yes, I am very cognizant of the consequences of my choice. And please trust me when I say I did not make that decision lightly. I perceived there might be fatalities. I hoped there wouldn't be, but I'm a pragmatic man. The losses seemed somehow acceptable compared to the potential loss of life because of a cataclysmic pandemic. It sounds like I'm a heartless asshole, but I'm not. I guarantee you that the possibility for calamity here is real. Maybe you're not as concerned about the world's future as I am, I don't know. But something like this could destroy us. If you accept nothing else about what I tell you today, believe that."

"Why not just leave Thomas and Aidan where they were and let everyone come home? Why not send them right before Wallingford is there, not months before?"

"That would be far too suspicious. I realize that sounds horrible, I do. I tried to establish another alternative, but there wasn't any other way to do it. I predicted they'd likely run into complications; it would be unrealistic to think they wouldn't. It was medieval England, after all. They needed enough time to plan and organize their strategy. I knew of two confirmed times and places where we would find Wallingford. I wanted a back-up plan should they miss him at the first location."

He puts his head in his hands, and when he looks up, his eyes have welled up with tears.

"I couldn't determine another approach. I understand three American transporters died, and six others across the globe. I accept responsibility for that, and I plan to take care of the surviving families financially—anonymously. I choose not to do it in my name, because that would make me a hero in the public's eye. They won't realize I'm responsible for the deaths. And I am far from a hero. It's the least I can do for them, and you are the only two besides my senior financial officer who will ever know where the money came from. I must live with the burden of knowing I'm answerable for the deaths of nine people. That's harder than you can fathom."

I sigh and hang my head for a second, trying to absorb it all.

"There are many things those families will never get back. And the survivors have suffered beyond belief. What will you do for them? I'm not asking for myself, nor do I want your money, but the others will need some help," I suggest.

"I aim to set up a fund that would compensate each transporter or their surviving beneficiary three times the amount I was to pay Thomas and Aidan. I never imagined you or anyone would transport away from their original drop point. I don't understand how the transponders crossed, but I'll make sure it never happens again. I am impressed with M. Thomas, the programmer who figured that out. I tracked his work, and it's very impressive. I will establish a hard play for him and try to recruit him over here. Again, I recognize that sounds harsh."

I laugh out loud. "M. Thomas is a girl. Her name is Maddie. She's my son's girlfriend."

"Oh, I apologize, I had no way of identifying if they were male or female. That was rather sexist of me to assume, wasn't it?"

I roll my eyes this time; I just can't help myself. Ethan looks over at me and then down at my purse on the floor. I feel certain of his choice, and I agree with him: the chapter must go to Hoyt so he can present his research to WHO. There isn't any path around it. If there's any chance he is right, this must get to the appropriate people. I reach into my purse and hand it to Jonathan.

He gets up and crosses to the desk where he picks up two pieces of paper and takes out a lighter.

He touches the flame to the corner of the papers and lets them fall into the aluminum waste can.

"The checks for Thomas and Aidan," he states. "I give you my word, I will pay everyone who deserves compensation. I took hours of notes and recordings about my investigation and stashed them in my safe. I equipped it with technology I hoped would keep the contents immune from changes in the timeline. If Thomas and Aidan retrieved the writings, I knew the Albion treatise may no longer be part of history. If they had to bring the entire book back, I didn't want to risk not knowing why I did this. This is all new to me, so I wasn't sure if the memory of my analysis would remain intact once the timeline changed. Even if I remembered, would I distinguish what the Albion was? I couldn't work out how changing the past would affect me and my memory now, if at all. So, I set a reminder on my calendar to direct me to all my analysis the day I slated the system to come back online. My memory of sending Thomas and Aidan back was intact, but not the memory of my probe of the Albion. I guess when you two took part of the treatise out of 1335 England, it wiped the Albion from my memory because it never existed as of that moment. I reviewed my research last week after my calendar prompt. I'm more convinced than ever this is the right thing to do. I stand by the accuracy of my software."

Once the checks finish burning, he drops into his chair looking defeated.

"So, where do we go from here? Are you two going to the press? What about Thomas and Aidan?"

Ethan and I exchange a glance, and I defer to him to answer.

"No Jonathan, we aren't running to the press. This conversation never leaves this room. We stand to lose as much as you since we've turned the writings over. Just give your research to WHO and let them take the lead. As far as Thomas and Aidan, I'm certain Aidan just wants to return to his life and forget he was ever a part of this. But I want to confirm he gets his share of money from the fund. He helped when we needed him the most, and he needs the cash. I don't, however, think Thomas deserves anything but a prison sentence. All he ever wanted was the payment, and that drove his decisions. He is responsible for the death of the French transporter, Estera Bargeron. I need you to be certain he receives nothing. I don't care how you do that. Put him on the list so you don't raise suspicion. But make sure he collects no money. His share should reroute to Jacques Bargeron, Estera's husband. We've reported Thomas, but it may take some time for the government to investigate and make him answer for her death. In the interim, if he rears his ugly head, please notify me. It would give me great satisfaction to handle him."

"Understood. What a disappointment he was. On another subject, let me ask you both a question. And I may be way off base here. What would you say if I guaranteed to never delay another transporter who isn't willingly extending their stay on a transport? Would you two be interested in any future projects with me?"

"You cannot be serious," I say, narrowing my eyes.

"Define 'projects'," says Ethan.

My head snaps toward Ethan and I frown at him. He shrugs his shoulders.

"Well, I think we may be onto something here. What about other matters we can fix for the greater good of mankind? I'm not suggesting changing circumstances to our own preference or altering history. I'm talking about preventing future catastrophes such as the type we discussed here today."

My gaze hasn't left Ethan, and he looks as serious as I've ever seen him.

"Listen mate. It was one thing to do this after stumbling upon it like we did, but I'd have to know every detail about any subsequent projects. I would need to understand why and what the consequences could be. I'd also need to know it would involve no one else. Any project should affect no transporter without their prior collaboration. Or put them in any danger whatsoever. I speak only for myself," Ethan says, as he turns to face me.

He studies me closely, waiting for my response and I hear myself say, "Ditto. The same criteria would have to be a guarantee for me to consider it."

What? I have lost my damn mind.

"Excellent. Well, I have some ideas. I'll be in touch."

He stands up to shake our hands. I turn to walk away and stop when a thought occurs to me.

"Wait, one—no, two more points. I want you to take care of Annabelle Harris' girls. A college fund or a Hoyt Enterprises scholarship, something of that nature. And I need your word that Estera Bargeron's husband will get a house by the ocean in Cyprus."

"Done, I can manage that," he adds.

I nod and shake his hand again. We walk out of the office without looking back, taking the elevator to the lobby. Ethan reaches to take my hand in his.

"We did it," he says.

"Yes, it's over."

"I suspect this is just the beginning, Christine. Can I take you to a nice dinner this evening? You realize you never accepted my invitation."

"I accept, and you may. Go on ahead, I'll meet you outside. I have a call to make first."

I've delayed this for too long. And now that our meeting with Hoyt is behind me, I can't make any more excuses to myself. I should have called before now, but this will be difficult for us both. If I'm being honest, I needed the time to prepare myself to get through this call with the respect and grace it deserves. I walk to a quiet corner of the corridor and connect to the number I saved in my phone when I got home. I press call and hear a man with a beautiful accent answer.

"Hello, Jacques? Hi, my name is Christine Stewart. I was with your wife Estera in England, and I promised her I would deliver a message to you. Do you have a moment to talk?"

* * *

A week later, I'm lying on a lounge chair, the sun warming me. The sound of the waves lulls me into a state of relaxation I can't ever seem to achieve anywhere but on the beach.

"Joe, look at your daughter, she's eating sand again! Please go get her. I swear that kid will eat anything," Annabelle adds, shaking her head and laughing.

"Willow, stop eating sand!" Joe shouts as he springs up from his chair and jogs across the sand toward the giggling little girl.

I glance at Annabelle and smile. She tips her drink at me before taking a sip.

"Ah, nectar of the Gods, my friend," she responds.

"Christine, do you want another rum drink?" Maddie peeks out from under her oversized straw hat. "I'm going to get one for Michael and I."

"Yes, Maddie, I would love one, thank you."

"Mom, you might turn over, you're looking kinda red."

"Mmm-hmmm. In a minute."

"I could stay here forever," Ethan says.

I peer at him and squint against the sunlight.

"Well, we could, I suppose. Aruba is beautiful, I agree. But we work next week. Plus, I'm sure Joe will insist that Annabelle go home, eventually. And your unit will want you back if you intend to keep your job Ethan."

"Let him try," Annabelle responds laughing and sipping her drink.

"Maybe I'll try a lateral transfer to the Los Angeles unit," he says.

I close my eyes and lift my face toward the sun, smiling.

"Well, Jonathan would find us and make us come back anyway, since we've all agreed to help him with his future time travel projects. It's not as if I won't see you both regularly, working on his projects. But I like the sound of that transfer, Ethan. You both know we have places to go, people to see, and important matters to attend to, thanks to him."

Ethan reaches for my hand, taking it in his. "That we do, my dear. That we do."

THE END

ABOUT THE AUTHOR

Christy Cooper-Burnett is an author based in California with a degree in Administration of Justice. She retired early after spending most of her career in new home construction management and now divides her time between northern and southern California. Her work focuses on creating relatable stories and characters that transcend genres and encourage readers to imagine what they would do if thrown into the unique, imaginative situations her protagonists end up in.

NOTE FROM THE AUTHOR

Word-of-mouth is crucial for any author to succeed. If you enjoyed *No Way Home*, please leave a review online—anywhere you are able. Even if it's just a sentence or two. It would make all the difference and would be very much appreciated.

Thanks!
Christy

Thank you so much for reading one of our
Time Travel novels.
If you enjoyed our book, please check out our recommendation
for your next great read!

The Scent of Time by Alan T. McKean

"Alan McKean's distinctive voice presents epic drama and spiritual
discovery through time."
—Leslie P. García, author of *Wildflower Redemption*

View other Black Rose Writing titles at
www.blackrosewriting.com/books and use promo code
PRINT to receive a **20% discount** when purchasing.